HUNTER
QUATERMAIN'S
STORY

H. RIDER HAGGARD

HUNTER QUATERMAIN'S STORY

The Uncollected Adventures of Allan Quatermain

Edited and with an introduction by
Peter Haining

PETER OWEN
London and Chester Springs

PETER OWEN PUBLISHERS
73 Kenway Road, London SW5 0RE

Peter Owen books are distributed in the USA by
Dufour Editions Inc., Chester Springs, PA 19425-0007

This collection first published in Great Britain 2003 by
Peter Owen Publishers

Text illustrations by Samuel Carter, Russell Flint,
Maurice Greiffenhagen, Charles Kerr and A.C. Michael

ISBN 0 7206 1182 2

A catalogue record for this book is available from the British Library

Printed and bound in Great Britain by
Bookmarque Ltd, Croydon, Surrey

Rider Haggard was able to weave the magic carpet and I was swept along by it and inspired by it, too. It made me realize what an enormous treasure chest of stories Africa was and it has stayed with me over the years of my own writing, In fact, there are echoes of *King Solomon's Mines* in a lot of my own books.

Wilbur Smith, *The Times*, 17 March 2001

Contents

Introduction

Garsington is a typical little English village, lying in a stretch of beautiful hilly countryside bounded by the A40 and the B480 as they converge towards Oxford. It is not, though, generally known as the place which inspired the name of one of the most famous characters in British fiction, a man on a par with Robinson Crusoe and Sherlock Holmes. For Allan Quatermain, the brave and resourceful hunter–explorer who became an icon after his appearance in *King Solomon's Mines* and seventeen other tales of high adventure written by Sir Henry Rider Haggard, was actually named after a local farmer who once worked in the surrounding fields.

The village has not changed greatly since the ten-year-old Rider Haggard arrived in 1866 to be a boarder at the small school run by the Reverend H.J. Graham at Garsington Rectory. Graham served as the local rector as well as teaching a small group of youngsters whose parents believed they needed extra tuition to prepare them for higher education. Haggard, who had been sent there because he was a slow learner, was to enjoy three idyllic years in the low, grey building, with its seventeenth-century dovecote and an ancient, hollow elm tree standing in the grounds. Originally constructed three centuries earlier as an asylum for members of an Oxford college where the plague raged, the old rectory was to be pulled down a few years after Haggard's residency and replaced by a new building.

The young Rider enjoyed wandering about the lanes and meadow paths of the village and made several friends. One was a farmer, who he was to describe later in these words: "He was a fine, handsome man of about fifty, with grey hair and aristocratic features, that came to him probably enough with his Norman blood . . . He was called Quatermain, a name that I used in *King Solomon's Mines* and other books in after years."

A sketch by Rider Haggard of Allan Quatermain based on the Garsington farmer he knew as a child

William Quatermain lived in a small cottage close to Garsington's Norman church, and when Haggard returned to the scenes of his youth in 1887 to write an article entitled "On Going Back" for *Longman's Magazine* he found two tombstones in the graveyard, one erected to the memory of William Quatermain and the other to his "beloved wife". On one a recent visitor had placed a bouquet of sweet-briar. The old man had died eleven years earlier, Haggard discovered, completely unaware that his name was destined for immortality.

Apart from the name, Haggard carried away other memories from the Oxfordshire village that found their way into the adventures of Allan Quatermain. Garsington Rectory, for instance, was appropriated by Haggard as the birthplace of his hero and renamed "Garsingham Rectory". Here Quatermain's father had been the curate and later a missionary. The Reverend Graham himself inspired one of the most unforgettable scenes in *King Solomon's Mines*. Unusually for a man of the cloth he wore a thick gold ring engraved with sun symbols that stuck in Haggard's memory. An inveterate diarist throughout his life, he recalled the piece or jewellery in an entry dated 15 November 1920:

Mr. Graham told me that an old friend of his who had business in Peru had opened some burial place and in it found a chamber wherein, round a stone table, sat a dead and mummified man at the head and about a dozen other persons ranged round the table – whether male or female or both, I do not remember, if indeed Mr. Graham knew. All I can recollect of the rest of the story is that the man at the head of the table wore this ring upon his hand and that the discoverer of the tomb took it thence and gave it to Mr. Graham in after years. The tale made a deep impression on my youthful mind and I used it in *King Solomon's Mines* when I depicted the White Dead sitting round the Stone Board under the presidency of the White Death.

One of Rider Haggard's friends in Garsington was Blanche, the pretty, fair-haired little sister of the rector's wife. She often used to play with him in the large hollow trunk of the old elm, "where we taught each other the rudiments of flirtation", he confessed somewhat coyly. The girl was almost certainly the model for Stella Carson, the squire's daughter, whom the young Allan Quatermain loves and marries in the story "Allan's Wife", which appears in this collection.

Almost certainly unaware of her pupil's ripening sexuality, Mrs. Graham encouraged Haggard's love of reading and years later wrote congratulating him on his literary success. She was, she wrote, "scarcely able to believe that the little, quiet boy who used to drive with me about the Garsington lanes could have written such clever books". The author himself never forgot her postscript to this letter of praise: "I was told the other day that you had never been abroad yourself but had married a Zulu lady and got all your information from her."

Henry Rider Haggard was born on 22 June 1856, the sixth son and eighth child of William and Ella Haggard of Bradenham Hall, near Thetford in Norfolk. The boy's father was a moderately wealthy landowner who could claim descent from Sir Andrew Ogard, a Dane, who had settled in England during the reign of Henry VI. William Haggard was a barrister, a local justice of the peace and acknowledged squire of the district who "reigned at Bradenham like a king, blowing everybody up and making rows innumerable", according to his son Rider.

"Squire" Haggard was a paternal despot to his family – which composed ten in all: seven boys and three girls – and frequently harsh and abusive to his servants in the house and on the estate. The children's mother, however, was a calming influence, and the boy was to recall her as an "angel that had lost her way and found herself in pandemonium". Ella Haggard, the daughter of a civil servant, had been born in Bombay and delighted in telling her children stories of India – which particularly enthralled young Rider. She was also a writer, producing poetry and songs for magazines and newspapers, and in 1857 published *Myra; or, The Rose of the East*. This poem of nine cantos concerned the Afghan War of 1852 and reflected on the "mysterious laws of the universe". It was undoubtedly from his mother that Rider inherited his literary talents, and the theme of *Myra* was also to surface in a number of Rider's own stories.

Growing up in Norfolk the boy learned to ride and shoot and enjoyed regular trips to Europe. However, in 1867 the family moved to London, and Rider began his formal education at a day school. He proved a poor scholar, lacking in concentration and with an inability

The "White Dead" incident from *King Solomon's Mines*, drawn by Walter Paget

to absorb general knowledge. Following a severe telling-off by his father – "You are only fit to be a greengrocer!" – the youngster was dispatched to Garsington and the kindly ministrations of the Reverend Graham.

After the happy years in the Oxfordshire countryside Rider spent another three unspectacular years at a grammar school in Ipswich, where he earned the nickname "Nosey" and captained the school's 2nd XI football team. He did, however, like the headmaster, Dr. H.A. Holden, and later became a friend when the teacher moved to London. For a short time Haggard considered a career as a soldier, but Squire Haggard had already decided that his "dunderhead" son should join the Foreign Office and in 1875 obtained for him a post as a general factotum on the staff of his friend, Sir Henry Bulwer, who had been appointed Lieutenant-Governor of Natal in South Africa. The young man was just nineteen years old.

The years that followed in Africa were to shape Haggard's life and career. His tall, thin build earned him the Zulu name, Lundanda u Ndandokalweni ("The Tall One Who Travels in the Heights" or, more succinctly, Indanda) and he quickly grew to love the country-side and admire the indigenous population.

The label that has since been attached to Haggard by his critics as an arch-imperialist and racist who created only literary stereotypes and dismissed all blacks as ignorant natives is actually not substant-iated by the facts. In 1997 a handwritten account that Haggard had kept during a return journey to South Africa in 1914 came to light in the Norfolk Records Office in Norwich, to which the author had donated many of his papers. The man who discovered the papers was Mark Cheyne, Haggard's last surviving grandson, and in it was clear evidence that his grandfather had supported black South Africans in their struggle for land rights and that he had met the Reverend John Dube, the first president of the African National Congress (ANC). Haggard sympathized with Dube's views on the plight of the Zulus and the other tribes under British rule. Writing his account in the very year that the First World War broke out in Europe, he prophesied the future in Africa with uncanny foresight. After recording that he reluc-tantly believed the "impressive" Reverend Dube's case for repealing the law against dispossessed black landowners from buying back their land from Europeans was destined to fail, he went on:

But what will be the end of it all? Seven million black folk cannot be permanently neglected (or is oppressed the word?) by one million and a quarter whites . . . Perhaps one day their turn will come again, either with steel or bullet, or more probably by mere weight of numbers and the ballot box.

Whatever other impressions of Africa Rider Haggard brought back with him when he returned to London in August 1881, the people – black in particular – their languages, customs and rituals as well as the exotic, mysterious and dangerous nature of the terrain, were for ever imprinted on his brain. The bloody wars with the Zulus and the violent troubles with the Boers in the Transvaal also echoed in his mind. And when, at the beginning of the twentieth century, he used this as a source of inspiration for his stories, he as surely invented Africa as a subject for fiction in the British imagination as H.G. Wells was then inventing science fiction. His tales of Allan Quatermain opened up the last remaining "Dark Continent" on Earth.

During his time in South Africa Haggard had also begun developing his writing skills by contributing articles about the country and its people to magazines in Britain. These included "The Transvaal" for *Macmillan's Magazine* and two for The *Gentlemen's Magazine*, "A Zulu War Dance" and "A Visit to Chief Secocoeni", all in 1877. However, the payment for such essays could not possibly keep him and his new wife, Louie, whom he had recently married, and so with the financial assistance of his father Haggard decided to study to be a lawyer. In his spare time, though, he would continue writing.

To aid his studies, Haggard moved with his young wife to her family's home, Ditchingham House in Norfolk, where they would remain for the rest of their lives. In these charming surroundings he tackled his first novel, *Dawn*, a romance about a young girl's triumph over adversity. It was an unlikely theme for a man steeped in Africa and the lore of the wild, and although he did find a publisher two years later the book received poor reviews and did not sell well. Not deterred, he produced a second book, *The Witch's Head* – subtitled

A Tale of Love and War – which appeared in 1885 to a rather better reception.

In the January of that year Rider Haggard passed his examinations, and returning to London began to specialize in probate and divorce law. His career was barely under way, however, when a chance conversation with one of his brothers changed the course of his life for ever. The two men had been arguing the merits of *Treasure Island* by Robert Louis Stevenson, which Rider considered "not so remarkable". At this his brother bet him that he could not "write anything half as good". The wager was for just one shilling (5p), but the tiro author felt his creative juices rise to the challenge.

For six weeks Haggard spent his evenings and weekends writing an adventure story he entitled *King Solomon's Mines*, drawing on some of his most vivid experiences in Africa. Once again his work was turned down by a number of publishers. By chance, however, the manuscript about the quest of explorer Allan Quatermain to find the legendary ancient Phoenician mines lost in the heart of Africa was seen by the Scottish writer and journalist Andrew Lang. Immediately impressed, Lang passed it to the chief editor at Cassell and Co., John Williams, with the apt recommendation – although the circumstances of its creation were unknown to him – that he "almost preferred it to *Treasure Island*", a book which that firm had published.

The story of Rider Haggard's interview with Williams and the editor's offer of £100 for the entire copyright of the book or a 10 per cent royalty on sales has been frequently told. The struggling young author, to whom the ready cash seemed like a godsend, was about to accept the first offer when a clerk, sitting unobtrusively in the corner of the publisher's office, whispered: "Mr. Haggard, if I were you I would take the other agreement." Taking this advice, which ultimately made his fortune, was probably the wisest decision of his life.

Far less well known is the sequel to this story, which occurred when many years later Haggard made a subsequent visit to Cassell's offices on 19 November 1917. He wrote in his diary:

"He" of "She."

A cartoon of Rider Haggard by Will Farrow, from *Sport & Fiction*, May 1924

At the request of Mr. [Desmond] Flower, the editor, I identified the room in which I had my famous interview of 32 years ago with the editor when, inspired by a clerk in the corner, I suddenly changed my mind and took the royalty agreement instead of the sum down. They were much interested and suggested that the place should be labelled, "The Room Where Sir Rider Haggard Saved His Bacon".

Although tales of high adventure were not altogether new when *King Solomon's Mines* was published in September 1885, it was perfectly timed to launch a fresh public craze. The development of the telegraph and the appointment by newspapers of foreign correspondents was already bringing descriptions of wars and inter-national incidents to the firesides of British readers – and they were hungry for more. The advertisements that Cassell's plastered across London on publication day, declaring *"King Solomon's Mines* – The Most Amazing Story Ever Written", promised to satisfy this demand for heroic deeds. Almost overnight Rider Haggard became a best-seller, and the name of his very able, strong and wise hero Allan

Quatermain was to be heard on the lips of thousands of delighted readers.

The author's knowledge of Africa was evident from the very first page and immediately prompted enquiries about the man Rider Haggard. He became the focus of attention for feature writers and a popular model with cartoonists. The *succès d'estime* also began what would prove almost endless speculation as to who the original of the great white hunter really was.

One of the first candidates put forward was Sir Theophilus Shepstone, who had been the Secretary of Native Affairs in Natal from 1856. It was discovered that he had been a friend of the young Haggard and often told him stories about his life after his arrival in the Cape in 1820 as a baby of three in the arms of his missionary father. Later Haggard recalled:

> He [Shepstone] had the power of silence, but he observed everything and forgot little. To me, however, when the mood was on him, he would talk a great deal – the stories I have heard from him would fill half a volume – and sometimes even unfold to me the secret springs of his actions.

Although Haggard undoubtedly endowed Quatermain with a few of Shepstone's earlier biographical details – as is evident in the story "Allan's Wife" – and the Secretary himself actually appears in *The Witch's Head*, he was not the inspiration for the hunter. Nor was another candidate, the famous explorer and big-game hunter F.C. Selous. According to the *Dictionary of National Biography* Selous possessed "indomitable courage, enduring energy and great tenacity" and had become something of a celebrity through his books, in particular *A Hunter's Wanderings in Africa* (1881).

The adventure-loving American Theodore Roosevelt, who was destined to become the twenty-sixth president of the USA in 1901 and was for some years a friend of Haggard's, was among those who subscribed to this view until disabused of the fact by the author himself. Writing in his diary in July 1916 following a meeting between the two men, Haggard states:

> I found that he [Roosevelt] is fond of my stories, reminding me of incidents in passages in them I had almost forgotten. Allan Quatermain, he said, he had always taken to be me, clothed in the body of Selous – as many others have done. I told him that he was right as to the first but not as to the second, since at the time I conceived Allan Quatermain I did not know Selous. He said he was especially fond of the old boy's [Quatermain's] reflections and moralizings, and seemed to think that some of my work would live.

The truth is that Haggard was Quatermain, as he endeavoured to set right once and for all in his autobiography, *The Days of My Life*, published in 1926:

> To be honest, I always find it easy to write of Allan Quatermain, who, after all, is only myself set in a variety of imagined situations, thinking my thoughts and looking at life through my eyes. Indeed, there are several subjects with which I always find it not difficult to deal – for instance Old Egypt, Norsemen and African savages. Of these last, however, I prefer to write in the company of Allan Quatermain.

Even before *King Solomon's Mines* appeared in the bookshops in the autumn of 1885 Haggard began another book about Quatermain, which he intended to be the hunter's last adventure. Starting on 17 July he again wrote at great speed and completed *Allan Quatermain* on 28 September. The work would not, however, be published for almost two years, during which time an extraordinary cult had developed around Haggard's hero.

As has proved the case with a number of the immortal characters of fiction, Quatermain soon began to take on a life of his own beyond the pages that Haggard had written. In Africa, for example, a road leading to some excavations in Zimbabwe was named Allan Quatermain's

Road, although Haggard maintained that all the ruins in *King Solomon's Mines* were the fruit of his imagination. In the sequel, *Allan Quatermain*, Haggard invented a mission station at an unexplored spot on the Tana River that was attacked by the Masai. In subsequent editions of the book he was forced to insert the following self-explanatory note:

> By a very strange and sad coincidence, since this book was written, the Masai, in April 1886, massacred a missionary and his wife – Mr. and Mrs. Houghton – on this same Tana River and at the spot described. These are, I believe, the first white people who are known to have fallen victims to this cruel tribe.

In the third of the hunter's adventures, *Maiwa's Revenge* (1888), Haggard describes in detail the struggle his hero had with some natives who pursue him up the face of a cliff and one of whom grabs hold of his ankle. Quatermain escapes by firing down on the man along the line of his leg with a pistol. Referring to this scene in *The Days of My Life*, he wrote:

> Some years later a gentleman arrived at my house in Norfolk whose name, I think, was Ebbage, and on whose card was printed the vague and remote address, "Matabeleland". He informed me that he had travelled specially from London to inquire how on earth I had learned the details of his escape from certain savages, as he had never mentioned them to a single soul. Before he left I satisfied myself that his adventure and that invented by myself and described in the tale, which I had thought one of a somewhat original sort, were in every particular identical.

In 1919 Allan Quatermain made the front pages of the British newspapers because of a superstition that had apparently become attached to it. Haggard again provides the details in a diary entry for 29 March:

Quatermain's escape in *Maiwa's Revenge*, drawn by Hookway Cowles

Superstitions of every sort are rampant now-a-days. Here is an instance which I take from the *Daily News* of 26th March. It seems that whenever a certain battery were sent any of my books, the S.O.S. signal was immediately received, three of them coming when one of the battery was reading *Allan Quatermain*. So poor Allan and the rest were always burned upon arrival, with the result that the S.O.S. calls declined. As the *Daily News* remarks: "The story might not be so surprising if the books had not been Sir Rider Haggard's and the battery itself had appealed for help." Also I may point out that the prodigy might be read otherwise. Allan was always a helpful person and his spirit on these occasions obviously indicated when and where help was needed! In the Twentieth Century can anything be more childish and ridiculous than this burning of books for such a reason?

There are, of course, several other memorable characters to be found among the total of eighteen novels and short stories that record Allan Quatermain's life from 1817 to 1885. (See the "Allan Quatermain Saga" on page 33.) There are his friends, Sir Henry Curtis, a tall, blond-haired English gentlemen, and Captain John Good, the punctilious retired naval officer, who are first encountered in *King Solomon's Mines*. Umslopogaas, the mighty Zulu warrior, who more than once comes to the white hunter's aid, was based on a Swazi warrior who befriended the young Haggard and told him many stories about his people. (Andrew Lang, who was the first reader of many of the author's manuscripts and who was a great admirer of the African, said of him in 1892: "Umslopogaas is one of my dearest friends in fiction – I will never desert him.") And, perhaps most memorable of all, Zikali, the dwarfish witch-doctor who is intent on destroying the Zulu Nation: the Moriarty, indeed, to Quatermain's Sherlock Holmes.

All of these characters are to be found, albeit sometimes in minor roles, in the stories that are reprinted in these pages. "Hunter Quartermain's Story" is an ideal opener because it takes the form of an after-dinner hunting tale recounted by Allan Quatermain to Sir Henry Curtis and Captain John Good in the immediate aftermath of their famous exploits at King Solomon's mines. Haggard in fact wrote the gripping little adventure shortly after the success of his best-seller as a result of a request by Olive Schreiner – the South African novelist and champion of women's rights – to contribute a story to a book being published to raise funds for the North-Eastern

Hospital for Children in Hackney Road, London. The anthology, *In A Good Cause*, contained several other stories – including Schreiner's own "African Moonshine" – plus poetry and illustrations, and it was published in time for Christmas 1885. Haggard's tale is unique

Hunter Quatermain with his trio of friends, Captain John Good, Sir Henry Curtis and the Swazi warrior Umslopogaas

among the Quatermain canon in that it is the only one in which he is described as having a "curious little accent, which made his speech noticeable".

The following year Haggard produced another excellent anecdotal tale of his hero, "Long Odds", once again in the company of Curtis and Good. It was snapped up by *Macmillan's Magazine* – which had been responsible some nine years earlier for publishing the author's very first article, "The Transvaal" – and appeared in the February 1886 issue. (When "Long Odds" was first published in America in 1899 in the *Household Library* it appeared under the title "The Spring of a Lion".)

The return visit to Garsington in 1887 for his article "On Going

Back" inspired Haggard's third Quatermain short story, "A Tale of Three Lions". It is the account of a desperate hunt for gold and the savagery of a trio of lions. Despite the brevity of the tale it was first published in three parts in the October, November and December 1887 issues of *Atalanta Magazine*, apparently as a gimmick to increase sales. It was the first of the Quatermain short stories to be published in America in December 1887 by J.W. Lovell of New York in their *Lovell's Library* series, cumbersomely retitled "Allan the Hunter: A Tale of Three Lions (and Prince, another Lion)".

The fourth Quatermain short story did not materialize from Haggard's pen for almost twenty-five years, so busy was he kept on his novels about the hunter and other literary and public service for which he was awarded a knighthood in 1912. "Magepa the Buck" was, though, well worth the wait and had evolved once again from the author's generosity towards children's charities. This had become all the keener following the tragic death of his only son, "Jock" Rider Haggard, who had died in 1891 at the tender age of ten. Haggard was a keen supporter of the National Society for the Prevention of Cruelty to Children, and at the organization's annual meeting in May 1895 he seconded a resolution tabled by the Earl of Iddesleigh that still resounds as strongly today as it did over a century ago:

> That this meeting of the NSPCC having regard alike to the interests of the unhappy children of the country, and to the country's domestic and social welfare, would respectfully impress upon the Magistrates of the land the importance of their supporting the Society's endeavour to enforce upon neglectful parents the discharge of parental duty.

In seconding the resolution Haggard spoke about the need for parents to play a full part in the raising and education of their children and told a story from his African experiences to illustrate his argument. The writer's speech was later reprinted with that of other speakers in a pamphlet issued by the NSPCC, and the story can be quite clearly identified as the basis for "Magepa the Buck". It describes the amazing feat of endurance by a Zulu warrior in the same mould as Haggard's friend Umslopogaas, risking his own life to save that of a child. The final version of the tale was published in *Pears' Christmas Annual* for 1912 and reprinted two years later in another charity publication, *Princess Mary's Gift Book*.

The witch-doctor Zikali has, however, none of the finer feelings of Umslopogaas or Magepa. He is hell-bent in his determination to bring about the downfall of the Zulu Nation by the use of plotting and magic. Haggard first introduced this evil mastermind in the Quatermain novel *Marie* (1912), although his presence is mentioned only in a few remarks. But in four further adventures – *Child of Storm* (1913), *Heu-Hue; or The Monster* (1924), *She and Allan* (1921) and *Finished* (1917) – Zikali's machinations have a considerable effect on the hunter's life. The wizard dies finally with his vengeance accomplished in the aptly named *Finished*, having become a character that millions of readers loved to hate. So much so, in fact, that when the first Quatermain story was adapted for the stage in 1914 the souvenir programme contained an episode "Zikali the Wizard" by Haggard to introduce both his hero and his arch-rival to those theatre goers new to the characters.

The play was called *Mameena*, and it was an adaptation of *Child of the Storm* – Haggard's favourite among all his books – dramatized by the actor-manager Oscar Asche at the Globe Theatre, London, opening on 7 October 1914. Despite the war clouds hovering over London, the show was lavishly produced with three Zulu kraals and numerous African costumes being hired to lend authenticity. Two Zulu chieftains were also brought to London to appear alongside Harcourt Beatty and Herbert Grimwood, who played Quatermain and Zikali respectively. The hunter's bravery in defeating a plot by the witch-doctor against the Zulu beauty Mameena (Lily Brayton), played out against the backdrop of a torrid wasteland, captured the public's imagination, and the production ran for over one hundred and thirty performances.

The final story here, "Allan's Wife", published as a booklet by

Spencer Blackett in 1889, rounds off the saga of the white hunter. It completes the story after his death in June 1885 as described in *Allan Quatermain*. Haggard's decision to kill off his character in the second book rebounded on him – a similar reaction greeted Arthur Conan Doyle when he dispatched Sherlock Holmes and Professor Moriarty over the Reichenbach Falls in *The Final Problem* in 1893; he was then forced by an outraged public's demand to "resurrect" the sleuth of Baker Street. Rider Haggard in his turn had to satisfy the clamour of his readers by continuing for the rest of his life to recount the earlier adventures of Quatermain – the final adventure, *Allan and the Ice Gods*, not, in fact, appearing until after the author's death.

"Allan's Wife," the longest tale in this collection, answers questions about Quatermain's early life in Garsington and introduces Stella Carson, whom he rescues from a fire and later makes his wife. One question which remains unanswered is whether Haggard himself rescued his flirtatious friend, Blanche – the model for Stella Carson – from an untimely end and thereafter nursed a passion for the girl which may or may not have been consummated. Sadly, there is no evidence to substantiate or refute the theory.

Allan and the Ice Gods, the last Quatermain novel, published post-humously in May 1927, was something of a collaboration between Haggard and his friend Rudyard Kipling, whom he had first met at the Savile Club in London. The two men had struck up a friendship after the publication of Haggard's brilliant pioneer "Lost Race" novel, *She*, in 1887. The tale of a fabulously beautiful Egyptian princess, Ayesha, "She-Who-Must-Be-Obeyed", it had cemented his fame and also earned him acclaim in the popular press as "King Romance". (Later, in 1919, Haggard could not resist the temptation to bring together his two most famous characters in *She and Allen*, not one of the most successful of the series.)

During one of their meetings Kipling startled his new friend by declaring that the success they had both enjoyed was down to them being "telephone wires". He explained, "*You* didn't write *She*, you know – something wrote it through you!" The men's shared interest

in mysticism and ancient history lead to them discussing many of
their later projects. In January 1922 Haggard confided in his diary
after a day spent with Kipling:

> As usual Kipling and I talked till we were tired about everything in
> heaven above and earth beneath. Incidentally, too, we hammered out
> the skeleton plot for a romance I propose to write under some such
> title as *Allan and the Ice Gods* which is to deal with the terrible
> advance of one of the Ice Ages upon a little handful of the primitive
> inhabitants of the earth. He has a marvellously fertile mind and I
> never knew anyone quite so quick at seizing and developing an idea.
> We spent a most amusing two hours over this plot and I have brought
> home the results in several sheets of MS written by him and myself.

Comparison of these sheets of paper with the published book provides a clear indication as to just how substantial was Kipling's
contribution to this final Quatermain story. If Haggard had not died
on 14 May 1925, peacefully at his home in Ditchingam, who is to say
that he might not have given his friend credit for his part in this *Tale
of Beginnings*, as he subtitled his hero's last foray
into history?

Allan Quatermain's fame was, however, estab-
lished long before this date, and the only surprise
is that he has had to wait until now for all the

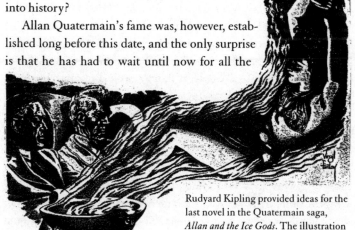

Rudyard Kipling provided ideas for the
last novel in the Quatermain saga,
Allan and the Ice Gods. The illustration
is by Virgil Finlay.

short stories about him to be collected together. In complete contrast, however, within a matter of months of the appearance of *King Solomon's Mines* other authors were busy using the Dark Continent as the background for their stories and books – many failing miserably because of their lack of Haggard's hard-won personal knowledge – while Quatermain himself was being given the accolade of scores of imitations and parodies, notably *Punch's* comic "Adam Slaughter-man" by "Walker Weird, author of *Hee Hee, Solomon's Ewers &c.*" (August, 1887); John De Morgan's *King Solomon's Treasures* (published in New York in 1887); and "From Mr. Allan Quatermain to Sir Henry Curtis" (1899) by Haggard's mentor Andrew Lang, in which several characters from the books attempt to lure the white hunter out of what they fear to be his early retirement to an African farm. (*Vide* Sherlock Holmes' retreat to Sussex to keep bees!)

Film-makers were not slow in realizing the appeal of Allan Quatermain, either. In 1919 both *King Solomon's Mines* and *Allan Quatermain* were turned into silent black-and-white movies directed by H. Lisle Lucoque. Appropriately they were made by the African Film Production Company and filmed partly in their Killarney Studios in Johannesburg and partly on location. The youthful English actor Albert Lawrence played Quatermain in both pictures, complete with a heavy beard and the usual histrionic acting style of the era. The hunter's two friends also appeared in both pictures, Holford J. Hamlin playing Sir Henry Curtis and Ray Brown as Captain Good.

Almost twenty years passed before Quatermain returned to the screen, with the great theatrical actor Sir Cedric Hardwicke in the lead role of the Gaumont British Pictures version of *King Solomon's Mines* (1937). John Loder and Roland Young co-starred as Curtis and Good, with Anna Lee as an additional and totally unnecessary female lead. Although primarily shot in the company's English studios by director Robert Stevenson some location shooting was done in the Umgeni Valley in Natal, with the American actor–singer Paul Robeson making an impressive Umbopa. The Hollywood leading man Stewart Granger appeared in MGM's version of the same story

produced after another lengthy break by Sam Zimbalist in 1950.
Helen Deutsch's screenplay introduced Deborah Kerr as Sir Henry's
daughter, Elizabeth Curtis.

The best-selling novelist James Clavell took even greater liberties

The "Adam Slaughterman" parody from *Punch*, 27 August 1887

with Haggard's original in MGM's 1959 remake entitled *Watusi*. Al
Zimbalist, son of the aforementioned Sam, produced the film, which
starred George Montgomery as "Harry" Quatermain, son of Allan,
retracing his father's footsteps to the famous mines. In 1963 Italian
director Piero Regnoli abandoned virtually every shred of the original

story for the Panda Company's *Nelle Miniere di Re Salomoni* (*Samson in King Solomon's Mines*), starring muscle-man Reg Park and the pulchritudinous Wandisa Guida.

Richard Chamberlain, a heart-throb of films and television since the 1960s, brought a handsome but often brutal Quatermain to the screen in the bloodstained Cannon extravaganza, *King Solomon's Mines* (1985), which was described by the *Daily Mail* at the time as "an Indiana Jones-type romp through Mumbo-Jumbo land". Directed by J. Lee Thompson, it was scripted by Gene Quintano and James R. Silke, who had audiences in uproar with lines such as, "Soon the girl will be ours and Quatermain will be grovelling at my feet." The girl in question was the American beauty Sharon Stone, and the man with the evil intentions towards her that master of screen villainy Herbert Lom.

One further version of *Allan Quatermain* has been made in the interim, in 1979, by producers Alvin Rakoff and Susan Lewis, who retitled the story *King Solomon's Treasure*. Rakoff himself directed the Technicolor saga, starring John Colico as the hunter with David McCullum and Patrick Macnee as Curtis and Good respectively. The sex-symbol actress, Britt Ekland, appeared as the beautiful Queen Nyaleptha. Since that date there have been no further travesties of the Quatermain saga, but hopes are again high among admirers of Haggard's work that Sean Connery, the former James Bond, now in his seventies and recognized as one of the world's great actors, will add a new dimension to the immortal hunter in *The League of Extraordinary Gentlemen* (2003), the tale of a group of literary heroes who serve Queen Victoria.

Both Rider Haggard and Allan Quatermain will, I am sure, continue to be highly regarded by readers hungry for unadorned tales of rugged and colourful adventure. I am supported in this conviction by Graham Greene, who devoted a special article to "Rider Haggard's Secret", in which he wrote: "Rider Haggard was perhaps the greatest of all the writers who enchanted us when we were young. Enchantment was just what he exercised: he fixed pictures in our minds that the years have been unable to wear away." Another famous writer, C.S. Lewis, was equally convinced: "Haggard's best work will survive because it is based on an appeal well above the high-water mark. The fullest tides of fashion cannot demolish it. A great myth is relevant as long as the predicament of humanity lasts; as long as humanity itself lasts."

Hammond Innes, who until his death in 1998 was one of the most popular contemporary novelists writing in the Rider Haggard tradition, was also a great admirer of Allan Quatermain. He lived in the same East Anglian countryside where Haggard spent much of his life and like him travelled extensively in Africa in order to collect material for his own brand of high adventure. It was during a meal we shared together in the Suffolk village where he lived that "Ralph" Innes, as he was known to his friends, encouraged me to collect together all the Quatermain short stories. "It can only have one result," he said with an acknowledgement to the genius of the man who had inspired his own career. "It will encourage lots of readers to plunge once more into his incredible mine of romanticism." I hope that his words will come true, because Rider Haggard is a writer who should never be neglected nor allowed to go out of fashion: a true storyteller.

Peter Haining
Boxford, Suffolk, 2003

Readers should note that the "Editor" alluded to in the footnotes within this book is not the present editor and that the notes are taken from the original editions of the stories.

The Allan Quatermain Saga

A chronology of the novels and short stories, including original publication dates and the years in which the adventures take place

1817	Birth of Allan Quatermain, Garsingham, Oxfordshire
1835–8	*Marie* [novel] (1912)
1842–69	"Allan's Wife" [short story] (1889)
1854–6	*Child of Storm* [novel] (1913)
1854	"Zikali the Wizard" [short story] (1914)
1858	"A Tale of Three Lions" [short story] (1887)
1859	*Maiwa's Revenge* [novel] (1888)
1868	"Hunter Quatermain's Story" [short story] (1885)
1869	"Long Odds" [short story] (1886)
1870	*The Holy Flower* [novel] (1915)
1871	*Heu-Heu, or The Monster* [novel] (1924)
1872	*She and Allan* [novel] (1921)
1873	*The Treasure of the Lake* [novel] (1926)
1874	*The Ivory Child* [novel] (1916)
1879	*Finished* [novel] (1917)
1879	"Magepa the Buck" [short story] (1912)
1880	*King Solomon's Mines* [novel] (1885)
1882	*The Ancient Allan* [novel] (1920)
1883	*Allan and the Ice Gods* [novel] (1927)
1884–5	*Allan Quatermain* [novel] (1887)
June, 1885	Death of Allan Quatermain, Zu-Vendis, Africa

The "official" portrait of Allan Quatermain, drawn by Charles Kerr

Hunter Quatermain's Story

Sir Henry Curtis is, as everybody acquainted with him knows, one of the most hospitable men on earth. It was in the course of the enjoyment of his hospitality at his place in Yorkshire the other day that I heard the hunting story which I am now about to transcribe. Many of those who read it will no doubt have heard some of the strange rumours that are flying about to the effect that Sir Henry Curtis and his friend Captain Good, R.N., found a vast treasure of diamonds out in the heart of Africa the other day, supposed to have been hidden by the Egyptians, or King Solomon, or somebody. I first saw the matter alluded to in a paragraph in one of the society papers the day before I started for Yorkshire to pay my visit to Curtis, and arrived, needless to say, burning with curiosity; for there is something very fascinating to the mind in the idea of hidden treasure. When I got to the Hall, I at once tackled Curtis about it, and he did not deny the truth of the story; but on my pressing him to tell it he would not, nor would Good, who was also staying in the house.

"You would not believe me if I did," he said with one of the hearty laughs which seem to come right out of those great lungs of his. "You must wait till Hunter Quatermain comes; he will arrive here from Africa to-night, and I am not going to say a word about the matter, or Good either, until he turns up. Quatermain was with us all through; he has known about the business for years and years, and if it had not been for him we should not have been here to-day. I am off to meet him presently."

I could not get a word more out of him, nor could anybody else, though we were all dying of curiosity, especially some of the ladies. I shall never forget their faces in the drawing-room before dinner when Good produced a great rough diamond, weighing fifty carats or more, and told them that he had many larger than that. If ever I saw curiosity and envy printed on fair faces, I saw it then.

It was just at that moment that the door was opened, and Mr. Allan Quatermain announced, whereupon Good shovelled the diamond into his pocket, and sprang at a little man who came limping shyly into the room, convoyed by Sir Henry Curtis himself.

"Here he is, Good, safe and sound," said Sir Henry, gleefully. "Ladies and gentlemen, let me introduce you to one of the oldest hunters and the very best shot in Africa, who has killed more elephants and lions than any other man alive."

Everybody turned and stared politely at the curious-looking little lame man, and though his size was insignificant, he was quite worth staring at. He had short grizzled hair, which stood about an inch above his head like the bristles of a brush, large brown eyes, that seemed to notice everything, and a withered face, tanned absolutely the colour of mahogany from exposure to the weather. He spoke, too, when he returned Good's enthusiastic greeting, with a curious little accent, which made his speech noticeable.

It so happened that I sat next to Mr. Allan Quatermain at dinner, and, of course, did my best to draw him; but he was not to be drawn. He admitted that he had recently been a long journey into the interior of Africa with Sir Henry Curtis and Captain Good, and that they had found treasure, and then politely turned the subject and began to ask me questions about England, where he had never been before. Of course, I did not find this very interesting, and so cast about for some means to bring the conversation round again.

Now, we were dining in a sort of oak-panelled vestibule, and on the wall opposite to me were fixed two gigantic elephant tusks, and under them a pair of buffalo horns, very rough and knotted, showing that they came off an old bull, and with the tip of one horn split and chipped. I noticed that Hunter Quatermain's eyes kept glancing at these trophies, and took an occasion to ask him if he knew anything about them.

"I ought to," he answered, with a little laugh; "the elephant to which those tusks belonged tore one of our party right in two about eighteen months ago, and as for the buffalo horns, they were nearly the death of me, and were the end of a servant of mine to whom I was much attached. I gave them to Sir Henry when he left Natal some months ago"; and Mr. Quatermain sighed and turned to answer a question from the lady whom he had taken down to dinner, and who, needless to say, was also employed in trying to pump him about the diamonds.

Indeed, all round the table there was a simmer of scarcely suppressed excitement, which, when the servants had left the room, could no longer be restrained.

"Now, Mr. Quatermain," said the lady next him, "we have been kept in an agony of suspense by Sir Henry and Captain Good, who have persistently refused to tell us a word of this story about the hidden treasure till you came, and we simply can bear it no longer; so, please, begin at once."

"Yes," said everybody, "go on please."

Hunter Quatermain glanced round the table apprehensively; he did not seem to appreciate finding himself the object of so much curiosity.

"Ladies and gentlemen," he said at last, with a shake of his grizzled head, "I am very sorry to disappoint you, but I cannot do it. It is this way. At the request of Sir Henry and Captain Good I have written down a true and plain account of King Solomon's Mines and how we found them, so you will soon all be able to learn all about that wonderful adventure for yourselves; but until then I will say nothing about it, not from any wish to disappoint your curiosity, or to make myself important, but simply because the whole story partakes so much of the marvellous, that I am afraid to tell it in a piecemeal, hasty fashion, for fear I shall be set down as one of those common fellows of whom there are so many in my profession, who are not ashamed to narrate things they have not seen, and even to tell wonderful stories about wild animals they have never killed. And I think that my companions in adventure, Sir Henry Curtis and Captain Good, will bear me out in what I say."

"Yes, Quatermain, I think you are quite right," said Sir Henry. "Precisely the same considerations have forced Good and myself to hold our tongues. We did not wish to be bracketed with – well, with other famous travellers."

There was a murmur of disappointment at these announcements.

"I believe you are all hoaxing us," said the young lady next to Mr. Quatermain, rather sharply.

"Believe me," answered the old hunter, with a quaint sort of courtesy and a little bow of his grizzled head; "though I have lived all my life in the wilderness, and amongst savages, I have neither the heart, nor the want of manners, to wish to deceive one so lovely."

Whereat the young lady, who was pretty, looked appeased.

"This is very dreadful," I broke in. "We ask for bread and you give us a stone, Mr. Quatermain. The least that you can do is to tell us the story of the tusks opposite and the buffalo horns underneath. We won't let you off with less."

"I am but a poor story-teller," put in the old hunter, "but if you will forgive my want of skill, I shall be happy to tell you, not the story of the tusks, for it is part of the history of our journey to King Solomon's Mines, but that of the buffalo horns beneath them, which is now ten years old."

"Bravo, Quatermain!" said Sir Henry. "We shall all be delighted. Fire away! Fill up your glass first."

The little man did as he was bid, took a sip of claret, and began: "About ten years ago, I was hunting up in the far interior of Africa, at a place called Gatgarra, not a great way from the Chobe River. I had with me four native servants, namely, a driver and voorlooper, or leader, who were natives of Matabeleland, a Hottentot called Hans, who had once been the slave of a Transvaal Boer, and a Zulu hunter, who had for five years accompanied me upon my trips, and whose name was Mashune. Now near Gatgarra I found a fine piece of healthy, park-like country, where the grass was very good, considering the time of year; and here I made a little camp or head-quarter settlement, from whence I went on expeditions on all sides in search of game, especially elephant. My luck, however, was bad; I got but little ivory. I was therefore very glad when some natives brought me news that a large herd of elephants were feeding in a valley about thirty miles away. At first I thought of trekking down to the valley, waggon and all, but gave up the idea on hearing that it was infested with the deadly 'tsetse' fly, which is certain death to all animals, except man, donkeys, and wild game. So I reluctantly determined to leave the waggon in the charge of the Matabele leader and driver, and to start on a trip into the thorn country, accompanied only by the Hottentot Hans and Mashune.

"Accordingly on the following morning we started, and on the evening of the next day reached the spot where the elephants were reported to be. But here again we were met by ill luck. That the elephants had been there was evident enough, for their spoor was plentiful, and so were other traces of their presence in the shape of mimosa trees torn out of the ground, and placed topsy-turvy on their flat crowns, in order to enable the great beasts to feed on their sweet roots; but the elephants themselves were conspicuous by their absence, having elected to move on. This being so, there was only one thing to do, and that was to move after them, which we did, and a pretty hunt they led us. For a fortnight or more we dodged about after those elephants, coming up with them on two occasions, and a splendid herd they were – only, however, to lose them again. At length we came up with them a third time, and I managed to shoot one bull, and then they made right off again, where it was useless to try and follow them. After this I gave it up in disgust, and we made the best of our way back to the camp, not in the sweetest of tempers, carrying the tusks of the elephant I had shot. It was on the afternoon of the fifth day of our tramp that we reached the little Koppie overlooking the spot where the waggon stood, and I confess that I climbed it with a pleasurable sense of home-coming, for his waggon is the hunter's home, as much as his house is a civilized person's. I reached the top of the Koppie, and looked in the direction where the friendly white tent of the waggon should be, and there was no waggon, nothing but a black burnt plain stretching away as far as the eye could reach. I rubbed my eyes and looked again, and made out on the spot of the camp not my waggon, but some charred beams of wood. Half wild with grief and anxiety, I ran at full speed down the slope of the Koppie, and across the bit of plain below to the spring of water, where my camp had been, followed by Hans and Mashune. I was soon there, only to find that my worst suspicions were confirmed. The waggon and all its contents, including my spare guns and ammunition, had been destroyed by a grass fire.

"Now before I started, I had left orders with the driver to burn off the grass round the camp, in order to guard against accidents of this nature, and this was the reward of my folly: a very proper illustration of the necessity, especially where natives are concerned, of doing a thing oneself if one wants it done at all. Evidently the lazy rascals had not burnt round the waggon; most probably, indeed, they had themselves carelessly fired the tall and resinous tambouki grass near by; the wind had driven the flames on to the waggon tent, and there was quickly an end of the whole thing. As for the driver and leader, I know not what became of them: probably fearing my anger, they bolted, taking the oxen with them. I have never seen them from that hour to this. I sat down there on the black veldt by the spring, and gazed at the charred axles and disselboom of my waggon, and I can assure you, ladies and gentlemen, I felt inclined to cry. As for Mashune and Hans they cursed away vigorously, one in Zulu and the other in Dutch. Ours was a pretty position. We were nearly three hundred miles away from Bamangwato, the capital of Khama's country, which was the nearest spot where we could get any help, and our ammunition, spare guns, clothing, food, and everything else were all totally destroyed. I had just what I stood in, which was a flannel shirt, a pair of "veldt-schoons" or shoes of raw hide, my eight-bore rifle, and a few cartridges. Hans and Mashune had also each a Martini rifle and some cartridges, not many. And it was with this equipment that we had to undertake a journey of three hundred miles through a desolate and almost uninhabited region. I can assure you that I have never been in a worse position, and I have been in some queer ones. However, these things are the natural incidents of a hunter's life, and the only thing to do was to make the best of them.

"Accordingly, after passing a comfortless night by the remains of my waggon, we started next morning on our long journey towards civilization. Now if I were to set to work to tell you all the troubles and incidents of that dreadful journey I should keep you listening here till midnight; so I will, with your permission, pass on to the particular adventure of which the pair of buffalo horns opposite are the melancholy memento.

"We had been travelling for about a month, living and getting along as best we could, when one evening we camped some forty miles from Bamangwato. By this time we were indeed in a melancholy plight, footsore, half starved, and utterly worn out; and, in addition, I was suffering from a sharp attack of fever, which half blinded me and made me as weak as a babe. Our ammunition, too, was exhausted; I had only one cartridge left for my eight-bore rifle, and Hans and Mashune, who were armed with Martini Henrys, had three between them. It was about an hour from sundown when we halted and lit a fire, for luckily we had still a few matches. It was a charming spot to camp, I remember. Just off the game track we were following was a little hollow, fringed about with flat-crowned mimosa trees, and at the bottom of the hollow, a spring of clear water welled up out of the earth, and formed a pool, round the edges of which grew an abundance of watercresses of an exactly similar kind to those which were handed round the table just now. Now we had no food of any kind left, having that morning devoured the last remains of a little oribe antelope, which I had shot two days previously. Accordingly Hans, who was a better shot than Mashune, took two of the three remaining Martini cartridges, and started out to see if he could not kill a buck for supper. I was too weak to go myself.

"Meanwhile Mashune employed himself in dragging together

some dead boughs from the mimosa trees to make a sort of 'skerm', or shelter for us to sleep in, about forty yards from the edge of the pool of water. We had been greatly troubled with lions in the course of our long tramp, and only on the previous night had very nearly been attacked by them, which made me nervous, especially in my weak state. Just as we had finished the skerm, or rather something which did duty for one, Mashune and I heard a shot apparently fired about a mile away.

"'Hark to it!' sung out Mashune in Zulu, more I fancy by way of keeping his spirits up than for any other reason, for he was a sort of black Mark Tapley, and very cheerful under difficulties. 'Hark to the wonderful sound with which the "Maboona" (the Boers) shook our fathers to the ground at the battle of the Blood River. We are hungry now, my father; our stomachs are small and withered up like a dried ox's paunch, but they will soon be full of good meat. Hans is a Hottentot, and an "umfagozan" (a low fellow), but he shoots straight – ah! he certainly shoots straight. Be of a good heart, my father, there will soon be meat upon the fire, and we shall rise up men.'

"And so he went on talking nonsense till I told him to stop, because he made my head ache with his empty words.

"Shortly after we heard the shot the sun sank in his red splendour, and there fell upon earth and sky the awful hush of the African wilderness. The lions were not up as yet, they would probably wait for the moon, and the birds and beasts were all at rest. I cannot describe the intensity of the quiet of the night: to me in my weak state, and fretting as I was over the non-return of the Hottentot Hans, it seemed almost ominous – as though Nature were brooding over some tragedy which was being enacted in her sight.

"It was quiet – quiet as death, and lonely as the grave.

"'Mashune,' I said at last, 'where is Hans; my heart is heavy for him.'

"'Nay, my father, I know not; mayhap he is weary, and sleeps, or mayhap he has lost his way.'

"'Mashune, art thou a boy to talk folly to me? Tell me, in all the years thou hast hunted by my side, didst thou ever know a Hottentot to lose his path or to sleep upon the way to camp?'

"'Nay, Macumazahn' (that is my native name, and means the man who "gets up by night", or who "is always awake"), 'I know not where he is.'

"But though we talked thus, we neither of us liked to hint at what was in both our minds, namely, that misfortune had overtaken the poor Hottentot.

"'Mashune,' I said at last, 'go down to the water and bring me of those green herbs that grow there. I am hungered, and must eat something.'

"'Nay, my father; surely there are ghosts there; they come out of the water at night, and sit upon the banks to dry themselves. An Isanusi told it me.'*

"Mashune was, I think, one of the bravest men I ever knew in the daytime, but he had a more than civilized dread of the supernatural.

"'Must I go myself, thou fool?' I said sternly.

"'Nay, Macumazahn, if thy heart yearns for strange things like a sick woman, I go, even if the ghosts devour me.'

"And accordingly he went, and soon returned with a large bundle of watercresses, of which I ate greedily.

"'Art thou not hungry?' I asked the great Zulu presently, as he sat eyeing me eating.

"'Never was I hungrier, my father.'

"'Then eat,' and I pointed to the watercresses.

"'Nay, I cannot eat those herbs.'

"'If thou dost not eat thou wilt starve: eat, Mashune.'

"He stared at the watercresses doubtfully for a while, and at last seized a handful and crammed them into his mouth, crying out as he did so, 'Oh, why was I born that I should live to feed on green weeds like an ox; surely if my mother could have known it she would have killed me when I was born'; and so he went on lamenting between

---

* Isanusi, witch-finder

each fistful of watercresses till all were finished, when he declared that he was full indeed of stuff, but it lay very cold on his stomach, 'like snow upon a mountain'. At any other time I should have laughed, for it must be admitted he had a ludicrous way of putting things. Zulus do not like green food.

"Just after Mashune had finished his watercress, we heard the loud 'woof woof' of a lion, who was evidently promenading round our little skerm much nearer than was pleasant. Indeed, on looking into the darkness and listening intently, I could hear his snoring breath, and catch the light of his great yellow eyes. We shouted loudly, and Mashune threw some sticks on the fire to frighten him, which apparently had the desired effect, for we saw no more of him for a while.

"Just after we had had this fright from the lion, the moon rose in her fullest splendour, throwing a robe of silver light over all the earth. I never saw a more beautiful moonrise. I remember that sitting there in the skerm I could with ease read faint pencil notes in my pocket-book. As soon as the moon was up game began to trek down to the water just below us. I could, from where I sat, see all sorts of them passing along a little ridge that ran to our right on their way to the drinking place. Indeed, one buck – a large eland – came within twenty yards of the skerm, and stood at gaze, staring at it suspiciously, his beautiful head and twisted horns standing out clearly against the sky. I had, I recollect, every mind to have a pull at him on the chance of providing ourselves with a good supply of beef; but remembering that we had but two cartridges left, and the extreme uncertainty of a shot by moonlight, I at length decided to refrain. The eland presently moved on to the water, and a minute or two afterwards there arose a great sound of splashing, followed by the quick fall of galloping hoofs.

" 'What's that, Mashune?' I asked.

" 'That dam lion; buck smell him,' replied the Zulu in English, of which he had a very superficial knowledge.

"Scarcely were the words out of his mouth before we heard a

sort of whine over the other side of the pool, which was instantly answered by a loud coughing roar close to us.

"'By Jove!' I said, 'there are two of them. They have lost the buck; we must look out they don't nobble us.' And again we made up the fire, and set to and shouted, with the result that the lions moved off.

"'Mashune,' I said, 'you watch till the moon gets over that tree, when it will be the middle of the night. Then wake me. Watch well now, or the lions will be picking those worthless bones of yours before you are three hours older. I must rest a little, or I shall die.'

"'Koos,' (chief) answered the Zulu. 'Sleep, my father, sleep in peace; my eyes shall be open as the stars; and like the stars shall watch over you.'

"Although I was so weak, I could not at once follow his advice. To begin with, my head ached with fever, and I was torn with anxiety as to the fate of the Hottentot Hans; and, indeed, as to our own fate, left with sore feet, empty stomachs, and two cartridges, to find our way to Bamangwato, forty miles off. Then the mere sensation of knowing that there are one or more hungry lions prowling round you somewhere in the dark is disquieting, however well one may be used to it, and, by keeping the attention on the stretch, tends to prevent one from sleeping. In addition to all these troubles, too, I was, I remember, seized with a dreadful longing for a pipe of tobacco, whereas, under the circumstances, I might as well have longed for the moon.

"At last, however, I got off into an uneasy sleep as full of bad dreams as a prickly pear is of points, one of which, I recollect, was that I was setting my naked foot upon a cobra that rose upon its tail and hissed my name, 'Macumazahn', into my ear. Indeed, the cobra hissed with such persistency that at last I roused myself.

"'*Macumazahn, nanzia, nanzia!*' (there, there!) whispered Mashune's voice into my drowsy ears. Raising myself, I opened my eyes, and I saw Mashune kneeling by my side and pointing towards the water. Following the line of his outstretched hand, my eyes fell upon a sight that, old hunter as I was even in those days, made me jump. About twenty paces from the little skerm was a large ant-heap, and on the summit of the ant-heap, her four feet rather close together, so as to find standing space, stood the massive form of a big lioness. Her head was towards the skerm, and in the bright moonlight I saw her lower it and lick her paws.

"Mashune thrust the Martini rifle into my hands, whispering that it was loaded. I lifted it and covered the lioness, but found that even in that light I could not make out the fore-sight of the Martini. As it would be madness to fire without doing so, for the result would probably be that I should wound the lioness, if, indeed, I did not miss her altogether, I lowered the rifle; and, hastily tearing a fragment of paper from one of the leaves of my pocket-book, which I had been consulting just before I went to sleep, I proceeded to fix it on to the front sight. But all this took a little time, and before the paper was satisfactorily arranged, Mashune again gripped me by the arm, and pointed to a dark heap under the shade of a small mimosa tree which grew not more than ten paces from the skerm.

"'Well, what is it?' I whispered; 'I can see nothing.'

"'It is another lion,' he answered.

"'Nonsense, thy heart is dead with fear, thou seest double'; and I bent forward over the edge of the surrounding fence, and stared at the heap.

"Even as I said the words, the dark mass rose and stalked out into the moonlight. It was a magnificent, black-maned lion, one of the largest I had ever seen. When he had gone two or three steps he caught sight of me, halted, and stood there gazing straight towards us; he was so close that I could see the firelight reflected in his wicked, greenish eyes.

"'Shoot, shoot!' said Mashune. 'The devil is coming – he is going to spring!'

"I raised the rifle, and got the bit of paper on the fore-sight, straight on to a little patch of white hair just where the throat is set into the chest and shoulders. As I did so, the lion glanced back over his shoulder, as, according to my experience, a lion nearly always does before he springs. Then he dropped his body a little, and I saw his big paws spread out upon the ground as he put his weight on them to gather purchase. In haste I pressed the trigger of the Martini, and not an instant too soon; for, as I did so, he was in the act of springing. The report of the rifle rang out sharp and clear on the intense silence of the night, and in another second the great brute had landed on his head within four feet of us, and rolling over and over towards us, was sending the bushes which composed our little fence flying with convulsive strokes of his great paws. We sprang out of the other side of the 'skerm', and he rolled on to it and into it and then right through the fire. Next he raised himself and sat upon his haunches like a great dog, and began to roar. Heavens; how he roared! I never heard anything like it before or since. He kept filling his lungs with air, and then emitting it in the most heart-shaking volumes of sound. Suddenly, in the middle of one of the loudest roars, he rolled over on to his side and lay still, and I knew that he was dead. A lion generally dies upon his side.

"With a sigh of relief I looked up towards his mate upon the antheap. She was standing there apparently petrified with astonishment, looking over her shoulder, and lashing her tail; but, to our intense joy, when the dying beast ceased roaring, she turned, and, with one enormous bound, vanished into the night.

"Then we advanced cautiously towards the prostrate brute, Mashune droning an improvised Zulu song as he went, about how Macumazahn, the hunter of hunters, whose eyes are open by night as well as by day, put his hand down the lion's stomach when it came to devour him and pulled out his heart by the roots, &c., &c., by way of expressing his satisfaction at the turn events had taken in his hyperbolical Zulu way.

"There was no need for caution; the lion was as dead as though he had already been stuffed with straw. The Martini bullet had entered within an inch of the white spot I had aimed at, and travelled right through him, passing out at the right buttock, near the root of the tail. The Martini has wonderful driving power, though the shock it gives to the system is, comparatively speaking, slight, owing to the smallness of the hole it makes. But fortunately the lion is an easy beast to kill.

"I passed the rest of that night in a profound slumber, my head reposing upon the deceased lion's flank, a position that had, I thought, a beautiful touch of irony about it, though the smell of his singed hair was disagreeable. When I woke again the faint primrose lights of dawn were flushing in the eastern sky. For a moment I could not understand the chill sense of anxiety that lay like a lump of ice at my heart, till the feel and smell of the skin of the dead lion beneath my head recalled the circumstances in which we were placed. I rose, and eagerly looked round to see if I could discover any signs of Hans, who, if he had escaped accident, would surely return to us at dawn, but there were none. Then hope grew faint, and I felt that it was not well with the poor fellow. Setting Mashune to build up the fire I hastily removed the hide from the flank of the lion, which was indeed a splendid beast, and cutting off some lumps of flesh, we toasted and ate them greedily. Lion's flesh, strange as it may seem, is very good eating, and tastes more like veal than anything else.

"By the time that we had finished our much-needed meal the sun was getting up, and after a drink of water and a wash at the pool, we started to try and find Hans, leaving the dead lion to the tender mercies of the hyænas. Both Mashune and myself were, by constant practice, pretty good hands at tracking, and we had not much difficulty in following his spoor, faint as it was. We had gone on in this way for half-an-hour or so, and were, perhaps, a mile or more from the site of our camping-place, when we discovered the spoor of a solitary bull buffalo mixed up with the spoor of Hans, and were able, from various indications, to make out that he had been tracking the buffalo. At length we reached a little glade in which there grew a stunted old mimosa thorn, with a peculiar and overhanging formation of root, under which a porcupine, or an ant-bear, or some such animal, had hollowed out a wide-lipped hole. About ten or fifteen paces from this thorn-tree there was a thick patch of bush.

"'See, Macumazahn! see!' said Mashune, excitedly, as we drew near the thorn; 'the buffalo has charged him. Look here, he stood to fire at him; look how firmly he planted his feet upon the earth; there is the mark of his crooked toe (Hans had one bent toe). Look! here the bull came like a boulder down the hill, his hoofs turning up the earth like a hoe. Hans had hit him: he bled as he came; there are the blood spots. It is all written down there, my father – there upon the earth.'

" 'Yes,' I said; 'yes; but *where is Hans?*'

"Even as I said it Mashune clutched my arm, and pointed to the stunted thorn just by us. Even now, gentlemen, it makes me feel sick when I think of what I saw.

"For fixed in a stout fork of the tree some eight feet from the ground was Hans himself, or rather his dead body, evidently tossed there by the furious buffalo. One leg was twisted round the fork, probably in a dying convulsion. In the side, just beneath the ribs, was a great hole, from which the entrails protruded. But this was not all. The other leg hung down to within five feet of the ground. The skin and most of the flesh were gone from it. For a moment we stood aghast, and gazed at this horrifying sight. Then I understood what had happened. The buffalo, with that devilish cruelty, which distinguishes the animal, had after his enemy was dead, stood underneath his body, and licked the flesh off the pendant leg with his file-like tongue. I had heard of such a thing before, but had always treated the stories as hunters' yarns; but I had no doubt about it now. Poor Hans' skeleton foot and ankle were an ample proof.

"We stood aghast under the tree, and stared and stared at this awful sight, when suddenly our cogitations were interrupted in a painful manner. The thick bush about fifteen paces off burst asunder with a crashing sound, and uttering a series of ferocious, pig-like grunts, the bull buffalo himself came charging out straight at us. Even as he came I saw the blood mark on his side where poor Hans' bullet had struck him, and also that, as is often the case with particularly savage buffaloes, his flanks had recently been terribly torn in an encounter with a lion.

"On he came, his head well up (a buffalo does not generally lower his head till he does so to strike); those great black horns – as I look at them before me, gentlemen, I seem to see them come charging at me as I did ten years ago, silhouetted against the green bush behind; on, on! With a shout Mashune bolted off sideways towards the bush. I had instinctively lifted my eight-bore, which I had in my hand. It would have been useless to fire at his head, for the dense horns would have turned the bullet; but as Mashune bolted, the bull slewed a little, with the momentary idea of following him, and as this gave me a ghost of a chance, I let drive my only cartridge at his shoulder. The bullet struck the shoulder blade and smashed it up, and then travelled on under the skin into his flank; but it did not stop him, though for a second he staggered. Throwing myself on to the ground I rolled, with the energy of despair, under the shelter of the projecting root of the thorn, crushing myself as far into the mouth of the ant-bear hole as I could. In a single instant he was after me. Kneeling down on his uninjured knee – for one leg, that of which I had broken the shoulder, was swinging helplessly to and fro – he set to work to try and hook me out of the hole with his crooked horn. At first he struck at me furiously, and it was one of the blows against the base of the tree which splintered the tip of the horn in the way that you see. Then he got more cunning, and shoving his head as far under the root as possible, made long semicircular sweeps at me, grunting furiously, and blowing saliva and hot steamy breath all over me. I was just out of reach of the horn, though every stroke, by widening the hole and making more room for his head, brought it closer to me, but every now and again I got heavy blows in the ribs from his muzzle. Feeling that I was being knocked silly, I made an effort, and seizing his rough tongue, which was hanging from his jaws, I twisted it with all my force. The great brute bellowed with pain and fury, and jerked himself backwards so strongly, that he dragged me some inches further from the mouth of the hole, and again made a sweep at me, catching me this time round the shoulder-joint in the hook of his horn.

"I felt that it was all up now, and began to holloa.

"'He has got me,' I shouted in mortal terror. '*Gwasa, Mashune, gwasa*' (stab, Mashune, stab).

"One hoist of the great head, and out of the hole I came like a periwinkle out of his shell. But even as I did so, I caught sight of Mashune's stalwart form advancing with his 'bangwan', or broad stabbing assegai raised above his head. In another quarter of a second I had fallen from the horn, and heard the blow of the spear, followed by the indescribable sound of steel shearing its way through flesh. I had fallen on my back, and looking up I saw that the gallant Mashune had driven the assegai two foot or more into the carcase of the buffalo, and was turning to fly.

"Alas! it was too late. Bellowing madly, and spouting blood from the mouth and nostrils, the devilish brute was on him, and had thrown him up like a feather, and then gored him twice as he lay. I struggled up with some wild idea of affording help, but before I had gone a step the buffalo gave one long sighing bellow, and rolled over dead by the side of his victim.

"Mashune was still living, but a single glance at him told me that his hour had come. The buffalo's horn had driven a great hole in his right lung, and inflicted other injuries.

"I knelt down beside him in the uttermost distress, and took his hand.

"'Is he dead, Macumazahn?' he whispered. 'My eyes are blind; I cannot see.'

"'Yes, he is dead.'

"'Did the devil hurt thee, Macumazahn?'

"'No, my poor fellow, I am not much hurt.'

"'Ow! I am glad,'

"Then came a long silence, broken only by the sound of the air whistling through the hole in his lung as he breathed.

"'Macumazahn, art thou there? I cannot feel thee.'

"'I am here, Mashune.'

"'I die, Macumazahn, the world flies round and round. I go ... I go out into the dark. Surely, my father, at times in days to come, thou wilt think of Mashune who stood by thy side . . . when thou killest elephants, as we used . . . as we used . . .'

"They were his last words, his brave spirit passed with them. I dragged his body to the hole under the tree, and pushed it in, placing his broad assegai by him, as is the custom of his people, that he might not go defenceless on his long journey; and then, gentlemen – I am not ashamed to confess – I stood alone there before it, and wept like a woman."

Long Odds

The story which is narrated in the following pages came to me from the lips of my old friend Allan Quatermain, or Hunter Quatermain, as we used to call him in South Africa. He told it to me one evening when I was stopping with him at the place he bought in Yorkshire. Shortly after that, the death of his only son so unsettled him, that he immediately left England, accompanied by two companions, who were old fellow-voyagers of his, Sir Henry Curtis and Captain Good, and has now utterly vanished into the dark heart of Africa. He is persuaded that a white people, of which he has heard rumours all his life, exists somewhere on the highlands in the vast, still unexplored interior, and his great ambition is to find them before he dies. This is the wild quest upon which he and his companions have departed, and from which I shrewdly suspect they never will return. One letter only have I received from the old gentleman, dated from a mission-station high up the Tana, a river on the east coast, about three hundred miles north of Zanzibar; in it he says they have gone through many hardships and adventures, but are alive and well, and have found traces which go far towards making him hope that the results of their wild quest may be a "magnificent and unexampled discovery". I greatly fear, however, that all he has discovered is death; for this letter came a long while ago, and nobody has heard a single word of the party since. They have totally vanished.

It was on the last evening of my stay at his house that he told the ensuing story to me and Captain Good, who was dining with him. He had eaten his dinner and drunk two or three glasses of old port, just to help Good and myself to the end of the second bottle. It was an unusual thing for him to do, for he was a most abstemious man, having conceived, as he used to say, a great horror of drink from observing its effects upon the class of men – hunters, transport riders, and others – amongst whom he had passed so many years of his life. Consequently the good wine took more effect on him than it would have done on most men, sending a little flush into his wrinkled cheeks, and making him talk more freely than usual.

Dear old man! I can see him now, as he went limping up and down the vestibule, with his grey hair sticking up in scrubbing-brush fashion, his shrivelled yellow face, and his large dark eyes, that were as keen as any hawk's, and yet soft as a buck's. The whole room was hung with trophies of his numerous hunting expeditions, and he had some story about every one of them, if only you could get him to tell them. Generally he would not, for he was not very fond of narrating his own adventures, but to-night the port wine made him more communicative.

"Ah, you brute!" he said, stopping beneath an unusually large skull of a lion, which was fixed just over the mantelpiece, beneath a long row of guns, its jaws distended to their utmost width. "Ah, you brute! you have given me a lot of trouble for the last dozen years, and will, I suppose, to my dying day."

"Tell us the yarn, Quatermain," said Good. "You have often promised to tell me, and you never have."

"You had better not ask me to," he answered, "for it is a longish one."

"All right," I said, "the evening is young, and there is some more port."

Thus adjured, he filled his pipe from a jar of coarse-cut Boer tobacco that was always standing on the mantelpiece, and still walking up and down the room, began:

"It was, I think, in the March of '69 that I was up in Sikukuni's country. It was just after old Sequati's time, and Sikukuni had got into power – I forget how. Anyway, I was there. I had heard that the Bapedi people had got down an enormous quantity of ivory from the

interior, and so I started with a waggon-load of goods, and came
straight away from Middelburg to try and trade some of it. It was a
risky thing to go into the country so early, on account of the fever; but
I knew that there was one or two others after that lot of ivory, so I
determined to have a try for it, and take my chance of fever. I had got
so tough from continual knocking about that I did not set it down at
much. Well, I got on all right for a while. It is a wonderfully beautiful
piece of bush veldt, with great ranges of mountains running through
it, and round granite koppies starting up here and there, looking out
like sentinels over the rolling waste of bush. But it is very hot – hot as
a stew-pan – and when I was there that March, which, of course, is
autumn in that part of Africa, the whole place reeked of fever. Every
morning, as I trekked along down by the Oliphant River, I used to
creep out of the waggon at dawn and look out. But there was no river
to be seen – only a long line of billows of what looked like the finest
cotton wool tossed up lightly with a pitchfork. It was the fever mist.
Out from among the scrub too came little spirals of vapour, as though
there were hundreds of tiny fires alight in it – reek rising from thousands of tons of rotting vegetation. It was a beautiful place, but the
beauty was the beauty of death; and all those lines and blots of vapour

wrote one great word across the surface of the country, and that word was 'fever'.

"It was a dreadful year of illness that. I came, I remember, to one little kraal of Knobnoses, and went up to it to see if I could get some *maas* (curdled butter-milk) and a few mealies. As I got near I was struck with the silence of the place. No children began to chatter, and no dogs barked. Nor could I see any native sheep or cattle. The place, though it had evidently been recently inhabited, was as still as the bush round it, and some guinea fowl got up out of the prickly pear bushes right at the kraal gate. I remember that I hesitated a little before going in, there was such an air of desolation about the spot. Nature never looks desolate when man has not yet laid his hand upon her breast; she is only lonely. But when man has been, and has passed away, then she looks desolate.

"Well, I passed into the kraal, and went up to the principal hut. In front of the hut was something with an old sheep-skin *kaross* (rug) thrown over it. I stooped down and drew off the rug, and then shrank back amazed, for under it was the body of a young woman recently dead. For a moment I thought of turning back, but my curiosity overcame me; so going past the woman, I went down on my hands and knees and crept into the hut. It was so dark that I could not see anything, though I could smell a great deal – so I lit a match. It was a 'tand-stickor' match, and burnt slowly and dimly, and as the light gradually increased I made out what I thought was a lot of people, men, women, and children, fast asleep. Presently it burnt up brightly, and I saw that they too, five of them altogether, were quite dead. One was a baby. I dropped the match in a hurry, and was making my way out of the hut as hard as I could go, when I caught sight of two bright eyes staring out of a corner. Thinking it was a wild cat, or some such animal, I redoubled my haste, when suddenly a voice near the eyes began first to mutter, and then to send up a succession of awful yells. Hastily I lit another match, and perceived that the eyes belonged to an old woman, wrapped up in a greasy leather garment. Taking her by the arm, I dragged her out, for she could not, or would not, come by herself, and the stench was overpowering me. Such a sight as she was – a bag of bones, covered over with black shrivelled parchment. The only white thing about her was her wool, and she seemed to be pretty well dead except for her eyes and her voice. She thought that I was a devil come to take her, and that is why she yelled so. Well, I got her down to the waggon, and gave her a 'tot' of Cape smoke, and then, as soon as it was ready, poured about a pint of beef-tea down her throat, made from the flesh of a blue vilderbeeste I had killed the day before, and after that she brightened up wonderfully. She could talk Zulu – indeed, it turned out that she had run away from Zululand in T'Chaka's time – and she told me that all the people that I had seen had died of fever. When they had died, the other inhabitants of the kraal had taken the cattle and gone away, leaving the poor old woman, who was helpless from age and infirmity, to perish of starvation or disease, as the case might be. She had been sitting there for three days among the bodies when I found her. I took her on to the next kraal, and gave the headman a blanket to look after her, promising him another if I found her well when I came back. I remember that he was much astonished at my parting with two blankets for the sake of such a worthless old creature. 'Why did I not leave her in the bush?' he asked. Those people carry the doctrine of the survival of the fittest to its extreme, you see.

"It was the night after I had got rid of the old woman that I made my first acquaintance with my friend yonder," and he nodded towards the skull that seemed to be grinning down at us in the shadow of the wide mantelshelf. "I had trekked from dawn till eleven o'clock – a long trek – but I wanted to get on; and then had the oxen turned out to graze, sending the voorlooper to look after them, meaning to inspan again about six o'clock, and trek with the moon till ten. Then I got into the waggon and had a good sleep till half-past two or so in the afternoon, when I got up and cooked some meat, and had my dinner, washing it down with a pannikin of black coffee – for it was difficult to get preserved milk in those days. Just as I had finished, and the driver, a man called Tom, was washing up the things, in comes the young scoundrel of a voorlooper driving one ox before him.

"'Where are the other oxen?' I asked.

"'Koos!' he said, 'Koos! (chief) the other oxen have gone away. I turned my back for a minute, and when I looked round again they were all gone except Kaptein, here, who was rubbing his back against a tree.'

"'You mean that you have been asleep, and let them stray, you villain. I will rub your back against a stick,' I answered, feeling very angry, for it was not a pleasant prospect to be stuck up in that fever trap for a week or so while we were hunting for the oxen. 'Off you go, and you too, Tom, and mind you don't come back till you have found them. They have trekked back along the Middelburg Road, and are a dozen miles off by now, I'll be bound. Now, no words; go both of you.'

"Tom, the driver, swore and caught the lad a hearty kick, which he richly deserved, and then, having tied old Kaptein up to the disselboom with a reim, they got their assegais and sticks and started. I would have gone too, only I knew that somebody must look after the waggon, and I did not like to leave either of the boys with it at night. I was in a very bad temper, indeed, although I was pretty well used to these sort of occurrences, and soothed myself by taking a rifle and going to kill something. For a couple of hours I poked about without seeing anything that I could get a shot at, but at last, just as I was again within seventy yards of the waggon, I put up an old Impala ram from behind a mimosa thorn. He ran straight for the waggon, and it was not till he was passing within a few feet of it that I could get a decent shot at him. Then I pulled, and caught him half-way down the spine; over he went, dead as a door-nail, and a pretty shot it was, though I ought not to say it. This little incident put me into rather a better temper, especially as the buck had rolled over right against the after part of the waggon, so I had only to gut him, fix a reim round his legs and haul him up. By the time I had done this, the sun was down, and the full moon was up, and a beautiful moon it was. And then there came down that wonderful hush that sometimes falls over the African bush in the early hours of the night. No beast was moving, and no bird called. Not a breath of air stirred the quiet trees, and the shadows did not even quiver; they only grew. It was very oppressive and very lonely, for there was not a sign of the cattle or the boys. I was quite thankful for the society of old Kaptein, who was lying down contentedly against the disselboom, chewing the cud with a good conscience.

"Presently, however, Kaptein began to get restless. First he snorted, then he got up and snorted again. I could not make it out, so like a fool I got down off the waggon-bog to have a look round, thinking it might be the lost oxen coming.

"Next instant I regretted it, for all of a sudden I heard an awful roar and saw something yellow flash past me and light on poor Kaptein. Then came a bellow of agony from the ox, and a crunch as the lion put his teeth through the poor brute's neck, and I began to realize what had happened. My rifle was in the waggon, and my first thought was to get hold of it, and I turned and made a bolt for it. I got my foot on the wheel and flung my body forward on to the waggon, and there I stopped as if I were frozen, and no wonder, for as I was about to spring up I heard the lion behind me, and next second I felt the brute, ay, as plainly as I can feel this table. I felt him, I say, sniffing at my left leg that was hanging down.

"My word! I did feel queer; I don't think that I ever felt so queer before. I dared not move for the life of me, and the odd thing was that I seemed to lose power over my leg, which had an insane sort of inclination to kick out of its own mere motion – just as hysterical people want to laugh when they ought to be particularly solemn. Well, the lion sniffed and sniffed, beginning at my ankle and slowly nosing away up to my thigh. I thought that he was going to get hold then, but he did not. He only growled softly, and went back to the ox. Shifting my head a little I got a full view of him. He was the biggest lion I ever saw, and I have seen a great many, and he had a most tremendous black mane. What his teeth were like you can see – look there, pretty big ones, ain't they? Altogether he was a magnificent animal, and as I lay there sprawling on the fore-tongue of the waggon, it occurred to me that he would look uncommonly well in a cage. He stood there by the carcase of poor Kaptein, and deliberately disembowelled him as neatly as a butcher could have done. All this while I dare not move, for he kept lifting his head and keeping an eye on me as he licked his bloody chops. When he had cleaned Kaptein out, he opened his mouth and roared, and I am not exaggerating when I say that the sound shook the waggon. Instantly there came back an answering roar.

" 'Heavens!' I thought, 'there is his mate.'

"Hardly was the thought out of my head when I caught sight in the moonlight of the lioness bounding along through the long grass, and after her a couple of cubs about the size of mastiffs. She stopped within a few feet of my head, and stood, and waved her tail, and fixed me with her glowing yellow eyes; but just as I thought that it was all over she turned, and began to feed on Kaptein, and so did the cubs. There were the four of them within eight feet of me, growling and quarrelling, rending and tearing and crunching poor Kaptein's bones; and there I lay shaking with terror, and the cold perspiration pouring out of me, feeling like another Daniel come to judgment in a new sense of the phrase. Presently the cubs had eaten their fill, and began to get restless. One went round to the back of the waggon, and pulled at the Impala buck that hung there, and the other came round my way and began the sniffing game at my leg. Indeed, he did more than that, for, my trouser being hitched up a little, he began to lick the bare skin with his rough tongue. The more he licked the more he liked it, to judge from his increased vigour and the loud purring noise he made. Then I knew that the end had come, for in another second his file-like tongue would have rasped through the skin of my leg – which was luckily pretty tough – and have got to the blood, and then there would be no chance for me. So I just lay there and thought of my sins, and prayed to the Almighty, and thought that after all life was a very enjoyable thing.

"And then all of a sudden I heard a crashing of bushes and the shouting and whistling of men, and there were the two boys coming back with the cattle which they had found trekking along all together. The lions lifted their heads and listened, and then without a sound bounded off – and I fainted.

"The lions came back no more that night, and by the next morning my nerves had got pretty straight again; but I was full of wrath when I thought of all that I had gone through at the hands, or rather noses, of those four lions, and of the fate of my after-ox Kaptein. He was a splendid ox, and I was very fond of him. So wroth was I that like a fool I determined to go for the whole family of them. It was worthy of a greenhorn out on his first hunting trip; but I did it nevertheless. Accordingly after breakfast, having rubbed some oil upon my leg, which was very sore from the cub's tongue, I took the driver, Tom, who did not half like the job, and having armed myself with an ordinary double No. 12 smoothbore, the first breech-loader I ever had, I started. I took the smoothbore because it shot a bullet very well; and my experience has been that a round ball from a smooth-bore is quite as effective against a lion as an express bullet. The lion is soft and not a difficult animal to finish if you hit him anywhere in the body. A buck takes far more killing.

"Well, I started, and the first thing I set to work to do was to try to make out whereabouts the brutes lay up for the day. About three hundred yards from the waggon was the crest of a rise covered with single mimosa trees, dotted about in a park-like fashion, and beyond this was a stretch of open plain running down to a dry pan, or water-hole, which covered about an acre of ground, and was densely clothed with reeds, now in the sere and yellow leaf. From the further edge of this pan the ground sloped up again to a great cleft, or nullah, which had been cut out by the action of water, and was pretty thickly sprinkled with bush, amongst which grew some large trees, I forget of what sort.

"It at once struck me that the dry pan would be a likely place to find my friends in, as there is nothing a lion is fonder of than lying up in reeds, through which he can see things without being seen himself. Accordingly thither I went and prospected. Before I had got half-way round the pan I found the remains of a blue vilderbeeste that had evidently been killed within the last three or four days and partially devoured by lions; and from other indications about I was soon assured that if the family were not in the pan that day, they spent a good deal of their spare time there. But if there, the question was how to get them out; for it was clearly impossible to think of going in after them unless one was quite determined to commit suicide. Now there was a strong wind blowing from the direction of the waggon, across the reedy pan towards the bush-clad kloof or donga, and this first gave me the idea of firing the reeds, which, as I think I told you, were pretty dry. Accordingly Tom took some matches and began starting little fires to the left, and I did the same to the right. But the reeds were still green at the bottom, and we should never have got them well alight had it not been for the wind, which got stronger and stronger as the sun got higher, and forced the fire into them. At last, after half-an-hour's trouble, the flames got a hold, and began to spread out like a fan, whereupon I got round to the further side of the pan to wait for the lions, standing well out in the open, as we stood at the copse to-day where you shot the woodcock. It was a rather risky thing to do, but I used to be so sure of my shooting in those days that I did not so much mind the risk. Scarcely had I got round when I heard the reeds parting before the onward rush of some animal. 'Now for it,' said I. On it came. I could see that it was yellow, and prepared for action, when instead of a lion out bounded a beautiful reit bok which had been lying in the shelter of the pan. It must, by the way, have been a reit bok of a peculiarly confiding nature to lay itself down with the lion like the lamb of prophesy, but I suppose that the reeds were thick, and that it kept a long way off.

"Well, I let the reit bok go, and it went like the wind, and kept my eyes fixed upon the reeds. The fire was burning like a furnace now; the flames crackling and roaring as they bit into the reeds, sending spouts of fire twenty feet and more into the air, and making the hot air dance above it in a way that was perfectly dazzling. But the reeds were still half green, and created an enormous quantity of smoke, which came rolling towards me like a curtain, lying very low on account of the wind. Presently, above the crackling of the fire, I heard a startled roar, then another and another. So the lions were at home.

"I was beginning to get excited now, for, as you fellows know, there is nothing in experience to warm up your nerves like a lion at close quarters, unless it is a wounded buffalo; and I got still more so when I made out through the smoke that the lions were all moving about on the extreme edge of the reeds. Occasionally they would pop their heads out like rabbits from a burrow, and then, catching sight of me standing about fifty yards out, draw them back again. I knew that it must be getting pretty warm behind them, and that they could not keep the game up for long; and I was not mistaken, for suddenly all four of them broke cover together, the old black-maned lion leading by a few yards. I never saw a more splendid sight in all my hunting experience than those four lions bounding across the veldt, over-shadowed by the dense pall of smoke and backed by the fiery furnace of the burning reeds.

"I reckoned that they would pass, on their road to the bushy kloof, within about five and twenty yards of me, so, taking a long breath, I got my gun well on to the lion's shoulder – tbe black-maned one – so as to allow for an inch or two of motion, and catch him through the heart. I was on, dead on, and my finger was just beginning to tighten on the trigger, when suddenly I went blind – a bit of reed-ash had drifted into my right eye. I danced and rubbed, and got it more or less clear just in time to see the tail of the last lion vanishing round the bushes up the kloof.

"If ever a man was mad I was that man. It was too bad; and such a shot in the open, too! However, I was not going to be beaten, so I just turned and marched for the kloof. Tom, the driver, begged and implored me not to go, but though as a general rule I never pretend to be very brave (which I am not), I was determined that I would either kill those lions or they should kill me. So I told Tom that he need not come unless he liked, but I was going; and being a plucky fellow, a Swazi by birth, he shrugged his shoulders, muttered that I was mad or bewitched, and followed doggedly in my tracks.

"We soon got to the kloof, which was about three hundred yards in length and but sparsely wooded, and then the real fun began. There might be a lion behind every bush – there certainly were four lions somewhere; the delicate question was, where. I peeped and poked and looked in every possible direction, with my heart in my mouth, and was at last rewarded by catching a glimpse of something yellow moving behind a bush. At the same moment, from another bush opposite me out burst one of the cubs and galloped back towards the burnt-out pan. I whipped round and let drive a snap shot that tipped him head over heels, breaking his back within two inches of the root of the tail, and there he lay helpless but glaring. Tom afterwards killed him with his assegai. I opened the breech of the gun and hurriedly pulled out the old case, which, to judge from what ensued, must I suppose have burst and left a portion of its fabric sticking to the barrel. At any rate, when I tried to get in the new case it would only enter half way; and – would you believe it? – this was the moment that the lioness, attracted no doubt by the outcry of her cub, chose to put in an appearance. There she stood, twenty paces or so from me, lashing her tail and looking just as wicked as it is possible to conceive. Slowly I stepped backwards, trying to push in the new case, and as I did so she moved on in little runs, dropping down after each run. The danger was imminent, and the case would not go in. At the moment I oddly enough thought of the cartridge maker, whose name I will not mention, and earnestly hoped that if the lion got me some condign punishment would overtake him. It would not go in, so I tried to pull it out. It would not come out either, and my gun was useless if I could not shut it to use the other barrel. I might as well have had no gun. Meanwhile I was walking backward, keeping my eye on the lioness, who was creeping forward on her belly without a sound, but lashing her tail and keeping her eye on me; and in it I saw that she was coming in a few seconds more. I dashed my wrist and the palm of my hand against the brass rim of the cartridge till the blood poured from them – look there are the scars of it to this day!"

Here Quatermain held up his right hand to the light and showed us seven or eight white cicatrices just where the wrist is set into the hand.

"But it was not of the slightest use," he went on; "the cartridge would not move. I only hope that no other man will ever be put in such an awful position. The lioness gathered herself together, and I gave myself up for lost, when suddenly Tom shouted out from somewhere in my rear:

" 'You are walking on to the wounded cub; turn to the right.'

"I had the sense, dazed as I was, to take the hint, and slewing round at right-angles, but still keeping my eyes on the lioness, I continued my backward walk.

"To my intense relief, with a low growl she straightened herself, turned, and bounded off further up the kloof.

" 'Come on, Inkoos,' said Tom, 'let's get back to the waggon.'

" 'All right, Tom,' I answered. 'I will when I have killed those three other lions,' for by this time I was bent on shooting them as I never remember being bent on anything before or since. 'You can go if you like, or you can get up a tree.'

"He considered the position a little, and then he very wisely got up a tree. I wish that I had done the same.

"Meanwhile I had got out my knife, which had an extractor in it, and succeeded after some difficulty in hauling out the case which had so nearly been the cause of my death, and removing the obstruction in the barrel. It was very little thicker than a postage-stamp; certainly not thicker than a piece of writing-paper. This done I loaded the gun, bound my handkerchief round my wrist and hand to staunch the flowing of the blood, and started on again.

"I had noticed that the lioness went into a thick green bush, or rather cluster of bushes, growing near the water, for there was a little stream running down the kloof, about fifty yards higher up, and for this I made. When I got there, however, I could see nothing, so I took up a big stone and threw it into the bushes. I believe that it hit the other cub, for out it came with a rush, giving me a broadside shot of which I promptly availed myself, knocking it over dead. Out, too, came the lioness like a flash of light, but quick as she went I managed to put the other bullet into her ribs, so that she rolled right over three times like a shot rabbit. I instantly got two more cartridges into the gun, and as I did so the lioness got up again and came crawling towards me on her fore-paws, roaring and groaning, and with such an expression of diabolical fury on her countenance as I have not often seen. I shot her again through the chest, and she fell over on to her side quite dead.

"That was the first and last time that I ever killed a brace of lions right and left, and, what is more, I never heard of anybody else doing it. Naturally I was considerably pleased with myself, and having again loaded up, went on to look for the black-maned beauty who had killed Kaptein. Slowly and with the greatest care I proceeded up the kloof, searching every bush and tuft of grass as I went. It was wonderfully exciting work, for I never was sure from one moment to another but that he would be on me. I took comfort, however, from the reflection that a lion rarely attacks a man – rarely, I say; sometimes he does, as you will see – unless he is cornered or wounded. I must have been nearly an hour hunting after the lion. Once I thought I saw something move in a clump of tambouki grass, but I could not be sure, and when I trod out the grass I could not find him.

"At last I got up to the head of the kloof, which made a *cul-de-sac*. It was formed of a wall of rock about fifty feet high. Down this rock trickled a little waterfall, and in front of it, some seventy feet from its face, was a great piled-up mass of boulders, in the crevices and on the top of which grew ferns and grass and stunted bushes. This mass was about twenty-five feet high. The sides of the kloof here were also very steep. Well, I got up to the top of the nullah and looked all round. No signs of the lion. Evidently I had either overlooked him further down, or he had escaped right away. It was very vexatious; but still three lions were not a bad bag for one gun before dinner, and I was fain to be content. Accordingly I departed back again, making my way round the isolated pillar of boulders, and beginning to feel that I was pretty well done up with excitement and fatigue, and should be more so before I had skinned those three lions. When I had got, as nearly as I could judge, about eighteen yards past the pillar or mass of boulders, I turned to have another look round. I have a pretty sharp eye, but I could see nothing at all.

"Then, on a sudden, I saw something sufficiently alarming. On the top of the mass of boulders, opposite to me, standing out clear against the rock beyond, was the huge black-maned lion. He had been crouching there, and now arose as though by magic. There he stood lashing his tail, just like a statue of the animal on the gateway of Northumberland House that I have seen a picture of. But be did not stand long. Before I could fire – before I could do more than get the gun to my shoulder – he sprang straight up and out from the rock, and driven by the impetus of that one mighty bound came hurtling through the air towards me.

"Heavens! how grand he looked, and how awful! High into the air he flew, describing a great arch. Just as he touched the highest point of his spring I fired. I did not dare to wait, for I saw that he would clear the whole space and land right upon me. Without a sight, almost without aim, I fired, as one would fire a snap shot at a snipe. The bullet told, for I distinctly heard its thud above the rushing sound caused by the passage of the lion through the air. Next second I was swept to the ground (luckily I fell into a low creeper-clad bush, which broke the shock), and the lion was on the top of me, and the next those great white teeth of his had met in my thigh – I heard them grate against the bone. I yelled out in agony, for I did not feel in the least benumbed and happy, like Dr. Livingstone – who, by the way, I knew very well – and gave myself up for dead. But suddenly, as I did so, the lion's grip on my thigh loosened, and he stood over me, swaying to and fro, his huge mouth, from which the blood was gushing, wide opened. Then he roared, and the sound shook the rocks.

"To and fro he swung, and suddenly the great head dropped on me, knocking all the breath from my body, and he was dead. My bullet had entered in the centre of his chest and passed out on the right side of the spine about half way down the back.

"The pain of my wound kept me from fainting, and as soon as I got my breath I managed to drag myself from under him. Thank heavens, his great teeth had not crushed my thigh-bone; but I was losing a great deal of blood, and had it not been for the timely arrival of Tom, with whose aid I got the handkerchief off my wrist and tied it round my leg, twisting it tight with a stick, I think I should have bled to death.

"Well, it was a just reward for my folly in trying to tackle a family of lions single-handed. The odds were too long. I have been lame ever since and shall be to my dying day; in the month of March the wound always troubles me a great deal, and every three years it breaks out raw. I need scarcely add that I never traded the lot of ivory at Sikukuni's. Another man got it – a German – and made five hundred pounds out of it after paying expenses. I spent the next month on the broad of my back, and was a cripple for six months after that. And now I've told you the yarn, so I will have a drop of Hollands and go to bed."

A Tale of Three Lions

The Interest on Ten Shillings

Most of you will have heard of Allan Quatermain, who was one of the
party that discovered King Solomon's mines some little time ago, and
who afterwards came to live in England near his friend Sir Henry
Curtis. He went back to the wilderness again, as these old hunters
almost invariably do, on one pretext or another.* They cannot endure
civilization for very long, its noise and racket and the omnipresence
of broad-clothed humanity proving more trying to their nerves than
the dangers of the desert. I think that they feel lonely here, for it is a
fact that is too little understood, though it has often been stated, that
there is no loneliness like the loneliness of crowds, especially to those
who are unaccustomed to them. "What is there in the world," old
Quatermain would say, "so desolate as to stand in the streets of a great
city and listen to the footsteps falling, falling, multitudinous as the
rain, and watch the white line of faces as they hurry past, you know
not whence, you know not whither? They come and go, their eyes
meet yours with a cold stare, for a moment their features are written
on your mind, and then they are gone for ever. You will never see
them again; they will never see you again; they come up out of the
unknown, and presently they once more vanish into the unknown,
taking their secrets with them. Yes, that is loneliness pure and unde-
filed; but to one who knows and loves it, the wilderness is not lonely,
because the spirit of nature is ever there to keep the wanderer company. He finds companions in the winds – the sunny streams babble

---

* This of course was written before Mr. Quatermain's account of the adventures in the
newly discovered country of Zu-Vendis of himself, Sir Henry Curtis and Capt. John Good
had been received in England. – Editor

like Nature's children at his feet; high above him, in the purple sunset, are domes and minarets and palaces, such as no mortal man has built, in and out of whose flaming doors the angels of the sun seem to move continually. And there, too, is the wild game, following its feeding-grounds in great armies, with the springbuck thrown out before for skirmishers; then rank upon rank of long-faced blesbuck, marching and wheeling like infantry; and last the shining troops of quagga, and the fierce-eyed shaggy vilderbeeste to take, as it were, the place of the cossack host that hangs upon an army's flanks.

"Oh, no," he would say, "the wilderness is not lonely, for, my boy, remember that the further you get from man, the nearer you grow to God," and though this is a saying that might well be disputed, it is one I am sure that anybody will easily understand who has watched the sun rise and set on the limitless desert plains, and seen the thunder chariots of the clouds roll in majesty across the depths of unfathomable sky.

Well, at any rate he went back again, and now for many months I have heard nothing at all of him, and to be frank, I greatly doubt if anybody will ever hear of him again. I fear that the wilderness, that has for so many years been a mother to him, will now also prove his grave and the grave of those who accompanied him, for the quest upon which he and they have started is a wild one indeed.

But while he was in England for those three years or so between his return from the successful discovery of the wise king's buried treasures, and the death of his only son, I saw a great deal of old Allan Quatermain. I had known him years before in Africa, and after he came home, whenever I had nothing better to do, I used to run up to Yorkshire and stay with him, and in this way I at one time and another heard many of the incidents of his past life, and most curious some of them were. No man can pass all those years following the rough existence of an elephant-hunter without meeting with many strange adventures, and of these in one way and another old Quatermain has certainly seen his share. Well, the story that I am going to tell you in the following pages is one of the more recent of these adventures, though I forget the exact year in which it happened. At any rate I know that it was the only trip upon which he took his son Harry (who is since dead) with him, and that Harry was then about fourteen. And now for the story, which I will repeat, as nearly as I can, in the words in which Hunter Quatermain told it to me one night in the old oak-panelled vestibule of his house in Yorkshire. We were talking about gold-mining –

"Gold-mining!" he broke in; "ah! yes, I once went gold-mining at Pilgrims' Rest in the Transvaal, and it was after that that we had the business about Jim-Jim and the lions. Do you know Pilgrims' Rest? Well, it is, or was, one of the queerest little places you ever saw. The town itself was pitched in a stony valley, with mountains all about it, and in the middle of such scenery as one does not often get the chance of seeing. Many and many is the time that I have thrown down my pick and shovel in disgust, clambered out of my claim, and walked a couple of miles or so to the top of some hill. Then I would lie down in the grass and look out over the glorious stretch of country – the smiling valleys, the great mountains touched with gold – real gold of the sunset, and clothed in sweeping robes of bush, and stare into the depths of the perfect sky above; yes, and thank Heaven I had got away from the cursing and the coarse jokes of the miners, and the voices of those Basutu Kaffirs as they toiled in the sun, the memory of which is with me yet.

"Well, for some months I dug away patiently at my claim, till the very sight of a pick or of a washing-trough became hateful to me. A hundred times a day I lamented my own folly in having invested eight hundred pounds, which was about all that I was worth at the time, in this gold-mining. But like other better people before me, I had been bitten by the gold bug, and now was forced to take the consequences. I bought a claim out of which a man had made a fortune – five or six thousand pounds at least – as I thought, very cheap; that is, I gave him five hundred pounds down for it. It was all that I had made by a very rough year's elephant-hunting beyond the Zambesi, and I sighed deeply and prophetically when I saw my successful friend, who was a Yankee, sweep up the roll of Standard Bank notes with the lordly air of the man who has made his fortune, and cram them into his breeches pockets. 'Well,' I said to him – the happy vendor – 'it is a magnificent property, and I only hope that my luck will be as good as yours has been.'

"He smiled; to my excited nerves it seemed that he smiled ominously, as he answered me in a peculiar Yankee drawl: 'I guess, stranger, as I ain't the one to make a man quarrel with his food, more especial when there ain't no more going of the rounds; and as for that there claim, well, she's been a good nigger to me; but between you and me, stranger, speaking man to man, now that there ain't any filthy lucre between us to obscure the features of the truth, I guess she's about worked out!'

"I gasped; the fellow's effrontery took the breath out of me. Only five minutes before he had been swearing by all his gods – and they appeared to be numerous and mixed – that there were half a dozen fortunes left in the claim, and that he was only giving it up because he was downright weary of shovelling the gold out.

"'Don't look so vexed, stranger,' went on my tormentor, 'perhaps there is some shine in the old girl yet; anyway you are a downright good fellow, you are, therefore you will, I guess, have a real A1 opportunity of working on the feelings of Fortune. Anyway it will bring the muscle up upon your arm, for the stuff is uncommon stiff, and, what is more, you will in the course of a year earn a sight more than two thousand dollars in value of experience.'

"Then he went just in time, for in another moment I should have gone for him, and I saw his face no more.

"Well, I set to work on the old claim with my boy Harry and half a dozen Kaffirs to help me, which, seeing that I had put nearly all my worldly wealth into it, was the least that I could do. And we worked, my word, we did work – early and late we went at it – but never a bit of gold did we see; no, not even a nugget large enough to make a scarf-pin out of. The American gentleman had secured it all and left us the sweepings.

Charles Kerr

"For three months this went on, till at last I had paid away all, or very near all, that was left of our little capital in wages and food for the Kaffirs and ourselves. When I tell you that Boer meal was sometimes as high as four pounds a bag, you will understand that it did not take long to run through our banking account.

"At last the crisis came. One Saturday night I had paid the men as usual, and bought a muid of mealie meal at sixty shillings for them to fill themselves with, and then I went with my boy Harry and sat on the edge of the great hole that we had dug in the hillside, and which in bitter mockery we had named Eldorado. There we sat in the moonlight with our feet over the edge of the claim, and were melancholy enough for anything. Presently I pulled out my purse and emptied its contents into my hand. There was a half-sovereign, two florins, ninepence in silver, no coppers – for copper practically does not circulate in South Africa, which is one of the things that make living so dear there – in all exactly fourteen and ninepence.

"'There, Harry, my boy!' I said, 'that is the sum total of our worldly wealth; that hole has swallowed all the rest.'

"'By George!' said Master Harry; 'I say, father, you and I shall have to let ourselves out to work with the Kaffirs and live on mealie pap,' and he sniggered at his unpleasant little joke.

"But I was in no mood for joking, for it is not a merry thing to dig like anything for months and be completely ruined in the process, especially if you happen to dislike digging, and consequently I resented Harry's light-heartedness.

"'Be quiet, boy!' I said, raising my hand as though to give him a cuff, with the result that the half-sovereign slipped out of it and fell into the gulf below.

"'Oh, bother,' said I, 'it's gone.'

"'There, Dad,' said Harry, 'that's what comes of letting your angry passions rise; now we are down to four and nine.'

"I made no answer to these words of wisdom, but scrambled down the steep sides of the claim, followed by Harry, to hunt for my little all. Well, we hunted and we hunted, but the moonlight is an uncertain thing to look for half-sovereigns by, and there was some loose soil about, for the Kaffirs had knocked off working at this very spot a couple of hours before. I took a pick and raked away the clods of earth with it, in the hope of finding the coin; but all in vain. At last in sheer annoyance I struck the sharp end of the pickaxe down into the soil, which was of a very hard nature. To my astonishment it sunk in right up to the haft.

"'Why, Harry,' I said, 'this ground must have been disturbed!'

"'I don't think so, father,' he answered; 'but we will soon see,' and he began to shovel out the soil with his hands. 'Oh,' he said presently, 'it's only some old stones; the pick has gone down between them, look!' and he began to pull at one of the stones.

"'I say, Dad,' he said presently, almost in a whisper, 'it's precious heavy, feel it'; and he rose and gave me a round, brownish lump about the size of a very large apple, which he was holding in both his hands. I took it curiously and held it up to the light. It *was* very heavy. The moonlight fell upon its rough and filth-encrusted surface, and as I looked, curious little thrills of excitement began to pass through me. But I could not be sure.

"'Give me your knife, Harry,' I said.

"He did so, and resting the brown stone on my knee I scratched at its surface. Great heavens, it was soft!

"Another second and the secret was out, we had found a great nugget of pure gold, four pounds of it or more. 'It's gold, lad,' I said, 'it's gold, or I'm a Dutchman!'

"Harry, with his eyes starting out of his head, glared down at the gleaming yellow scratch that I had made upon the virgin metal, and then burst out into yell upon yell of exultation, which went ringing away across the silent claims like the shrieks of somebody being murdered.

"'Be quiet!' I said; 'do you want every thief on the fields after you?'

"Scarcely were the words out of my mouth when I heard a stealthy footstep approaching. I promptly put the big nugget down and sat on it, and uncommonly hard it was. As I did so I saw a lean dark face poked over the edge of the claim and a pair of beady eyes searching us out. I knew the face, it belonged to a man of very bad character known as Handspike Tom, who had, I understood, been so named at the Diamond Fields because he had murdered his mate with a handspike. He was now no doubt prowling about like a human hyæna to see what he could steal.

"'Is that you, 'Unter Quatermain?' he said.

"'Yes, it's I, Mr. Tom,' I answered, politely.

"'And what might all that there yelling be?' he asked. I was walking along, a-taking of the evening air and a-thinking on the stars, when I 'ears 'owl after 'owl.'

"'Well, Mr. Tom,' I answered, 'that is not to be wondered at, seeing that like yourself they are nocturnal birds.'

"''Owl after 'owl!' he repeated sternly, taking no notice of my interpretation, 'and I stops and says, "That's murder," and I listens again and thinks, "No, it ain't; that 'owl is the 'owl of hexultation; some one's been and got his fingers into a gummy yeller pot, I'll swear, and gone off 'is 'ead in the sucking of them." Now, 'Unter Quatermain, is I right? is it nuggets? Oh, lor!' and he smacked his lips audibly – 'great big yellow boys – is it them that you have just been and tumbled across?'

"'No,' I said, boldly, 'it isn't' – the cruel gleam in his black eyes altogether overcoming my aversion to untruth, for I knew that if once he found out what it was that I was sitting on – and by the way I have heard of rolling in gold being spoken of as a pleasant process, but I certainly do not recommend anybody who values comfort to try sitting on it – I should run a very good chance of being 'handspiked' before the night was over.

"'If you want to know what it was, Mr. Tom,' I went on, with my politest air, although in agony from the nugget underneath – for I hold it is always best to be polite to a man who is so ready with a handspike – 'my boy and I have had a slight difference of opinion, and I was enforcing my view of the matter upon him; that's all.'

"'Yes, Mr. Tom,' put in Harry, beginning to weep, for Harry was a smart boy, and saw the difficulty we were in, 'that was it – I hallooed because father beat me.'

"'Well, now, did yer, my dear boy – did yer? Well, all I can say is that a played-out old claim is a wonderful queer sort of place to come to for to argify at ten o'clock of night, and what's more, my sweet youth, if ever I should 'ave the argifying of yer' – and he leered unpleasantly at Harry – 'yer won't 'oller in quite such a jolly sort o' way. And now I'll be saying good-night, for I don't like disturbing of a family party. No, I ain't that sort of man, I ain't. Good-night to yer, 'Unter Quatermain – good-night to yer, my argified young one'; and Mr. Tom turned away disappointed, and prowled off elsewhere, like a human jackal, to see what he could thieve or kill.

" 'Thank goodness!' I said, as I slipped off the lump of gold. 'Now, then, do you get up, Harry, and see if that consummate villain has gone.' Harry did so, and reported that he had vanished towards Pilgrims' Rest, and then we set to work, and very carefully, but trembling with excitement, with our hands hollowed out all the space of ground into which I had struck the pick. Yes, as I hoped, there was a regular nest of nuggets, twelve in all, running from the size of a hazel-nut to that of a hen's egg, though of course the first one was much larger than that. How they all came there nobody can say; it was one of those extraordinary freaks, with stories of which, at any rate, all people acquainted with alluvial gold-mining will be familiar. It turned out afterwards that the American who sold me the claim had in the same way made his pile – a much larger one than ours, by the way – out of a single pocket, and then worked for six months without seeing colour, after which he gave it up.

"At any rate, there the nuggets were, to the value, as it turned out afterwards, of about twelve hundred and fifty pounds, so that after all I took out of that hole four hundred and fifty pounds more than I put into it. We got them all out and wrapped them up in a handkerchief, and then, fearing to carry home so much treasure, especially as we knew that Mr. Handspike Tom was on the prowl, made up our minds to pass the night where we were – a necessity which, disagreeable as it was, was wonderfully sweetened by the presence of that handkerchief full of virgin gold – the interest of my lost half-sovereign.

"Slowly the night wore away, for with the fear of Handspike Tom before my eyes I did not dare to go to sleep, and at last the dawn came. I got up and watched its growth, till it opened like a flower upon the eastern sky, and the sunbeams began to spring in splendour from mountain-top to mountain-top. I watched it, and as I did so it flashed upon me, with a complete conviction which I had not felt before, that I had had enough of gold-mining to last me the rest of my natural life, and I then and there made up my mind to clear out of Pilgrims' Rest and go and shoot buffalo towards Delagoa Bay. Then I turned, took the pick and shovel, and although it was a Sunday morning, woke up Harry and set to work to see if there were any more nuggets about. As I expected, there were none. What we had got had lain together in a little pocket filled with soil that felt quite different from the stiff stuff round and outside the pocket. There was not another trace of gold. Of course it is possible that there were more pocketfuls somewhere about, but all I have to say is I made up my mind that, whoever found them, I should not; and, as a matter of fact, I have since heard that this claim has been the ruin of two or three people, as it very nearly was the ruin of me.

"'Harry,' I said presently, 'I am going away this week towards Delagoa to shoot buffalo. Shall I take you with me, or send you down to Durban?'

"'Oh, take me with you, father,' begged Harry, 'I want to kill a buffalo!'

"'And supposing that the buffalo kills you instead?' I asked.

"'Oh, never mind,' he said, gaily, 'there are lots more where I came from.'

"I rebuked him for his flippancy, but in the end I consented to take him.

CHAPTER II
What Was Found in the Pool

Something over a fortnight had passed since the night when I lost half-a-sovereign and found twelve hundred and fifty pounds in look-ing for it, and instead of that horrid hole, for which, after all, Eldorado was scarcely a misnomer, a very different scene stretched away before us clad in the silver robe of the moonlight. We were camped – Harry and I, two Kaffirs, a Scotch cart, and six oxen – on the swelling side of a great wave of bush-clad land. Just where we had made our camp, however, the bush was very sparse, and only grew about in clumps, while here and there were single flat-topped mimosa-trees. To our right a little stream, which had cut a deep channel for itself in the bosom of the slope, flowed musically on between banks green with maidenhair, wild asparagus, and many beautiful grasses. The bed-rock here was red granite, and in the course of centuries of patient washing the water had hollowed out some of the huge slabs in its path into great troughs and cups, and these we used for bathing-places. No Roman lady, with her baths of porphyry or alabaster, could have had a more delicious spot to bathe herself than we found within fifty yards of our skerm, or rough inclosure of mimosa thorn, that we had dragged together round the cart to protect us from the attacks of lions. That there were several of these brutes about, I knew from their spoor, though we had neither heard nor seen them.

"Our bath was a little nook where the eddy of the stream had washed away a mass of soil, and on the edge of it there grew a most beautiful old mimosa thorn. Beneath the thorn was a large smooth slab of granite fringed all round with maidenhair and other ferns, that sloped gently down to a pool of the clearest sparkling water, which lay in a bowl of granite about ten feet wide by five deep in the centre. Here to this slab we went every morning to bathe, and that delightful bath is among the most pleasant of my hunting reminiscences, as it is also, for reasons which will presently appear, among the most painful.

"It was a lovely night. Harry and I sat to the windward of the fire, where the two Kaffirs were busily employed in cooking some impala steaks off a buck which Harry, to his great joy, had shot that morning, and were as perfectly contented with ourselves and the world at large as two people could possibly be. The night was beautiful, and it would require somebody with more words on the tip of his tongue than I have to describe properly the chastened majesty of those moon-lit wilds. Away for ever and for ever, away to the mysterious north, rolled the great bush ocean over which the silence brooded. There beneath us a mile or more to the right ran the wide Oliphant, and mirror-like flashed back the moon, whose silver spears were shivered on its breast and tossed in twisted lines of light far and wide about the mountains and the plain. Down upon the river-banks grew great timber-trees that through the stillness pointed solemnly to Heaven, and the beauty of the night lay upon them like a cloud. Everywhere was silence – silence in the starred depths, silence on the bosom of the sleeping earth. Now, if ever, great thoughts might rise in a man's mind, and for a space he might forget his littleness in the sense that he partook of the pure immensity about him.

"Hark! what was that?

"From far away down by the river there comes a mighty rolling sound, then another, and another. It is the lion seeking his meat.

"I saw Harry shiver and turn a little pale. He was a plucky boy enough, but the roar of a lion heard for the first time in the solemn bush veldt at night is apt to shake the nerves of any lad.

"'Lions, my boy,' I said; 'they are hunting down by the river there; but I don't think that you need make yourself uneasy. We have been here three nights now, and if they were going to pay us a visit I believe that they would have done so before this. However, we will make up the fire.'

"'Here, Pharaoh, do you and Jim-Jim get some more wood before we go to sleep, else the cats will be purring round you before morning.'

"Pharaoh, a great brawny Swazi, who had been working for me at Pilgrims' Rest, laughed, rose, and stretched himself, then calling to Jim-Jim to bring the axe and a reim, he started off in the moonlight towards a clump of sugar-bush where we cut our fuel from some dead trees. He was a fine fellow in his way, was Pharaoh, and I think that he had been named Pharaoh because he had an Egyptian cast of countenance and a royal sort of swagger about him. But his way was a somewhat peculiar way, on account of the uncertainty of his temper, and very few people could get on with him; also if he could find liquor he would drink like a fish, and when he drank he became shockingly bloodthirsty. These were his bad points: his good ones were that, like most people of the Zulu blood, he became exceedingly attached if he took to you at all; he was a hard-working and intelligent man, and about as dare-devil and plucky a fellow at a pinch as I have ever had to do with. He was about five-and-thirty years of age or so, but not a 'keshla' or ringed man. I believe that he had got into trouble in some way in Swaziland, and the authorities of his tribe would not allow him to assume the ring, and that is why he came to work at the gold-fields. The other man, or rather lad, Jim-Jim, was a Mapoch Kaffir, or Knobnose, and even in the light of subsequent events I fear that I cannot speak very well of him. He was an idle and careless young rascal, and only that very morning I had to tell Pharaoh to give him a beating for letting the oxen stray, which Pharaoh did with the greatest gusto, although he was by way of being very fond of Jim-Jim. Indeed, I saw him consoling Jim-Jim afterwards with a pinch of snuff from his own ear-box, whilst he explained to him that the next time it came in the way of duty to flog him, he meant to thrash him with the other hand, so as to cross the old cuts and make a 'pretty pattern' on his back.

"Well, off they went, though Jim-Jim did not at all like leaving the camp at that hour, even when the moonlight was so bright, and in due course returned safely enough with a great bundle of wood. I laughed at Jim-Jim, and asked him if he had seen anything, and he said yes, he had; he had seen two large yellow eyes staring at him from behind a bush, and heard something snore.

"As, however, on further investigation the yellow eyes and the snore appeared to have existed only in Jim-Jim's lively imagination, I was not greatly disturbed by this alarming report; but having seen to the making-up of the fire, got into the skerm and went quietly to sleep with Harry by my side.

"Some hours afterwards I woke up with a start. I don't know what woke me. The moon had gone down, or at least was almost hidden behind the soft horizon of bush, only her red rim being visible. Also a wind had sprung up and was driving long hurrying lines of cloud across the starry sky, and altogether a great change had come over the mood of the night. By the look of the sky I judged that we must be about two hours from daybreak.

"The oxen, which were as usual tied to the disselboom of the Scotch cart, seemed very restless – they kept snuffling and blowing, and rising up and lying down again, so I at once suspected that they must wind something. Presently I knew what it was that they winded, for within fifty yards of us a lion roared, not very loud, but quite loud enough to make my heart come into my mouth.

"Pharaoh was sleeping on the other side of the cart, and, looking beneath it, I saw him raise his head and listen.

"'Lion, Inkoos,' he whispered, 'lion!'

"Jim-Jim also jumped up, and by the faint light I could see that he was in a very great fright indeed.

"Thinking that it was as well to be prepared for emergencies, I told Pharaoh to throw wood upon the fire, and woke up Harry, who I verily believe was capable of sleeping happily through the crack of doom. He was a little scared at first, but presently the excitement of the position came home to him, and he grew quite anxious to see his majesty face to face. I got my rifle handy and gave Harry his – a Westley Richards falling block, which is a very useful gun for a youth, being light and yet a good killing rifle, and then we waited.

"For a long time nothing happened, and I began to think that the best thing we could do would be to go to sleep again, when suddenly I heard a sound more like a cough than a roar within about twenty yards of the skerm. We all looked out, but could see nothing; and then followed another period of suspense. It was very trying to the nerves, this waiting for an attack that might be developed from any quarter or might not be developed at all; and though I was an old hand at this sort of business I was anxious about Harry, for it is wonderful how the presence of anybody to whom one is attached unnerves a man in moments of danger. I know, although it was now chilly enough, I could feel the perspiration running down my nose, and in order to relieve the strain on my attention employed myself in watching a beetle which appeared to be attracted by the firelight, and was sitting before it thoughtfully rubbing his antennæ against each other.

"Suddenly the beetle gave such a jump that he nearly pitched headlong into the fire, and so did we all – gave jumps, I mean, and no wonder, for from right under the skerm fence there came a most frightful roar – a roar that literally made the Scotch cart shake and took the breath out of me.

"Harry uttered an exclamation, Jim-Jim howled outright, while the poor oxen, who were terrified almost out of their hides, shivered and lowed piteously.

"The night was almost entirely dark now, for the moon had quite set, and the clouds had covered up the stars, so that the only light we had came from the fire, which by this time was burning up brightly again. But, as you know, firelight is absolutely useless to shoot by, it is so uncertain, besides, it penetrates but a very little way into the darkness, although if one is in the dark outside one can see it from so far away.

"Presently the oxen, after standing still for a moment, suddenly winded the lion and did what I feared they would do – began to 'skrek', that is, to try and break loose from the trektow to which they were tied, and rush off madly into the wilderness. Lions know of this habit on the part of oxen, which are, I do believe, the most foolish animals under the sun, a sheep being a very Solomon compared to them; and it is by no means uncommon for a lion to get in such a position that a herd or span of oxen may wind him, skrek, break their reims, and rush off into the bush. Of course, once there, they are helpless in the dark; and then the lion chooses the one that he loves best and eats him at his leisure.

"Well, round and round went our six poor oxen, nearly trampling us to death in their mad rush; indeed, had we not hastily tumbled out of the way, we should have been trodden to death, or at the least seriously injured. As it was, Harry was run over, and poor Jim-Jim being caught by the trektow somewhere beneath the arm, was hurled right across the skerm, landing by my side only some paces off.

"Snap went the disselboom of the cart beneath the transverse strain put upon it. Had it not broken the cart would have overset; as it was, in another minute, oxen, cart, trektow, reims, broken disselboom, and everything were tied in one vast heaving, plunging, bellowing, and seemingly inextricable knot.

"For a moment or two this state of affairs took my attention off from the lion that had caused it, but whilst I was wondering what on earth was to be done next, and how we should manage if the cattle broke loose into the bush and were lost – for cattle frightened in this manner will go straight away like mad things – my thoughts were suddenly recalled to the lion in a very painful fashion.

"For at that moment I perceived by the light of the fire a kind of gleam of yellow travelling through the air towards us.

"'The lion! the lion!' holloaed Pharaoh, and as he did so, he, or rather she, for it was a great gaunt lioness, half wild no doubt with hunger, lit right in the middle of the skerm, and stood there in the smoky gloom lashing her tail and roaring. I seized my rifle and fired it at her, but what between the confusion, my agitation, and the uncertain light, I missed her and nearly shot Pharaoh. The flash of the rifle, however, threw the whole scene into strong relief, and a wild sight it was I can tell you – with the seething mass of oxen twisted all round the cart, in such a fashion that their heads looked as though they were growing out of their rumps, and their horns seemed to protrude from their backs; the smoking fire with just a blaze in the heart of the smoke; Jim-Jim in the foreground, where the oxen had thrown him in their wild rush, stretched out there in terror; and then as a centre to the picture the great gaunt lioness glaring round with hungry yellow eyes, roaring and whining as she made up her mind what to do.

"It did not take her long, however, just the time that it takes a flash to die into darkness, for, before I could fire again or do anything, with a most fiendish snort she sprang upon poor Jim-Jim.

"I heard the unfortunate lad shriek, and then almost instantly I saw his legs thrown into the air. The lioness had seized him by the neck, and with a sudden jerk thrown his body over her back so that his legs hung down upon the further side.* Then, without the slightest hesitation, and apparently without any difficulty, she cleared the skerm fence at a single bound, and bearing poor Jim-Jim with her vanished into the darkness beyond, in the direction of the bathing-place that I have already described. We jumped up perfectly mad with horror and fear, and rushed wildly after her, firing shots at haphazard on the chance that she would be frightened by them into dropping her prey, but nothing could we see, and nothing could we hear. The lioness had vanished into the darkness, taking Jim-Jim with her, and to attempt to follow her till daylight was madness. We should only expose ourselves to the risk of a like fate.

"So with scared and heavy hearts we crept back to the skerm, and sat down to wait for the dawn, which now could not be much more than an hour off. It was absolutely useless to try even to disentangle the oxen till then, so all that was left for us to do was to sit and wonder how it came to pass that the one should be taken and the other left, and to hope against hope that our poor servant might have been mer-cifully delivered from the lion's jaws.

"At length the faint dawn came stealing like a ghost up the long slope of bush, and glinted on the tangled oxen's horns, and with white and frightened faces we got up and set to the task of disentangling the cattle, till such time as there should be light enough to enable us to follow the trail of the lioness which had gone off with Jim-Jim. And here a fresh trouble awaited us, for when at last with infinite difficulty we had loosened the great helpless brutes, it was only to find that one of the best of them was very sick. There was no mistake about the way he stood with his legs slightly apart and his head hanging down. He

---

* I have known a lion carry a two-year-old ox over a stone wall four feet high in this fashion, and a mile away into the bush beyond. He was subsequently poisoned by strychnine put into the carcass of the ox, and I still have his claws. – Editor

had got the redwater, I was sure of it. Of all the difficulties connected with life and travelling in South Africa those connected with oxen are perhaps the worst. The ox is the most exasperating animal in the world, a negro excepted. He has absolutely no constitution, and never neglects an opportunity of falling sick of some mysterious disease. He will get thin upon the slightest provocation, and from mere maliciousness die of 'poverty'; whereas it is his chief delight to turn round and refuse to pull whenever he finds himself well in the centre of a river, or the waggon-wheel nicely fast in a mud hole. Drive him a few miles over rough roads and you will find that he is footsore; turn him loose to feed and you will discover that he has run away, or if he has not run away he has of malice aforethought eaten 'tulip' and poisoned himself. There is always something wrong with him. The ox is a brute. It was of a piece with his accustomed behaviour for the one in question to break out – on purpose probably – with redwater just when a lion had walked off with his herd. It was exactly what I should have expected, and I was therefore neither disappointed nor surprised.

"Well, it was no use crying as I should almost have liked to do, because if this ox had redwater it was probable that the rest of them had it too, although they had been sold to me as 'salted', that is, proof against such diseases as redwater and lungsick. One gets hardened to this sort of thing in South Africa in course of time, for I suppose in no other country in the world is the waste of animal life so great.

"So taking my rifle and telling Harry to follow me (for we had to leave Pharaoh to look after the oxen – Pharaoh's lean kine, I called them), I started to see if anything could be found of or appertaining to the unfortunate Jim-Jim. The ground round our little camp was hard and rocky, and we could not hit off any spoor of the lioness, though just outside the skerm we saw a drop or two of blood. About three hundred yards from the camp, and a little to the right, was a patch of sugar bush mixed up with the usual mimosa, and for this I made, thinking that the lioness would have been sure to take her prey there to devour it. On we pushed through the long grass that was bent down beneath the weight of the soaking dew. In two minutes we were wet through up to the thighs, as wet as though we had waded through water. In due course, however, we reached the patch of bush, and by the grey light of the morning cautiously and slowly pushed our way into it. It was very dark under the trees, for the sun was not yet up, so we walked with the most extreme care, half expecting every minute to come across the lioness licking the bones of poor Jim-Jim. But no lioness could we see, and as for Jim-Jim there was not even a finger-joint of him to be found. Evidently they had not come here.

"So pushing through the bush we proceeded to hunt every other likely spot, but with the same result.

"'I suppose she must have taken him right away,' I said at last, sadly enough. 'At any rate he will be dead by now, so God have mercy on him, we can't help him. What's to be done now?'

"'I suppose that we had better wash ourselves in the pool, and then go back and get something to eat. I am filthy,' said Harry.

"This was a practical if a somewhat unfeeling suggestion. At least it struck me as unfeeling to talk of washing when poor Jim-Jim had been so recently eaten. However, I did not let my sentiment carry me away, so we went off to the beautiful spot that I have described, to wash. I was the first to reach it, which I did by scrambling down the ferny bank. Then I turned round, and started back with a yell – as well I might, for almost from beneath my feet there came a most awful snarl.

"I had lit nearly upon the back of the lioness, that had been sleeping on the slab where we always stood to dry ourselves after bathing. With a snarl and a growl, before I could do anything, before I could even cock my rifle, she had bounded right across the crystal pool, and vanished over the opposite bank. It was all done in an instant, as quick as thought.

"She had been sleeping on the slab, and oh, horror! what was that sleeping beside her? It was the red remains of poor Jim-Jim, lying on a patch of blood-stained rock.

"'Oh! father, father!' shrieked Harry, 'look in the water!'

"I looked. There, floating in the centre of the lovely, tranquil pool, was Jim-Jim's head. The lioness had bitten it right off, and it had rolled down the sloping rock into the water.

CHAPTER III
Jim-Jim Is Avenged

We never bathed in that pool again; indeed for my part I could never look at its peaceful purity fringed round with waving ferns without thinking of that ghastly head which rolled itself off through the water when we tried to catch it.

"Poor Jim-Jim! We buried what was left of him, which was not very much, in an old bread-bag, and though whilst he lived his virtues were not great, now that he was gone we could have wept over him. Indeed, Harry did weep outright; while Pharaoh used very bad language in Zulu, and I registered a quiet little vow on my account that I would let daylight into that lioness before I was forty-eight hours older, if by any means it could be done.

"Well, we buried him, and there he lies in the bread-bag (which I rather grudged him, as it was the only one we had), where lions will not trouble him any more – though perhaps the hyænas will, if they consider that there is enough of him left to make it worth their while to dig him up. However, he won't mind that; so there is an end of the book of Jim-Jim.

"The question that now remained was, how to circumvent his murderess. I knew that she would be sure to return as soon as she was hungry again, but I did not know when she would be hungry. She had left so little of Jim-Jim behind her that I should scarcely expect to see her the next night, unless indeed she had cubs. Still, I felt that it would not be wise to miss the chance of her coming, so we set about making preparations for her reception. The first thing that we did was to strengthen the bush wall of the skerm by dragging a large quantity of the tops of thorn-trees together, and laying them one on the other in such a fashion that the thorns pointed outwards. This, after our experience of the fate of Jim-Jim, seemed a very necessary precaution, since if where one goat can jump another can follow, as the Kaffirs say, how much more is this the case when an animal so active and so vigorous as the lion is concerned! And now came the further question, how were we to beguile the lioness to return? Lions are animals that have a strange knack of appearing when they are not wanted, and keeping studiously out of the way when their presence is required. Of course it was possible that if she had found Jim-Jim to her liking she would come back to see if there were any more of his kind about, but still it was not to be relied on.

"Harry, who as I have said was an eminently practical boy, suggested to Pharaoh that he should go and sit outside the skerm in the moonlight as a sort of bait, assuring him that he would have nothing to fear, as we should certainly kill the lioness before she killed him. Pharaoh however, strangely enough, did not seem to take to this suggestion. Indeed, he walked away, much put out with Harry for having made it.

"It gave me an idea, however.

"'By Jove!' I said, 'there is the sick ox. He must die sooner or later, so we may as well utilize him.'

"Now, about thirty yards to the left of our skerm, as one stood facing down the hill towards the river, was the stump of a tree that had been destroyed by lightning many years before, standing equidistant between, but a little in front of, two clumps of bush, which were severally some fifteen paces from it.

"Here was the very place to tie the ox; and accordingly a little before sunset the sick animal was led forth by Pharaoh and made fast there, little knowing, poor brute, for what purpose; and we began our long vigil, this time without a fire, for our object was to attract the lioness and not to scare her.

"For hour after hour we waited, keeping ourselves awake by pinching each other – it is, by the way, remarkable what a difference of opinion as to the force of pinches requisite to the occasion exists in the mind of pincher and pinched – but no lioness came. At last the moon went down, and darkness swallowed up the world, as the Kaffirs say, but no lion came to swallow us up. We waited till dawn, because we did not dare to go to sleep, and then at last with many bad thoughts in our hearts we took such rest as we could get, and that was not much.

"That morning we went out shooting, not because we wanted to, for we were too depressed and tired, but because we had no more meat. For three hours or more we wandered about in a broiling sun looking for something to kill, but with absolutely no results. For some unknown reason the game had grown very scarce about the spot, though when I was there two years before every sort of large game except rhinoceros and elephant was particularly abundant. The lions, of whom there were many, alone remained, and I fancy that it was the fact of the game they live on having temporarily migrated which made them so daring and ferocious. As a general rule a lion is an amiable animal enough if he is left alone, but a hungry lion is almost as dangerous as a hungry man. One hears a great many different opinions expressed as to whether or no the lion is remarkable for his courage, but the result of my experience is that very much depends upon the state of his stomach. A starving lion will not stick at a trifle, whereas a full one will flee at a very small rebuke.

"Well, we hunted all about, and nothing could we see, not even a duiker or a bush buck; and at last, thoroughly tired and out of temper, we started on our way back to camp, passing over the brow of a steepish hill to do so. Just as we climbed the crest of the ridge I came to a stand, for there, about six hundred yards to my left, his beautiful curved horns outlined against the soft blue of the sky, I saw a noble koodoo bull (*Strepsiceros kudu*). Even at that distance, for as you know my eyes are very keen, I could distinctly see the white stripes upon its side when the light fell upon it, and its large and pointed ears twitch as the files worried it.

"So far so good; but how were we to get at it? It was ridiculous to risk a shot at that great distance, and yet both the ground and the wind lay very ill for stalking. It seemed to me that the only chance would be to make a detour of at least a mile or more, and come up on the other side of the koodoo. I called Harry to my side, and explained to him what I thought would be our best course, when suddenly, without any delay, the koodoo saved us further trouble by suddenly starting off down the hill like a leaping rocket. I do not know what had frightened it, certainly we had not. Perhaps a hyæna or a leopard – a tiger as we call it there – had suddenly appeared; at any rate, off it went, running slightly towards us, and I never saw a buck go faster. I am afraid that forgetting Harry's presence I used strong language, and really there was some excuse. As for Harry, he stood watching the beautiful animal's course. Presently it vanished behind a patch of bush, to emerge a few seconds later about five hundred paces from us, on a stretch of comparatively level ground that was strewn with boulders. On it went, clearing the boulders in its path with a succession of great bounds that were beautiful to behold. As it fled I happened to look round at Harry, and perceived to my astonishment that he had got his rifle to his shoulder.

"'You young donkey!' I exclaimed, 'surely you are not going to –' and just at that moment the rifle went off.

"And then I think I saw what was in its way one of the most wonderful things I ever remember in my hunting experience. The koodoo was at the moment in the air, clearing a pile of stones with its fore-legs tucked up underneath it. All of an instant the legs stretched themselves out in a spasmodic fashion, it lit on them, and they doubled up beneath it. Down went the noble buck, down upon his head. For a moment he seemed to be standing on his horns, his hind-legs high in the air, and then over he rolled and lay still.

"'Great Heavens!' I said, 'why, you've hit him! He's dead.'

"As for Harry, he said nothing, but merely looked scared, as well he might, for such a marvellous, I may say such an appalling and ghastly fluke it has never been my lot to witness. A man, let alone a boy, might have fired a thousand such shots without ever touching the object; which, mind you, was springing and bounding over rocks quite five hundred yards away; and here this lad – taking a snap shot, and merely allowing for speed and elevation by instinct, for he did not put up his sights – had knocked the bull over as dead as a door-nail. Well, I made no further remark, the occasion was too solemn for talking, but merely led the way to where the koodoo had fallen. There he lay, beautiful and quite still; and there, high up, about half-way down his neck, was a neat round hole. The bullet had severed the spinal marrow, passing through the vertebrae and away on the other side.

"It was already evening when, having cut as much of the best meat as we could carry from the bull, and tied a red handkerchief and some tufts of grass to his spiral horns, which, by the way, must have been nearly five feet in length, in the hope of keeping the jackals and aasvögels (vultures) from him, we finally got back to camp, to find Pharaoh, who was getting rather anxious at our absence, ready to greet us with the pleasing intelligence that another ox was sick. But even this dreadful bit of intelligence could not dash Harry's spirits; the fact of the matter being, incredible as it may appear, I do verily believe that in his heart of hearts he set down the death of that koodoo to the credit of his own skill. Now, though the lad was a pretty shot enough, this of course was ridiculous, and I told him so very plainly.

"By the time that we had finished our supper of koodoo steaks (which would have been better if the koodoo had been a little younger), it was time to get ready for Jim-Jim's murderess. Accordingly we determined again to expose the unfortunate sick ox, that was now absolutely on its last legs, being indeed scarcely able to stand. All the afternoon Pharaoh told us it had been walking round and round in a circle as cattle in the last stage of redwater generally do. Now it had come to a standstill, and was swaying to and fro with its head hanging down. So we tied him up to the stump of the tree as on the previous night, knowing that if the lioness did not kill him he would be dead by morning. Indeed I was afraid that he would die at once, in which case he would be of but little use as a bait, for the lion is a sportsmanlike animal, and unless he is very hungry generally prefers to kill his own dinner, though when that is once killed he will come back to it again and again.

"Then we again went through our experience of the previous night, sitting there hoar after hour, till at last Harry fell fast asleep, and, though I am accustomed to this sort of thing, even I could scarcely keep my eyes open. Indeed I was just dropping off, when suddenly Pharaoh gave me a push.

"'*Listen!*' he whispered.

"I was awake in a second, and listening with all my ears. From the clump of bush to the right of the lightning-shattered stump to which the sick ox was tied came a faint crackling noise. Presently it was repeated. Something was moving there, faintly and quietly enough, but still moving perceptibly, for in the intense stillness or the night any sound seemed loud.

"I woke up Harry, who instantly said, 'Where is she? where is she?' and began to point his rifle about in a fashion that was more dangerous to us and the oxen than to any possible lioness.

"'Be quiet!' I whispered, savagely; and as I did so, with a low and hideous growl a flash of yellow light sped out of the clump of bush, past the ox, and into the corresponding clump upon the other side. The poor sick creature gave a sort of groan, staggered round and then began to tremble. I could see it do so clearly in the moonlight, which was now very bright, and I felt a brute for having exposed the unfortunate animal to such agony as he must undoubtedly be undergoing. The lioness, for it was she, passed so quickly that we could not even distinguish her movements, much less fire. Indeed at night it is absolutely useless to attempt to shoot unless the object is very close and standing perfectly still, and then the light is so deceptive and it is so difficult to see the fore-sight that the best shot will miss more often than he hits.

"'She will be back again presently,' I said; 'look out, but for Heaven's sake don't fire unless I tell you to.'

"Hardly were the words out of my mouth when back she came, and again passed the ox without striking him.

"'What on earth is she doing?' whispered Harry.

"'Playing with it as a cat does with a mouse, I suppose. She will kill it presently.'

"As I spoke, the lioness once more flashed out of the bush, and this time sprang right over the doomed and trembling ox. It was a beautiful sight to see her clear him in the bright moonlight, as though it were a trick which she had been taught.

"'I believe that she has escaped from a circus,' whispered Harry; 'it's jolly to see her jump.'

"I said nothing, but I thought to myself that if it was, Master Harry did not quite appreciate the performance, and small blame to him. At any rate, his teeth were chattering a little.

"Then came a longish pause, and I began to think that the lioness must have gone away, when suddenly she appeared again, and with one mighty bound landed right on to the ox, and struck it a frightful blow with her paw.

"Down it went, and lay on the ground kicking feebly. She put down her wicked-looking head, and, with a fierce growl of contentment, buried her long white teeth in the throat of the dying animal. When she lifted her muzzle again it was all stained with blood. She stood facing us obliquely, licking her bloody chops and making a sort of purring noise.

"'Now's our time,' I whispered, 'fire when I do.'

"I got on to her as well as I could, but Harry, instead of waiting for me as I told him, fired before I did, and that of course hurried me. But when the smoke cleared, I was delighted to see that the lioness was rolling about on the ground behind the body of the ox, which covered her in such a fashion, however, that we could not shoot again to make an end of her.

"'She's done for! she's dead, the yellow devil!' yelled Pharaoh in exultation; and at that very moment the lioness, with a sort of convulsive rush, half rolled, half sprang, into the patch of thick bush to the right. I fired after her as she went, but so far as I could see without result; indeed the probability is that I missed her clean. At any rate she got to the bush in safety, and once there, began to make such a diabolical noise as I never heard before. She would whine and shriek with pain, and then burst out into perfect volleys of roaring that shook the whole place.

"'Well,' I said, 'we must just let her roar; to go into that bush after her at night would be madness.'

"At that moment, to my astonishment and alarm, there came an answering roar from the direction of the river, and then another from behind the swell of bush. Evidently there were more lions about. The wounded lioness redoubled her efforts, with the object, I suppose, of summoning the others to her assistance. At any rate they came, and quickly too, for within five minutes, peeping through the bushes of our skerm fence, we saw a magnificent lion bounding along towards us, through the tall tambouki grass, that in the moonlight looked for all the world like ripening corn. On he came in great leaps, and a glorious sight it was to see him. When within fifty yards or so, he stood still in an open space and roared. The lioness roared too; then there came a third roar, and another great black-maned lion stalked majestically up, and joined number two, till really I began to realize what the ox must have undergone.

"'Now, Harry,' I whispered, 'whatever you do don't fire, It's too risky. If they let us be, let them be.'

"Well, the pair marched off to the bush, where the wounded lioness was now roaring double tides, and the three of them began to snarl and grumble away together there. Presently, however, the lioness ceased roaring, and the two lions came out again, the black-maned one first – to prospect, I suppose – walked to where the carcass of the ox lay, and sniffed at it.

"'Oh, what a shot!' whispered Harry, who was trembling with excitement.

"'Yes,' I said; 'but don't fire; they might all of them come for us.'

"Harry said nothing, but whether it was from the natural impetuosity of youth, or because he was thrown off his balance by excitement, or from sheer recklessness and devilment, I am sure I cannot tell you, never having been able to get a satisfactory explanation from him; but at any rate the fact remains, he, without word or warning, entirely disregarding my exhortations, lifted up his Westley Richards and fired at the black-maned lion, and, what is more, hit it slightly on the flank.

"Next second there was a most awful roar from the injured lion. He glared around him and roared with pain, for he was sadly stung; and then, before I could make up my mind what to do, the great black-maned brute, clearly ignorant of the cause of his hurt, sprang right at the throat of his companion, to whom he evidently attributed his misfortune. It was a curious sight to see the astonishment of the other lion at this most unprovoked assault. Over he rolled with an angry snarl, and on to him sprang the black-maned demon, and began to worry him. This finally awoke the yellow-maned lion to a sense of the situation, and I am bound to say that he rose to it in a most effective manner. Somehow or other he got to his feet, and, roaring and snarling frightfully, closed with his mighty foe.

"Then ensued a most tremendous scene. You know what a shocking thing it is to see two large dogs fighting with abandonment. Well, a whole hundred of dogs could not have looked half so terrible as those two great brutes as they rolled and roared and rent in their horrid rage. They gripped each other, they tore at each other's throats, till their manes came out in handfuls, and the red blood streamed down their yellow hides. It was an awful and a wonderful thing to see the great cats tearing at each other with all the fierce energy of their savage strength, and making the night hideous with their heart-shaking noise. And the fight was a grand one too. For some minutes it was impossible to say which was getting the best of it, but at last I saw that the black-maned lion, though he was slightly the bigger, was failing. I am inclined to think that the wound in his flank crippled him. Anyway he began to get the worst of it, which served him right, as he was the aggressor. Still I could not help feeling sorry for him, for he had fought a gallant fight, when his antagonist finally got him by the throat, and, struggle and strike out as he would, began to shake the life out of him. Over and over they rolled together, a hideous and awe-inspiring spectacle, but the yellow one would not loose his hold, and at length poor black-mane grew faint, his breath came in great snores and seemed to rattle in his nostrils, then he opened his huge mouth, gave the ghost of a roar, quivered, and was dead.

"When he was quite sure that the victory was his own, the yellow-maned lion loosed his grip and sniffed at the fallen foe. Then he licked the dead lion's eye, and next, with his fore-feet resting on the carcass, sent up his own chant of victory, that went rolling and pealing down the dark paths of the night. And at this point I interfered. Taking a careful sight at the centre of his body, in order to give the largest possible margin for error, I fired, and sent a 570 express bullet right through him, and down he dropped dead upon the carcass of his mighty foe.

"After that, fairly satisfied with our performances, we slept peaceably till dawn, leaving Pharaoh to keep watch in case any more lions should take it into their heads to come our way.

"When the sun was well up we arose, and went very cautiously – at least Pharaoh and I did, for I would not allow Harry to come – to see if we could find any trace of the wounded lioness. She had ceased roaring immediately on the arrival of the two lions, and had not made a sound since, from which we concluded that she was probably dead. I was armed with my express, while Pharaoh, in whose hands a rifle was indeed a dangerous weapon, to his companions, had an axe. On our way we stopped to look at the two dead lions. They were magnificent animals, both of them, but their pelts were entirely spoiled by the terrible mauling they had given to each other, which was a sad pity.

"In another minute we were following the blood spoor of the wounded lioness into the bush, where she had taken refuge. This, I need hardly say, we did with the utmost caution; indeed, I for one did not at all like the job, and was only consoled by the reflection that it was necessary, and that the bush was not thick. Well, we stood there, keeping as far from the trees as possible, searching and looking about, but no lioness could we see, though we saw plenty of blood.

"'She must have gone somewhere to die, Pharaoh,' I said in Zulu.

"'Yes, Inkoos,' he answered, 'she has certainly gone away.'

"Hardly were the words out of his mouth, when I heard a roar, and starting round saw the lioness emerge from the very centre of a bush, in which she had been curled up, just behind Pharaoh. Up she went on to her hind-legs, and I noticed that one of her fore-paws was broken near the shoulder, for it hung limply down. Up she went, towering right over Pharaoh's head, and lifting her uninjured paw to strike him to the earth. And then, before I could get my rifle round or do anything to avert the coming catastrophe, the Zulu did a very brave and clever thing. Realizing his own imminent danger, he bounded to one side, and swinging the heavy axe round his head, brought it down right on to the back of the lioness, severing the vertebrae and killing her instantaneously. It was wonderful to see her collapse all in a heap like an empty sack.

"'My word, Pharaoh!' I said, 'that was well done, and none too soon.'

"'Yes,' he answered, with a little laugh, 'it was a good stroke, Inkoos. Jim-Jim will sleep better now.'

"Then, calling Harry to us, we examined the lioness. She was old, if one might judge from her worn teeth, and not very large, but thickly made, and must have possessed extraordinary vitality to have lived so long, shot as she was; for, in addition to her broken shoulder, my express bullet had blown a great hole in her middle that one might have put a fist into.

"Well, that is the story of the death of poor Jim-Jim and how we avenged it. It is rather interesting in its way, because of the fight between the two lions, of which I never saw the like in all my experience, and I know something of lions and their manners."

"And how did you get back to Pilgrims' Rest?' I asked Hunter Quatermain when he had finished his yarn.

"Ah, we had a nice job with that," he answered. "The second sick ox died, and so did another, and we had to get on as best we could with three harnessed unicorn fashion, while we pushed behind. We did about four miles a day, and it took us nearly a month, during the last week of which we pretty well starved."

"I notice," I said, "that most of your trips ended in disaster of some sort or another, and yet you went on making them, which strikes one as a little strange."

"Yes, I dare say: but then, remember I got my living for many years out of hunting. Besides, half the charm of the thing lay in the dangers and disasters, though they were terrible enough at the time. Another thing is, my trips were not all disastrous. Some time, if you like, I will tell you a story of one which was very much the reverse, for I made several thousand pounds out of it, and saw one of the most extraordinary sights a hunter ever came across. It was on this trip that I met the bravest native woman I ever knew; her name was Maiwa. But it is too late now, and besides, I am tired of talking about myself. Pass the water, will you!"

Magepa the Buck

In a preface to a story of the early life of the late Allan Quatermain, known in Africa as Macumazahn, which has been published under the name of "Marie", Mr. Curtis, the brother of Sir Henry Curtis, tells of how he found a number of manuscripts that were left by Mr. Quatermain in his house in Yorkshire. Of these "Marie" was one, but in addition to it and sundry other completed records I, the Editor to whom it was directed that these manuscripts should be handed for publication, have found a quantity of unclassified notes and papers. Some of these deal with matters that have to do with sport and game, or with historical events, and some are memoranda of incidents connected with the career of the writer, or with remarkable occurrences that he had witnessed of which he does not speak elsewhere.

One of these notes – it is contained in a book much soiled and worn that evidently its owner had carried about with him for years – reminds me of a conversation that I had with Mr. Quatermain long ago when I was his guest in Yorkshire. The note itself is short; I think that he must have jotted it down within an hour or two of the event to which it refers. It runs thus:

"I wonder whether in the 'Land Beyond' any recognition is granted for acts of great courage and unselfish devotion – a kind of spiritual Victoria Cross. If so I think it ought to be accorded to that poor old savage, Magepa, as it would be if I had any voice in the matter. Upon my word he has made me feel proud of humanity. And yet he was nothing but a 'nigger', as so many call the Kaffirs."

For a while I, the Editor, wondered to what this entry could allude. Then of a sudden it all came back to me. I saw myself, as a young man, seated in the hall of Quatermain's house one evening after dinner. With me were Sir Henry Curtis and Captain Good. We were smoking, and the conversation had turned upon deeds of heroism. Each of us detailed such acts as he could remember which had made the most impression on him. When we had finished, old Allan said:

"With your leave I'll tell you a story of what I think was one of the bravest things I ever saw. It happened at the beginning of the Zulu War, when the troops were marching into Zululand. Now at that time, as you know, I was turning an honest penny transport-riding for Government, or rather for the military authorities. I hired them three waggons with the necessary voorloopers and drivers, sixteen good salted oxen to each waggon, and myself in charge of the lot. They paid me, well, never mind how much – I am rather ashamed to mention the amount. The truth is that the Imperial officers bought in a dear market during the Zulu War; moreover, things were not always straight. I could tell you stories of folk, not all of them Colonials, who got rich quicker than they ought, commissions and that kind of thing. But perhaps these are better forgotten. As for me, I asked a good price for my waggons, or rather for the hire of them, of a very well-satisfied young gentleman in uniform who had been exactly three weeks in the country, and to my surprise, got it. But when I went to those in command and warned them what would happen if they persisted in their way of advance, then in their pride they would not listen to the old hunter and transport-rider, but politely bowed me out. If they had, there would have been no Isandhlwana disaster."

He brooded awhile, for, as I knew, this was a sore subject with him, one on which he would rarely talk. Although he escaped himself, Quatermain had lost friends on that fatal field. He went on:

"To return to old Magepa. I had known him for many years. The first time we met was in the battle of the Tugela. I was fighting for the king's son, Umbelazi the Handsome, in the ranks of the Tulwana regiment – I mean to write all that story, for it should not be lost. Well, as I have told you before, the Tulwana were wiped out; of the three thousand or so of them I think only about fifty remained alive after they had annihilated the three of Cetewayo's regiments that set upon them. But as it chanced Magepa was one who survived.

"I met him afterwards at old King Panda's kraal and recognized him as having fought by my side. Whilst I was talking to him the Prince Cetewayo came by; to me he was civil enough, for he knew how I chanced to be in the battle, but he glared at Magepa, and said:

"'Why, Macumazahn, is not this man one of the dogs with which you tried to bite me by the Tugela not long ago? He must be a cunning dog also, one who can run fast, for how comes it that he lives to snarl when so many will never bark again? *Ow!* if I had my way I would find a strip of hide to fit his neck.'

"'Not so,' I answered, 'he has the King's peace and he is a brave man – braver than I am, any way, Prince, seeing that I ran from the ranks of the Tulwana, while he stood where he was.'

"'You mean that your horse ran, Macumazahn. Well, since you like this dog, I will not hurt him,' and with a shrug he went his way.

"'Yet soon or late he *will* hurt me,' said Magepa, when the Prince had gone. 'U'Cetewayo has a memory long as the shadow thrown by a tree at sunset. Moreover, as he knows well, it is true that I ran, Macumazahn, though not till all was finished and I could do no more by standing still. You remember how, after we had eaten up the first of Cetewayo's regiments, the second charged us and we ate that up also. Well, in that fight I got a tap on the head from a kerry. It struck me on my man's ring which I had just put on, for I think I was the youngest soldier in that regiment of veterans. The ring saved me; still, for a while I lost my mind and lay like one dead. When I found it again the fight was over and Cetewayo's people were searching for our wounded that they might kill them. Presently they found me and saw that there was no hurt on me.

"'Here is one who shams dead like a stink-cat,' said a big fellow, lifting his spear.

"'Then it was that I sprang up and ran, who was but just married and desired to live. He struck at me, but I jumped over the spear, and the others that they threw missed me. Then they began to hunt me, but Macumazahn, I who am named "The Buck" because I am swifter of foot than any man in Zululand, outpaced them all and got away safe.'

"'Well done, Magepa,' I said. 'Still, remember the saying of your people, "At last the strong swimmer goes with the stream and the swift runner is run down."'

"'I know it, Macumazahn,' he answered, with a nod, 'and perhaps in a day to come I shall know it better.'

"I took little heed of his words at the time, but more than thirty years afterwards I remembered them.

"Such was my first acquaintance with Magepa. Now, friends, I will tell you how it was renewed at the time of the Zulu War.

"As you know, I was attached to the centre column that advanced into Zululand by Rorke's Drift on the Buffalo River. Before war was declared, or at any rate before the advance began, while it might have been and many thought it would be averted, I was employed transport-riding goods to the little Rorke's Drift Station, that which became so famous afterwards, and incidentally in collecting what information I could of Cetewayo's intentions. Hearing that there was a kraal a mile or so the other side of the river, of which the people were said to be very friendly to the English, I determined to visit it. You may think this was rash, but I was so well known in Zululand, where for many years, by special leave of the king, I was allowed to go whither I would quite unmolested and, indeed, under the royal protection, that I felt no fear for myself so long as I went alone.

"Accordingly one evening I crossed the drift and headed for a kloof in which I was told the kraal stood. Ten minutes' ride brought me in sight of it. It was not a large kraal; there may have been six or eight huts and a cattle enclosure surrounded by the usual fence. The situation, however, was very pretty, a knoll of rising ground backed by the wooded slopes of the kloof. As I approached I saw women and children running to the kraal to hide, and when I reached the gateway for some time no one would come out to meet me. At length a small boy appeared who informed me that the kraal was 'empty as a gourd'.

"'Quite so,' I answered; 'still go and tell the headman that Macumazahn wishes to speak with him.'

"The boy departed, and presently I saw a face that seemed familiar to me peeping round the edge of the gateway. After a careful inspection its owner emerged.

"He was a tall, thin man of indefinite age, perhaps between sixty and seventy, with a finely-cut face, a little grey beard, kind eyes and very well-shaped hands and feet, the fingers, which twitched incessantly, being remarkably long.

"'Greeting Macumazahn,' he said, 'I see you do not remember me. Well, think of the battle of the Tugela, and of the last stand of the Tulwana, and of a certain talk at the kraal of our Father-who-is-dead' (that is King Panda), 'and of how he who sits in his place' (he meant Cetewayo) 'told you that if he had his way he would find a hide rope to fit the neck of a certain one.'

"'Ah!' I said, 'I know you now, you are Magepa the Buck. So the Runner has not yet been run down.'

"'No, Macumazahn, not yet, but there is still time. I think that many swift feet will be at work ere long.'

"'How have you prospered?' I asked him.

"'Well enough, Macumazahn, in all ways except one. I have three wives, but my children have been few and are dead, except one daughter, who is married and lives with me, for her husband, too, is dead. He was killed by a buffalo, and she has not yet married again. But enter and see.'

"So I went in and saw Magepa's wives, old women all of them. Also at his bidding, his daughter, whose name was Gita, brought me some maas, or curdled milk, to drink. She was a well-formed woman, very like her father, but sad-faced, perhaps with a prescience of evil to come. Clinging to her finger was a beautiful boy of something under two years of age, who, when he saw Magepa, ran to him and threw his little arms about his legs. The old man lifted the child and kissed him tenderly, saying:

"'It is well that this toddler and I should love one another, Macumazahn, seeing that he is the last of my race. All the other children here are those of the people who have come to live in my shadow.'

"'Where are their fathers?' I asked, patting the little boy who, his mother told me, was named Sinala, upon the cheek, an attention that he resented.

"'They have been called away on duty,' answered Magepa shortly; and I changed the subject.

"Then we began to talk about old times, and I asked him if he had any oxen to sell, saying that this was my reason for visiting his kraal.

"'Nay, Macumazahn,' he answered in a meaning voice. 'This year all the cattle are the king's.'

"I nodded and replied that, as it was so, I had better be going, whereon, as I half expected, Magepa announced that he would see me safe to the drift. So I bade farewell to the wives and the widowed daughter, and we started.

"As soon as we were clear of the kraal Magepa began to open his heart to me.

"'Macumazahn,' he said, looking up at me earnestly, for I was mounted and he walked beside my horse, 'there is to be war. Cetewayo will not consent to the demands of the great White Chief from the Cape' – he meant Sir Bartle Frere – 'he will fight with the English; only he will let them begin the fighting. He will draw them on into Zululand and then overwhelm them with his impis and stamp them flat, and eat them up; and I, who love the English, am very sorry. Yes, it makes my heart bleed. If it were the Boers now, I should be glad, for we Zulus hate the Boers; but the English we do not hate; even Cetewayo likes them; still, he will eat them up if they attack him.'

"'Indeed,' I answered; and then as in duty bound I proceeded to get what I could out of him, and that was not a little. Of course, however, I did not swallow it all, since that I suspected that Magepa was feeding me with news that he had been ordered to disseminate.

"Presently we came to the mouth of the kloof in which the kraal stood, and here, for greater convenience of conversation, we halted, for I thought it as well that we should not be seen in close talk on the open plain beyond. The path here, I should add, ran past a clump of green bushes; I remember they bore a white flower that smelt sweet, and were backed by some tall grass, elephant-grass I think it was, among which grew mimosa trees.

"'Magepa,' I said, 'if in truth there is to be fighting, why don't you move over the river one night with your people and cattle, and get into Natal?'"

"'I would if I could, Macumazahn, who have no stomach for this war against the English. But there I should not be safe, since presently the king will come into Natal too, or send thirty thousand assegais as his messengers. Then what will happen to those who have left him?'

"'Oh! if you think that,' I answered, laughing, 'you had better stay where you are.'

"'Also, Macumazahn, the husbands of those women at my kraal have been called up to their regiments, and if their wives fled to the English they would be killed. Again, the king has sent for nearly all our cattle "to keep them safe". He fears lest we Border Zulus might join our people in Natal, and that is why he is keeping our cattle "safe."'

"'Life is more than cattle, Magepa. At least you might come.'

"'What! And leave my people to be killed? Macumazahn, you did not use to talk so. Still, hearken. Macumazahn, will you do me a service? I will pay you well for it. I would get my daughter Gita and my little grandson Sinala into safety. If I and my wives are wiped out it does not matter, for we are old. But her I would save, and the boy I would save, so that one may live who will remember my name. Now if I were to send them across the drift, say at the dawn, not to-morrow and not the next day, but the day after, would you receive them into your waggon and deliver them safe to some place in Natal? I have money hidden, fifty pieces of gold, and you may take half of these and also half of the cattle if ever I live to get them back out of the keeping of the king.'

"'Never mind about the money, and we will speak of the cattle afterwards,' I said. 'I understand that you wish to send your daughter and your little grandson out of danger; and I think you wise, very wise. When once the advance begins, if there is an advance, who knows what may happen? War is a rough game, Magepa. It is not the custom of you black people to spare women and children; and there will be Zulus fighting on our side as well as on yours; do you understand?'

"'*Ow!* I understand, Macumazahn. I have known the face of war and seen many a little one like my grandson Sinala assegaied upon his mother's back.'

"'Very good. But if I do this for you, you must do something for me. Say, Magepa, does Cetewayo *really* mean to fight, and if so, how? Oh yes, I know all you have been telling me, but I want not words but truth from the heart.'"

"'You ask secrets,' said the old fellow, peering about him into the gathering gloom. 'Still, "a spear for a spear and a shield for a shield," as our saying runs. I have spoken no lie. The king *does* mean to fight, not because he wants to, but because the regiments swear that they will wash their assegais; they who have never seen blood since that battle of the Tugela in which we two played a part, and if he will not suffer it, well, there are more of his race! Also he means to fight thus,' and he gave me some very useful information, that is, information which would have been useful if those in authority had deigned to pay any attention to it when I passed it on.

"Just as he finished speaking I thought that I heard a sound in the dense green bush behind us. It reminded me of the noise a man makes when he tries to stifle a cough, and frightened me. For if we had been overhead by a spy, Magepa was as good as dead, and the sooner I was across the river the better.

"'What's that?' I asked.

"'A bush buck, Macumazahn. There are lots of them about here.'

"Not being satisfied, though it is true that buck do cough like this, I turned my horse to the bush, seeking an opening. Thereon something crashed away and vanished into the long grass. In those shadows, of course, I could not see what it was, but such light as remained glinted on what might have been the polished tip of the horn of an antelope or – an assegai.

"'I told you it was a buck, Macumazahn,' said Magepa. 'Still, if you smell danger, let us come away from the bush, though the orders are that no white man is to be touched as yet.'

"Then, while we walked on towards the ford, he set out with great detail, as Kaffirs do, the exact arrangements that he proposed to make for the handing over of his daughter and her child into my care. I remember that I asked him why he would not send her on the following morning, instead of two mornings later. He answered because he expected an outpost of scouts from one of the regiments at his kraal that night, who would probably remain there over the morrow and perhaps longer. While they were in the place it would be difficult, if not impossible, for him to send away Gita and her son without exciting suspicion.

"Near the drift we parted, and I returned to our provisional camp and wrote a beautiful report of all that I had learned, of which report, I may add, no one took the slightest notice.

"I think it was the morning before that whereon I had arranged to meet Gita and the little boy at the drift that just about dawn I went down to the river for a wash. Having taken my dip, I climbed on to a flat rock to dress myself, and looked at the billows of beautiful, pearly mist which hid the face of the water, and considered – I almost said listened to – the great silence, for as yet no live thing was stirring.

"Ah! if I had known of the hideous sights and sounds that were destined to be heard ere long in this same haunt of perfect peace! Indeed, at that moment there came a kind of hint or premonition of them, since suddenly through the utter quiet broke the blood-curdling wail of a woman. It was followed by other wails and shouts, distant and yet distinct. Then the silence fell again.

"Now, thought I to myself, that noise might very well have come from old Magepa's kraal; luckily, however, sounds are deceptive in mist.

"Well, the end of it was that I waited there till the sun rose. The first thing on which its bright beams struck was a mighty column of smoke rising to heaven from where Magepa's kraal had stood!

"I went back to my waggons very sad – so sad that I could scarcely eat my breakfast. While I walked I wondered hard whether the light had glinted upon the tip of a buck's horn in that patch of green bush with the sweet-smelling white flowers a night or two ago. Or had it perchance fallen upon the point of the assegai of some spy who was watching my movements! In that event yonder column of smoke and the horrible cries that preceded it were easy to explain. For had not Magepa and I talked secrets together, and in Zulu?

"On the following morning at the dawn I attended at the drift in the faint hope that Gita and her boy might arrive there as arranged. But nobody came, which was not wonderful, seeing that Gita lay dead, stabbed through and through, as I saw afterwards (she made a good fight for the child), and that her spirit had gone to wherever go the souls of the brave-hearted, be they white or black. Only on the farther bank of the river I saw some Zulu scouts who seemed to know my errand, for they called to me, asking mockingly where was the pretty woman I had come to meet?

"After that I tried to put the matter out of my head, which indeed was full enough of other things, since now definite orders had arrived as to the advance, and with these many troops and officers.

"It was just then that the Zulus began to fire across the river at such of our people as they saw upon the bank. At these they took aim, and, as a result, hit nobody. A raw Kaffir with a rifle, in my experience, is only dangerous when he aims at nothing, for then the bullet looks after itself and may catch you. To put a stop to this nuisance a regiment of the friendly natives – there may have been several hundred of them – was directed to cross the river and clear the kloofs and rocks of the Zulu skirmishers who were hidden among them. I watched them go off in fine style, and in the course of the afternoon heard a good deal of shouting and banging of guns on the farther side of the river.

"Towards evening someone told me that our *impi*, as he called it grandiloquently, was returning victorious. Having at the moment nothing else to do, I walked down to the river at a point where the water was deep and the banks were high. Here I climbed to the top of a pile of boulders, whence with my field-glasses I could sweep a great extent of plain which stretched away on the Zululand side till at length it merged into hills and bush.

"Presently I saw some of our natives marching homewards in a scattered and disorganizedfashion, but evidently very proud of them- selves, for they were waving their assegais and singing scraps of war-songs. A few minutes later, a mile or more away I caught sight of a man running.

"Watching him through the glasses I noted three things: First, that he was tall; secondly, that he ran with extraordinary swiftness; and, thirdly, that he had something tied upon his back. It was evident, further, that he had good reason to run, since he was being hunted by a number of our Kaffirs, of whom more and more continually joined in the chase. From every side they poured down upon him, trying to cut him off and kill him, for as they got nearer I could see the assegais which they threw at him flash in the sunlight.

"Very soon I understood that the man was running with a definite object and to a definite point; he was trying to reach the river. I thought the sight very pitiful, this one poor creature being hunted to death by so many. Also I wondered why he did not free himself from the bundle on his back, and came to the conclusion that he must be a witch-doctor, and that the bundle contained his precious charms or medicines.

"This was while he was yet a long way off, but when he came nearer, within three or four hundred yards, of a sudden I caught the outline of his face against a good background, and knew it for that of Magepa.

"'My God!' I said to myself, 'it is old Magepa the Buck, and the bundle in the mat will be his grandson, Sinala!'

"Yes, even then I felt certain that he was carrying the child upon his back.

"What was I to do? It was impossible for me to cross the river at that place, and long before I could get round by the ford all would be finished. I stood up on my rock and shouted to those brutes of Kaffirs to let the man alone. They were so excited that they did not hear my words; at least, they swore afterwards that they thought I was encouraging them to hunt him down.

"But Magepa heard me. At the moment he seemed to be failing, but the sight of me appeared to give him fresh strength. He gathered himself together and leapt forward at a really surprising speed. Now the river was not more than three hundred yards away from him, and for the first two hundred of these he quite outdistanced his pursuers, although they were most of them young men and comparatively fresh. Then once more his strength began to fail.

"Watching through the glasses, I could see that his mouth was wide open, and that there was red foam upon his lips. The burden on his back was dragging him down. Once he lifted his hands as though to loose it; then with a wild gesture let them fall again.

"Two of the pursuers who had outpaced the others crept up to him – lank, lean men of not more than thirty years of age. They had stabbing spears in their hands, such as are used at close quarters, and these of course they did not throw. One of them gained a little on the other.

"Now Magepa was not more than fifty yards from the bank, with the first hunter about ten paces behind him and coming up rapidly. Magepa glanced over his shoulder and saw, then put out his last strength. For forty yards he went like an arrow, running straight away from his pursuers, until he was within a few feet of the bank, when he stumbled and fell.

"'He's done,' I said, and, upon my word, if I had had a rifle in my hand I think I would have stopped one or both of those bloodhounds and taken the consequences.

"But, no! Just as the first man lifted his broad spear to stab him through the back on which the bundle lay, Magepa leapt up and wheeled round to take the thrust in his chest. Evidently he did not wish to be speared in the back – for a certain reason. He took it sure enough, for the assegai was wrenched out of the hand of the striker. Still, as he was reeling backwards, it did not go through Magepa, or perhaps it hit a bone. He drew out the spear and threw it at the man, wounding him. Then he staggered on, back and back to the edge of the little cliff.

"It was reached at last. With a cry of 'Help me, Macumazahn!' Magepa turned, and before the other man could spear him, leapt straight into the deep water. He rose. Yes, the brave old fellow rose and struck out for the other bank, leaving a little line of red behind him.

"I rushed, or rather sprang and rolled down to the edge of the stream to where a point of shingle ran out into the water. Along this I clambered, and beyond it up to my middle. Now Magepa was being swept past me. I caught his outstretched hand and pulled him ashore.

" 'The boy!' he gasped; 'the boy! Is he dead?'

"I severed the lashings of the mat that had cut right into the old fellow's shoulders. Inside of it was little Sinala, spluttering out water, but very evidently alive and unhurt, for presently he set up a yell.'

" 'No,' I said, 'he lives, and will live.'

" 'Then all is well, Macumazahn.' (*A pause.*) 'It *was* a spy in the bush, not a buck. He overheard our talk. The king's slayers came. Gita held the door of the hut while I took the child, cut a hole through the straw with my assegai, and crept out at the back. She was full of spears before she died, but I got away with the boy. Till your Kaffirs found me I lay hid in the bush, hoping to escape to Natal. Then I ran for the river, and saw you on the farther bank. *I* might have got away, but that child is heavy.' (*A pause.*) 'Give him food, Macumazahn, he must be hungry.' (*A pause.*) 'Farewell. That was a good saying of yours – the swift runner is outrun at last. Ah! yet I did not run in vain.' (*Another pause, the last.*) Then he lifted himself upon one arm and with the other saluted, first the boy Sinala and next me, muttering, 'Remember your promise, Macumazahn.'

"That is how Magepa the Buck died. I never saw anyone carrying weight who could run quite so well as he," and Quatermain turned his head away as though the memory of this incident affected him somewhat.

"What became of the child Sinala?" I asked presently.

"Oh! I sent him to an institution in Natal, and afterwards was able to get some of his property back for him. I believe that he is being trained as an interpreter."

Zikali the Wizard

It was, I think, in the month of May in the year 1854 that I went hunting in rough country between the White and Black Umvolosi Rivers, by permission of Panda – whom the Boers had made King of Zululand after the defeat and death of Dingaan his brother. The district was very feverish, and for this reason I had entered it in the winter months. There was so much bush that, in the total absence of roads, I thought it wise not to attempt to bring my waggons down, and as no horses would live in that veld I went on foot. My principal companions were a Kaffir of mixed origin, called Sikauli, commonly abbreviated into Scowl, the Zulu chief Saduko, and a headman of the Undwandwe blood named Umbezi, at whose kraal on the high land about thirty miles away I left my waggon and certain of my men in charge of the goods and some ivory that I had traded.

This Umbezi was a stout and genial-mannered man of about sixty years of age, and, what is rare among these people, one who loved sport for its own sake. Being aware of his tastes, also that he knew the country and was skilled in finding game, I had promised him a gun if he would accompany me and bring a few hunters. It was a particularly bad gun that had seen much service, and one which had an unpleasing habit of going off at half-cock; but even after he had seen it, and I in my honesty had explained its weaknesses, he jumped at the offer.

"O Macumazana [that is my native name, often abbreviated into Macumazahn, which means "One who stands out", or as many interpret it, I don't know how, "Watcher-by-Night "] a gun that goes off sometimes when you do not expect it is much better than no gun at all, and you are a chief with a great heart to promise it to me, for when I own the White Man's weapon I shall be looked up to and feared by everyone between the two rivers."

Now, while he was speaking he handled the gun, that was loaded, observing which I moved behind him. Off it went in due course, its recoil knocking him backwards – for that gun was a devil to kick – and its bullet cutting the top off the ear of one of his wives. The lady fled screaming, leaving a little bit of her ear upon the ground.

"What does it matter?" said Umbezi, as he picked himself up, rubbing his shoulder with a rueful look. "Would that the evil spirit in the gun had cut off her tongue and not her ear! It is the Worn-out-Old-Cow's own fault; she is always peeping into everything like a monkey. Now she will have something to chatter about and leave my things alone for a while. I thank my ancestral Spirit it was not Mameena, for then her looks would have been spoiled."

"Who is Mameena?" I asked. "Your last wife?"

"No, no, Macumazahn; I wish she were, for then I should have the most beautiful wife in the land. She is my daughter, though not that of the Worn-out-Old Cow; her mother died when she was born, on the night of the Great Storm. You should ask Saduko there who Mameena is," he added with a broad grin, lifting his head from the gun, which he was examining gingerly, as though he thought it might go off again, and nodding towards someone who stood behind him.

I turned, and for the first time saw Saduko, whom I recognized at once as a person quite out of the ordinary run of natives.

He was a tall and magnificently formed young man, who, although his breast was scarred with assegai wounds, showing that he was a warrior, had not yet attained to the honour of the "ring" of polished wax laid over strips of rush bound round with sinew and sewn to the hair, the *isicoco* which at a certain age or dignity, determined by the king, Zulus are allowed to assume. But his face struck me more even than his grace, strength and stature. Undoubtedly it was a very fine face, with little or nothing of the negroid type about it; indeed, he might have been a rather dark-coloured Arab, to which stock he

probably threw back. The eyes, too, were large and rather melancholy, and in his reserved, dignified air there was something that showed him to be no common fellow, but one of breeding and intellect.

"*Siyakubona* [that is, "we see you", *anglice* "good-morrow"],

Saduko," I said, eyeing him curiously. "Tell me, who is Mameena?"

"*Inkoosi*," he answered in his deep voice, lifting his delicately shaped hand in salutation, a courtesy that pleased me who, after all, was nothing but a white hunter. "*Inkoosi*, has not her father said that she is his daughter?"

"Aye," answered the jolly old Umbezi, "but what her father has not said is that Saduko is her lover, or, rather, would like to be. *Wow!* Saduko," he went on, shaking his fat finger at him, "are you mad, man, that you think a girl like that is for you? Give me a hundred cattle, not one less, and I will begin to think of it. Why, you have not ten, and Mameena is my eldest daughter, and must marry a rich man."

"She loves me, O Umbezi," answered Saduko, looking down, "and that is more than cattle."

"For you, perhaps, Saduko, but not for me who am poor and want cows. Also," he added, glancing at him shrewdly, "are you so sure that Mameena loves you though you be such a fine man? Now, I should have thought that, whatever her eyes may say, her heart loves no one but herself, and that in the end she will follow her heart and not her eyes. Mameena the beautiful does not seek to be a poor man's wife and do all the hoeing. But bring me the hundred cattle and we will see, for, speaking truth from my heart, if you were a big chief there is no one I should like better as a son-in-law, unless it were Macumazahn here," he said, digging me in the ribs with his elbow, "who would lift up my House on his white back."

Now, at this speech Saduko shifted his feet uneasily; it seemed to me as though he felt there was truth in Umbezi's estimate of his daughter's character. But he only said :

"Cattle can be acquired."

"Or stolen," suggested Umbezi.

"Or taken in war," corrected Saduko. "When I have a hundred head I will hold you to your word, O father of Mameena."

"And then what would you live on, fool, if you gave all your beasts to me? There, there, cease talking wind. Before you have a hundred head of cattle Mameena will have six children who will not call *you* father. Ah, don't you like that? Are you going away?"

"Yes, I am going," he answered, with a flash of his quiet eyes; "only then let the man whom they do call father beware of Saduko."

"Beware of how you talk, young man," said Umbezi in a grave voice. "Would you travel your father's road? I hope not, for I like you well; but such words are apt to be remembered."

Saduko walked away as though he did not hear.

"Who is he?" I asked.

"One of high blood," answered Umbezi shortly. "He might be a chief to-day had not his father been a plotter and a wizard. Dingaan smelt him out" – and he made a sideways motion with his hand that among the Zulus means much. "Yes, they were killed, almost every one; the chief, his wives, his children and his headmen – every one except Chosa his brother and his son Saduko, whom Zikali the dwarf, the Smeller-out-of-evil-doers, the Ancient, who was old before Senzangakona became a father of kings, hid him. There, that is an evil tale to talk of," and he shivered. "Come, White Man, and doctor that old Cow of mine, or she will give me no peace for months."

So I went to see the Worn-out Old Cow – not because I had any particular interest in her, for, to tell the truth, she was a very disagreeable and antique person, the cast-off wife of some chief whom at an unknown date in the past the astute Umbezi had married from motives of policy – but because I hoped to hear more of Miss Mameena, in whom I had become interested.

Entering a large hut, I found the lady so impolitely named "the Old Cow" in a parlous state. There she lay upon the floor, an unpleasant object because of the blood that had escaped from her wound, surrounded by a crowd of other women and of children. At regular intervals she announced that she was dying, and emitted a fearful yell, whereupon all the audience yelled also; in short, the place was a perfect pandemonium.

Telling Umbezi to get the hut cleared, I said that I would go to fetch my medicines. Meanwhile I ordered my servant, Scowl, a humorous-looking fellow, light yellow in hue, for he had a strong dash of Hottentot in his composition, to cleanse the wound. When I returned from the waggon ten minutes later the screams were more terrible than before, although the chorus now stood without the hut. Nor was this surprising, for on entering the place I found Scowl trimming up "the Old Cow's" ear with a pair of blunt nail-scissors.

"O Macumazana," said Umbezi in a hoarse whisper, "might it not perhaps be as well to leave her alone? If she bled to death, at any rate she would be quieter."

"Are you a man or a hyæna?" I answered sternly, and set about the job, Scowl holding the poor woman's head between his knees.

It was over at length; a simple operation in which I exhibited – I believe that is the medical term – a strong solution of caustic applied with a feather.

"There, Mother," I said, for now we were alone in the hut, whence Scowl had fled, badly bitten in the calf, "you won't die now."

"No, you vile White Man," she sobbed, "I shan't die, but how about my beauty?"

"It will be greater than ever," I answered; "no one else will have an ear with such a curve in it. But, talking of beauty, where is Mameena?"

"I don't know where she is," she replied with fury, "but I very well know where she would be if I had my way. That peeled willow-wand of a girl" – here she added certain descriptive epithets I will not repeat – "has brought this misfortune upon me. We had a slight quarrel yesterday, White Man, and, being a witch as she is, she prophesied evil. Yes, when by accident I scratched her ear, she said that before long mine should burn, and surely burn it does." (This, no doubt, was true, for the caustic had begun to bite.)

"O devil of a White Man," she went on, "you have bewitched me; you have filled my head with fire."

Then she seized an earthenware pot and hurled it at me, saying, "Take that for your doctor-fee. Go, crawl after Mameena like the others and get her to doctor you."

By this time I was half through the bee-hole of the hut, my

movements being hastened by a vessel of hot water which landed behind me.

"What is the matter, Macumazahn?" asked old Umbezi, who was waiting outside.

"Nothing at all, friend," I answered with a sweet smile, "except that your wife wants to see you at once. She is in pain, and wishes you to soothe her. Go in; do not hesitate."

After a moment's pause he went in – that is, half of him went in. Then came a fearful crash, and he emerged again with the rim of a pot about his neck and his countenance veiled in a coating of honey.

"Where is Mameena?" I asked him as he sat up spluttering.

"Where I wish I was," he answered in a thick voice; "at a kraal five hours' journey away."

Well, that was the first I heard of Mameena.

That night as I sat smoking my pipe under the flap lean-to attached to the waggon, laughing to myself over the adventure of "the Old Cow", falsely described as "worn out", and wondering whether Umbezi had got the honey out of his hair, the canvas was lifted, and a Kaffir wrapped in a kaross crept in and squatted before me.

"Who are you?" I asked, for it was too dark to see the man's face.

"*Inkoosi*," answered a deep voice, "I am Saduko."

"You are welcome," I answered, handing him a little gourd of snuff in token of hospitality. Then I waited while he poured some of the snuff into the palm of his hand and took it in the usual fashion.

"*Inkoosi*," he said, when he had scraped away the tears produced by the snuff, "I have come to ask you a favour. You heard Umbezi say to-day that he will not give me his daughter, Mameena, unless I give him a hundred head of cows. Now, I have not got the cattle, and I cannot earn them by work in many years. Therefore I must take them from a certain tribe I know which is at war with the Zulus. But this I cannot do unless I have a gun. If I had a good gun, *Inkoosi* – one that only goes off when it is asked, and not of its own fancy – I who have some name could persuade a number of men, who once were servants of my father, or their sons, to be my companions in this venture."

"Do I understand that you wish me to give you one of my good guns with two mouths to it [i.e. double-barrelled] a gun worth at least twelve oxen, for nothing, O Saduko?" I asked in a cold and scandalized voice.

"Not so, O Watcher-by-Night," he answered; "not so, O He-who-sleeps-with-one-eye-open [another free and difficult rendering of my native name, Macumazahn, or more correctly, Macumazana], I should never dream of offering such an insult to your high-born intelligence." He paused and took another pinch of snuff, then went on in a meditative voice: "Where I propose to get those hundred cattle there are many more; I am told not less than a thousand head in all. Now, *Inkoosi*," he added, looking at me sideways, "suppose you gave me the gun I ask for, and suppose you accompanied me with your own gun and your armed hunters, it would be fair that you should have half the cattle, would it not?"

"That's cool," I said. "So, young man, you want to turn me into a cow-thief and get my throat cut by Panda for breaking the peace of his Country?"

"Neither, Macumazahn, for these are my own cattle. Listen, now, and I will tell you a story. You have heard of Matiwane, the chief of the Amangwane?"

"Yes," I answered. "His tribe lived near the head of the Umzinyati, did they not? Then they were beaten by the Boers or the English, and Matiwane came under the Zulus. But afterwards Dingaan wiped him out, with his House, and now his people are killed or scattered."

"Yes, his people are killed and scattered, but his House still lives. Macumazahn, I am his House, I, the only son of his chief wife, for Zikali the Wise Little One, the Ancient, who is of the Amangwane blood, and who hated Chaka and Dingaan – yes, and Senzangakona their father before them – but whom none of them could kill because he is so great and has such mighty spirits for his servants, saved and sheltered me."

"If he is so great, why, then, did he not save your father also, Saduko?" I asked, as though I knew nothing of this Zikali.

"I cannot say, Macumazahn. Perhaps the spirits plant a tree for themselves, and to do so cut down many other trees. At least, so it happened. It happened thus: Bangu, chief of the Amakoba, whispered into Dingaan's ear that Matiwane, my father, was a wizard; also that he was very rich. Dingaan listened because he thought a sickness that he had came from Matiwane's witchcraft. He said: 'Go, Bangu, and take a company with you and pay Matiwane a visit of honour, and in the night, O in the night – ! Afterwards, Bangu, we will divide the cattle, for Matiwane is strong and clever, and you shall not risk your life for nothing.'"

Saduko paused and looked down at the ground, brooding heavily.

"Macumazahn, it was done," he said presently. "They ate my father's meat, they drank his beer; they gave him a present from the king, they praised him with high names; yes, Bangu took snuff with him and called him brother. Then in the night, O in the night – !

"My father was in the hut with my mother and I, so big only" – and he held his hand at the height of a boy of ten – "was with them. The cry arose, the flames began to eat; my father looked out and saw. 'Break through the fence and away, woman,' he said; 'away with Saduko, that he may live to avenge me. Begone while I hold the gate! Begone to Zikali, for whose witchcrafts I pay with my blood.'

"Then he kissed me on the brow, saying but one word, 'Remember', and thrust us from the hut.

"My mother broke a way through the fence; yes, she tore at it with her nails and teeth like a hyæna. I looked back out of the shadow of the hut and saw Matiwane my father fighting like a buffalo. Men went down before him, one, two, three, although he had no shield: only his spear. Then Bangu crept behind him and stabbed him in the back and he threw up his arms and fell. I saw no more, for by now we were through the fence. We ran, but they perceived us. They hunted us as wild dogs hunt a buck. They killed my mother with a throwing assegai; it entered at her back and came out at her heart. I went mad, I drew it from her body, I ran at them. I dived beneath the shield of the first, a very tall man, and held the spear, so, in both my little hands.

His weight came upon its point and it went through him as though he were but a bowl of buttermilk. Yes, he rolled over, quite dead, and the handle of the spear broke upon the ground. Now the others stopped astonished, for never had they seen such a thing. That a child should kill a tall warrior, oh! that tale had not been told. Some of them would have let me go, but just then Bangu came up and saw the dead man who was his brother.

"'*Wow!*' he said when he knew how the man had died. 'This lion's cub is a wizard also, for how else could he have killed a soldier who has known war? Hold out his arms that I may finish him slowly.'

"So two of them held out my arms, and Bangu came up with his spear."

Saduko ceased speaking, not that his tale was done, but because his voice choked in his throat. Indeed, seldom have I seen a man so moved. He breathed in great gasps, the sweat poured from him, and his muscles worked convulsively. I gave him a pannikin of water and he drank, then he went on:

"Already the spear had begun to prick – look, here is the mark of it" – and opening his kaross he pointed to a little white line just below the breast-bone – "when a strange shadow thrown by the fire of the burning huts came between Bangu and me, a shadow as that of a toad standing on its hind legs. I looked round and saw that it was the shadow of Zikali, whom I had seen once or twice. There he stood, though whence he came I know not, wagging his great white head that sits on the top of his body like a pumpkin on an ant-heap, rolling his big eyes and laughing loudly.

"'A merry sight,' he cried in his deep voice that sounded like water in a hollow cave. 'A merry sight, O Bangu, Chief of the Amakoba! Blood, blood, plenty of blood! Fire, fire, plenty of fire! Wizards dead here, there, and everywhere! Oh ! a merry sight! I have seen many such; one at the kraal of your grandmother, for instance – your grandmother the great *Inkosikazi*, when I myself escaped with my life because I was so old; but never do I remember a merrier one than that which this moon shines on,' and he pointed to the White Lady who just then broke through the clouds. 'But, great Chief Bangu, lord loved by the son of Senzangakona, brother of the Black One [Chaka] who has ridden hence on the assegai, what is the meaning of *this* play?' and he pointed to me and to the two soldiers who held out my little arms.

"'I kill the wizard's cub, Zikali, that is all,' answered Bangu.

"'I see, I see,' laughed Zikali. 'A gallant deed! You have butchered the father and the mother, and now you would butcher the child who has slain one of your grown warriors in fair fight. A very gallant deed, well worthy of the chief of the Amakoba! Well, loose his spirit – only –' He stopped and took a pinch of snuff from a box which he drew from a slit in the lobe of his great ear.

"'Only what?' asked Bangu, hesitating.

"'Only I wonder, Bangu, what you will think of the world in which you will find yourself before tomorrow's moon arises. Come back thence and tell me, Bangu, for there are so many worlds beyond the sun, and I would learn for certain which of them such a one as you inhabits: a man who for hatred and for gain murders the father and the mother and then butchers the child – the child that could slay a warrior who has seen war, with the spear hot from his mother's heart.'

"'Do you mean that I shall die if I kill this lad?' shouted Bangu in a great voice.

"'What else?' answered Zikali, taking another pinch of snuff.

"'This, Wizard; that we will go together.'

"'Good, good!' laughed the dwarf. 'Let us go together. Long have I wished to die, and what better companion could I find than Bangu, Chief of the Amakoba, Slayer of Children, to guard me on a dark and terrible road? Come, brave Bangu, come; kill me if you can,' and again he laughed at him.

"Now, Macumazahn, the people of Bangu fell back muttering, for they found this business horrible. Yes, even those who held my arms let go of them.

"'What will happen to me, Wizard, if I spare the boy?' asked Bangu.

"Zikali stretched out his hand and touched the scratch that the assegai had made in me here. Then he held up his finger red with my blood, and looked at it in the light of the moon; yes, and tasted it with his tongue.

"'I think this will happen to you, Bangu,' he said. 'If you spare this boy he will grow into a man who will kill you and many others one day. But if you do not spare him I think that his spirit, working as spirits can do, will kill you to-morrow. Therefore the question is, will you live a while or will you die at once, taking me with you as your companion? For you must not leave me behind, brother Bangu.'

"Now Bangu turned and walked away, stepping over the body of my mother, and all his people walked away after him, so that presently Zikali the Wise and Little and I were left alone.

"'What! have they gone?' said Zikali, lifting up his eyes from the ground. 'Then we had better be going also, Son of Matiwane, lest he should change his mind and come back. Live on, Son of Matiwane, that you may avenge Matiwane.'"

"A nice tale," I said. "But what happened afterwards?"

"Zikali took me away and nurtured me at his kraal in the Black Kloof, where he lived alone save for his servants, for in that kraal he would suffer no woman to set foot, Macumazahn. He taught me much wisdom and many secret things, and would have made a great doctor of me had I so willed. But I willed it not who find spirits ill company, and there are many of them about the Black Kloof, Macumazahn. So in the end he said: 'Go where your heart calls, and be a warrior, Saduko. But know this: You have opened a door that can never be shut again, and across the threshold of that door spirits will pass in and out for all your life, whether you seek them or seek them not.'

"'It was you who opened the door, Zikali,' I answered angrily.

"'Mayhap,' said Zikali, laughing after his fashion, 'for I open when I must and shut when I must. Indeed, in my youth, before the Zulus were a people, they named me Opener of Doors; and now, looking through one of those doors, I see something about you, O Son of Matiwane.'

" 'What do you see, my father?' I asked.

" 'I see two roads, Saduko: the Road of Medicine, that is the spirit road, and the Road of Spears, that is the blood road. I see you travelling on the Road of Medicine, that is my own road, Saduko, and growing wise and great, till at last, fat, far away, you vanish over the precipice to which it leads, full of years and honour and wealth, feared yet beloved by all men, white and black. Only that road you must travel alone, since such wisdom may have no friends, and, above all, no woman to share its secrets. Then I look at the Road of Spears and see you, Saduko, travelling on that road, and your feet are red with blood, and women wind their arms about your neck, and one by one your enemies go down before you. You love much, and sin much for the sake of the love, and she for whom you sin comes and goes and comes again. And the road is short, Saduko, and near the end of it are many spirits; and though you shut your eyes you see them, and though you fill your ears with clay you hear them, for they are the ghosts of your slain. But the end of your journeying I see not. Now choose which road you will, Son of Matiwane, and choose swiftly, for I speak no more of this matter.'

"Then, Macumazahn, I thought a while of the safe and lonely path of wisdom, also of the blood-red path of spears where I should find love and war, and my youth rose up in me and – I chose the path of spears and the love and the sin and the unknown death."

"A foolish choice, Saduko, supposing that there is any truth in this tale of roads, which there is not."

"Nay, a wise one, Macumazahn, for since then I have seen Mameena and know why I chose that path."

"Ah!" I said. "Mameena – I forgot her. Well, after all, perhaps there is some truth in your tale of roads. When *I* have seen Mameena I will tell you what I think."

"When you have seen Mameena, Macumazahn, you will say that the choice was very wise. Well, Zikali, Opener of Doors, laughed loudly when he heard it. 'The ox seeks the fat pasture, but the young bull the rough mountain-side where the heifers graze,' he said; 'and after all, a bull is better than an ox. Now begin to travel your own road, Son of Matiwane, and from time to time return to the Black Kloof and tell me how it fares with you. I will promise you not to die before I know the end of it.'

Allan's Wife

Early Days

It may be remembered that in the last pages of his diary, written just before his death, Allan Quatermain makes allusion to his long dead wife, stating that he has written of her fully elsewhere.

When his death was known, his papers were handed to myself as his literary executor. Among them I found various manuscripts, of which the following is one. With the others we have nothing to do at present.

I have often thought (Mr. Quatermain's manuscript begins) that I would set down on paper the events connected with my marriage, and the loss of my most dear wife. Many years have now passed since that event, and to some extent time has softened the old grief, though Heaven knows it is still keen enough. On two or three occasions I have even begun the record. Once I gave it up because the writing of it depressed me beyond bearing, once because I was suddenly called away upon a journey, and the third time because a Kaffir boy found my manuscript convenient for lighting the kitchen fire.

But now that I am at leisure here in England, I will make a fourth attempt. If I succeed, the story may serve to interest some one in after years when I am dead and gone; before that I should not wish it to be published. It is a wild tale enough, and suggests some curious reflections.

I am the son of a missionary. My father was originally curate in charge of a small parish in Oxfordshire. He had already been some years married to my dear mother when he went there, and he had four children, of whom I was the youngest. I remember faintly the place where we lived. It was an ancient long grey house, facing the road. There was a very large tree of some sort in the garden. It was hollow, and we children used to play about inside of it, and knock knots of wood from the rough bark. We all slept in a kind of attic, and my mother always came and kissed us when we were in bed. I used to wake up and see her bending over me, a candle in her hand. There was a curious kind of pole projecting from the wall over my bed. Once I was dreadfully frightened because my eldest brother made me hang to it by my hands. That is all I remember about our old home. It has been pulled down long ago, or I would journey there to see it.

A little further down the road was a large house with big iron gates to it, and on the top of the gate pillars sat two stone lions, which were so hideous that I was afraid of them. Perhaps this sentiment was prophetic. One could see the house by peeping through the bars of the gates. It was a gloomy-looking place, with a tall yew hedge round it; but in the summer-time some flowers grew about the sun-dial in the grass plat. This house was called the Hall, and Squire Carson lived there. One Christmas – it must have been the Christmas before my father emigrated, or I should not remember it – we children went to a Christmas-tree festivity at the Hall. There was a great party there, and footmen wearing red waistcoats stood at the door. In the dining-room, which was panelled with black oak, was the Christmas-tree. Squire Carson stood in front of it. He was a tall, dark man, very quiet in his manners, and he wore a bunch of seals on his waistcoat. We used to think him old, but as a matter of fact he was then not more than forty. He had been, as I afterwards learned, a great traveller in his youth, and some six or seven years before this date he married a lady who was half a Spaniard – a papist, my father called her. I can remember her well. She was small and very pretty, with a rounded figure, large black eyes, and glittering teeth. She spoke English with a curious accent. I suppose that I must have been a funny child to look at, and I know that my hair stood up on my head then as it does now, for I still have a sketch of myself that my mother made of me, in which this peculiarity is strongly marked. On this occasion of the Christmas-tree I remember that Mrs. Carson turned to a tall, foreign-looking gentleman who stood beside her, and, tapping him affectionately on the shoulder with her gold eye-glasses, said:

"Look, cousin – look at that droll little boy with the big brown eyes; his hair is like a – what you call him? – scrubbing-brush. Oh, what a droll little boy!"

The tall gentleman pulled at his moustache, and, taking Mrs. Carson's hand in his, began to smooth my hair down with it till I heard her whisper:

"Leave go my hand, cousin. Thomas is looking like – like the thunderstorm."

Thomas was the name of Mr. Carson, her husband.

After that I hid myself as well as I could behind a chair, for I was shy, and watched little Stella Carson, who was the squire's only child, giving the children presents off the tree. She was dressed as Father Christmas, with some soft white stuff round her lovely little face, and she had large dark eyes, which I thought more beautiful than anything I had ever seen. At last it came to my turn to receive a present – oddly enough, considered in the light of future events, it was a large monkey. Stella reached it down from one of the lower boughs of the tree and handed it to me, saying:

"Dat is my Christmas present to you, little Allan Quatermain."

As she did so her sleeve, which was covered with cotton wool, spangled over with something that shone, touched one of the tapers and caught fire – how I do not know – and the flame ran up her arm towards her throat. She stood quite still. I suppose that she was paralysed with fear; and the ladies who were near screamed very loud, but did nothing. Then some impulse seized me – perhaps instinct would be a better word to use, considering my age. I threw myself upon the child, and, beating at the fire with my hands, mercifully succeeded in extinguishing it before it really got hold. My wrists were so badly scorched that they had to be wrapped up in wool for a long time afterwards, but with the exception of a single burn upon her throat, little Stella Carson was not much hurt.

This is all that I remember about the Christmas-tree at the Hall. What happened afterwards is lost to me, but to this day in my sleep I sometimes see little Stella's sweet face and the stare of terror in her dark eyes as the fire ran up her arm. This, however, is not wonderful, for I had, humanly speaking, saved the life of her who was destined to be my wife.

The next event which I can recall clearly is that my mother and three brothers all fell ill of fever, owing, as I afterwards learned, to the poisoning of our well by some evil-minded person, who threw a dead sheep into it.

It must have been while they were ill that Squire Carson came one day to the vicarage. The weather was still cold, for there was a fire in the study, and I sat before the fire writing letters on a piece of paper with a pencil, while my father walked up and down the room talking to himself. Afterwards I knew that he was praying for the lives of his wife and children. Presently a servant came to the door and said that some one wanted to see him.

"It is the squire, sir," said the maid, "and he says he particularly wishes to see you."

"Very well," answered my father, wearily, and presently Squire Carson came in. His face was white and haggard, and his eyes shone so fiercely that I was afraid of him.

"Forgive me for intruding on you at such a time, Quatermain," he said, in a hoarse voice, "but to-morrow I leave this place for ever, and I wish to speak to you before I go – indeed, I must speak to you."

"Shall I send Allan away?" said my father, pointing to me.

"No; let him bide. He will not understand." Nor, indeed, did I at the time, but I remembered every word, and in after years their meaning grew on me.

"First tell me," he went on, "how are they?" and he pointed upwards with his thumb.

"My wife and two of the boys are beyond hope," my father answered, with a groan. "I do not know how it will go with the third. The Lord's will be done!"

"The Lord's will be done," the squire echoed, solemnly. "And now, Quatermain, listen – my wife's gone."

"Gone!" my father answered. "Who with?"

"With that foreign cousin of hers. It seems from a letter she left that she always cared for him, not for me. She married me because she thought me a rich English milord. Now she has run through my property, or most of it, and gone. I don't know where. Luckily, she did not care to encumber her new career with the child; Stella is left to me."

"That is what comes of marrying a papist, Carson," said my father. That was his fault; he was as good and charitable a man as ever lived, but he was bigoted. "What are you going to do – follow her?"

He laughed bitterly in answer.

"Follow her!" he said; "why should I follow her? If I met her I might kill her or him, or both of them, because of the disgrace they have brought upon my child's name. No, I never want to look upon her face again. I trusted her, I tell you, and she has betrayed me. Let her go and find her fate. But I am going too. I am weary of my life."

"Surely, Carson, surely," said my father, "you do not mean . . . ?"

"No, no; not that. Death comes soon enough. But I will leave this civilized world which is a lie. We will go right away into the wilds, I and my child, and hide our shame. Where? I don't know where. Anywhere, so long as there are no white faces, no smooth, educated tongues –"

"You are mad, Carson," my father answered. "How will you live? How will you educate Stella? Be a man and wear it down."

"I will be a man, and I will wear it down, but not here, Quatermain. Education! Was not she – that woman who was my wife – was not she highly educated? – the cleverest woman in the county forsooth. Too clever for me, Quatermain – too clever by half! No, no, Stella shall be brought up in a different school; if it be possible, she shall forget her very name. Good-bye, old friend, good-bye for ever. Do not try to find me out, henceforth I shall be like one dead to you, to you and all I knew," and he was gone.

"Mad," said my father, with a heavy sigh. "His trouble has turned his brain. But he will think better of it."

At that moment the nurse came hurrying in and whispered something in his ear. My father's face turned deadly pale. He clutched at the table to support himself, then staggered from the room. My mother was dying!

It was some days afterwards, I do not know exactly how long, that my father took me by the hand and led me upstairs into the big room which had been my mother's bedroom. There she lay, dead in her coffin, with flowers in her hand. Along the wall of the room were arranged three little white beds, and on each of the beds lay one of my brothers. They all looked as though they were asleep, and they all had flowers in their hands. My father told me to kiss them, because I should not see them any more, and I did so, though I was very frightened. I did not know why. Then he took me in his arms and kissed me.

"The Lord gave," he said, "and the Lord hath taken away; blessed be the name of the Lord."

I cried very much, and he took me downstairs, and after that I have only a confused memory of men dressed in black carrying heavy burdens towards the grey churchyard!

Next comes a vision of a great ship and wide tossing waters. My father could no longer bear to live in England after the loss that had fallen on him, and made up his mind to emigrate to South Africa. We must have been poor at the time – indeed, I believe that a large portion of our income went from my father on my mother's death. At any rate we travelled with the steerage passengers, and the intense discomfort of the journey with the rough ways of our fellow emigrants still remain upon my mind. At last it came to an end, and we reached Africa, which I was not to leave again for many, many years.

In those days civilization had not made any great progress in Southern Africa. My father went up the country and became a missionary among the Kaffirs, near to where the town of Cradock now stands, and here I grew to manhood. There were a few Boer farmers in the neighbourhood, and gradually a little settlement of whites gathered round our mission station – a drunken Scotch blacksmith and wheelwright was about the most interesting character among them, who, when sober, could quote the Scottish poet Burns and the Ingoldsby Legends, then recently published, literally by the page. It was from him that I contracted a fondness for the latter amusing writings, which has never left me. Burns I never cared for so much, probably because of the Scottish dialect which repelled me. What little education I got was from my father, but I never had much leaning towards books, nor he much time to teach them to me. On the other hand, I was always a keen observer of the ways of men and nature. By the time that I was twenty I could speak Dutch and three or four Kaffir dialects perfectly, and I doubt if there was anybody in South Africa who understood native ways of thought and action more completely than I did. Also I was really a very good shot and horseman, and I think – as, indeed, my subsequent career proves to have been the case – a great deal tougher than the majority of men. Though I was then, as now, light and small, nothing seemed to tire me. I could bear any amount of exposure and privation, and I never met the native who was my master in feats of endurance. Of course, all that is different now; I am speaking of my early manhood.

It may be wondered that I did not run absolutely wild in such surroundings, but I was held back from this by my father's society. He was one of the gentlest and most refined men that I ever met; even the most savage Kaffir loved him, and his influence was a very good one for me. He used to call himself one of the world's failures. Would that there were more such failures. Every evening when his work was done he would take his prayer-book and, sitting on the little stoep or verandah of our station, would read the evening psalms to himself. Sometimes there was not light enough for this, but it made no difference, he knew them all by heart. When he had finished he would look out across the cultivated lands where the mission Kaffirs had their huts.

But I knew it was not these he saw, but rather the grey English church, and the graves ranged side by side before the yew near the wicket gate.

It was there on the stoep that he died. He had not been well, and one evening I was talking to him, and his mind went back to

Oxfordshire and my mother. He spoke of her a good deal, saying that she had never been out of his mind for a single day during all these years, and that he rejoiced to think he was drawing near that land whither she had gone. Then he asked me if I remembered the night when Squire Carson came into the study at the vicarage, and told him that his wife had run away, and that he was going to change his name and bury himself in some remote land.

I answered that I remembered it perfectly.

"I wonder where he went to," said my father, "and if he and his daughter Stella are still alive. Well, well! I shall never meet them again. But life is a strange thing, Allan, and you may. If you ever do, give them my kind love."

After that I left him. We had been suffering more than usual from the depredations of the Kaffir thieves, who stole our sheep at night, and, as I had done before, and not without success, I determined to watch the kraal and see if I could catch them. Indeed, it was from this habit of mine of watching at night that I first got my native name of Macumazahn, which may be roughly translated as "he who sleeps with one eye open". So I took my rifle and rose to go. But he called me to him and kissed me on the forehead, saying, "God bless you, Allan! I hope that you will think of your old father sometimes, and that you will lead a good and happy life."

I remember that I did not much like his tone at the time, but set it down to an attack of low spirits, to which he grew very subject as the years went on. I walked down to the kraal and watched till within an hour of sunrise; then, as no thieves appeared, I returned to the station. As I came near I was astonished to see a figure sitting in my father's chair. At first I thought it must be a drunken Kaffir, then that my father had fallen asleep there.

And so he had, for he was dead!

The Fire-Fight

When I had buried my father, and seen a successor installed in his place – for the station was the property of the Society – I set to work to carry out a plan which I had long cherished, but been unable to execute because it would have involved separation from my father. Put shortly, it was to undertake a trading journey of exploration right through the countries now known as the Free State and the Transvaal, and as much further North as I could go. It was an adventurous scheme, for though the emigrant Boers had begun to occupy positions in these territories, they were still to all practical purposes unexplored. But I was now alone in the world, and it mattered little what became of me; so, driven on by the overmastering love of adventure, which, old as I am, will perhaps still be my cause of death, I determined to undertake the journey.

Accordingly I sold what stock and property we had upon the station, reserving only the two best waggons and two spans of oxen. The proceeds I invested in such goods as were then in fashion, for trading purposes, and in guns and ammunition. The guns would have moved any modern explorer to merriment; but such as they were I managed to do a good deal of execution with them. One of them was a single-barrelled smoothbore, fitted for percussion caps – a *roer* we called it – which threw a three-ounce ball, and was charged with a handful of coarse black powder. Many is the elephant that I killed with that *roer,* although it generally knocked me backwards when I fired it, which I only did under compulsion. The best of the lot, perhaps, was a double-barrelled No. 12 shot-gun, but it had flint locks. Also there were some old tower muskets, which might or might not throw straight at seventy yards. I took six Kaffirs with me, and three good horses, which were supposed to be salted – that is, proof against the sickness. Among the Kaffirs was an old fellow named Indaba-zimbi, which, being translated, means "tongue of iron". I suppose he got this name from his strident voice and exhaustless eloquence. This man was a great character in his way. He had been a noted witch-doctor among a neighbouring tribe, and came to the station under the following circumstances, which, as he plays a considerable part in this history, are perhaps worth recording.

Two years before my father's death I had occasion to search the country round for some lost oxen. After a long and useless quest it occurred to me that I had better go to the place where the oxen were bred by a Kaffir chief, whose name I forget, but whose kraal was about fifty miles from our station. Thither I journeyed, and found the oxen safe at home. The chief entertained me handsomely, and on the following morning I went to pay my respects to him before leaving, and was somewhat surprised to find a collection of some hundreds of men and women sitting round him anxiously watching the sky in which the thunder-clouds were banking up in a very ominous way.

"You had better wait, white man," said the chief, "and see the rain-doctors fight the lightning."

I inquired what he meant, and learned that this man, Indaba-zimbi, had for some years occupied the position of wizard-in-chief to the tribe, although he was not a member of it, having been born in the country now known as Zululand. But a son of the chief's, a man of about thirty, had lately set up as a rival in supernatural powers. This irritated Indaba-zimbi beyond measure, and a quarrel ensued between the two witch-doctors that resulted in a challenge to trial by lightning being given and accepted. These were the conditions. The rivals must await the coming of a serious thunderstorm, no ordinary tempest would serve their turn. Then, carrying assegais in their hands, they must take their stand within fifty paces of each other upon a certain patch of ground where the big thunderbolts were observed to strike continually, and by the exercise of their occult powers and invocations to the lightning, must strive to avert death from themselves and bring it on their rival. The terms of this singular match had been arranged a month previously, but no storm worthy of the occasion had arisen. Now the local weather prophets believed it to be brewing.

I inquired what would happen if neither of the men were struck, and was told that they must then wait for another storm. If they escaped the second time, however, they would be held to be equal in power, and be jointly consulted by the tribe upon occasions of importance.

The prospect of being a spectator of so unusual a sight overcame my desire to be gone, and I accepted the chief's invitation to see it out. Before mid-day I regretted it, for though the western heavens grew darker and darker, and the still air heralded the coming of the storm, yet it did not come. By four o'clock, however, it became obvious that it must burst soon – at sunset, the old chief said, and in the company of the whole assembly I moved down to the place of combat. The kraal was built on the top of a hill, and below it the land sloped gently to the banks of a river about half a mile away. On the hither side of the bank was the piece of land that was, the natives said, "loved of the lightning". Here the magicians took up their stand, while the spectators grouped themselves on the hillside about two hundred yards away – which was, I thought, rather too near to be pleasant. When we had sat there for a while my curiosity overcame me, and I asked leave of the chief to go down and inspect the arena. He said I might do so at my own risk. I told him that the fire from above would not hurt white men, and went, to find that the spot was a bed of iron ore, thinly covered with grass, which of course accounted for its attracting the lightning from the storms as they travelled along the line of the river. At each end of this iron-stone area were placed the combatants, Indaba-zimbi facing the east, and his rival the west, and before each there burned a little fire made of some scented root. Moreover they were dressed in all the paraphernalia of their craft, snake-skins, fish bladders, and I know not what beside, while round their necks hung circlets of baboons' teeth and bones from human hands. First I went to the western end where the chief's son stood. He was pointing with his assegai towards the advancing storm, and invoking it in a voice of great excitement.

"Come, fire, and lick up Indaba-zimbi!

"Hear me, Storm Devil, and lick Indaba-zimbi with your red tongue!

"Spit on him with your rain!

"Whirl him away in your breath!

"Make him as nothing – melt the marrow in his bones!

"Run into his heart and burn away the lies!

"Show all the people who is the true Witch Finder!

"Let me not be put to shame in the eyes of this white man!"

Thus he spoke, or rather chanted, and all the while rubbed his broad chest – for he was a very fine man – with some filthy compound of medicine or *mouti*.

After a while, getting tired of his song, I walked across the iron-stone, to where Indaba-zimbi sat by his fire. He was not chanting at all, but his performance was much more impressive. It consisted in staring at the eastern sky, which was perfectly clear of cloud, and every now and again beckoning at it with his finger, then turning round to point with the assegai towards his rival. For a while I looked at him in silence He was a curious wizened man, apparently over fifty years of age, with thin hands that looked as tough as wire. His nose was much sharper than is usual among these races, and he had a queer habit of holding his head sideways like a bird when he spoke, which, in addition to the humour that lurked in his eye, gave him a most comical appearance. Another strange thing about him was that he had a single white lock of hair among his black wool. At last I spoke to him:

"Indaba-zimbi, my friend," I said, "you may be a good witch-doctor, but you are certainly a fool. It is no good beckoning at the blue; sky while your enemy is getting a start with the storm."

"You may be clever, but don't think you know everything, white man," the old fellow answered, in a high, cracked voice, and with something like a grin.

"They call you Iron-tongue," I went on; "you had better use it, or the Storm Devil won't hear you."

"The fire from above runs down iron," he answered, "so I keep my tongue quiet. Oh, yes, let him curse away, I'll put him out presently. Look now, white man."

I looked, and in the eastern sky there grew a cloud. At first it was small, though very black, but it gathered with extraordinary rapidity.

This was odd enough, but as I had seen the same thing happen before it did not particularly astonish me. It is by no means unusual in Africa for two thunderstorms to come up at the same time from different points of the compass.

"You had better get on, Indaba-zimbi," I said, "the big storm is coming along fast, and will soon eat up that baby of yours," and I pointed to the west.

"Babies sometimes grow to giants, white man," said Indaba-zimbi, beckoning away vigorously. "Look now at my cloud-child."

I looked; the eastern storm was spreading itself from earth to sky, and in shape resembled an enormous man. There was its head, its shoulders, and its legs; yes, it was like a huge giant travelling across the heavens. The light of the setting sun escaping from beneath the lower edge of the western storm shot across the intervening space in a sheet of splendour, and, lighting upon the advancing figure of cloud, wrapped its middle in hues of glory too wonderful to be described; but beneath and above this glowing belt his feet and head were black as jet. Presently, as I watched, an awful flash of light shot from the head of the cloud, circled it about as though with a crown of living fire, and vanished.

"Aha," chuckled old Indaba-zimbi, "my little boy is putting on his man's ring," and he tapped the gum ring on his own head, which natives assume when they reach a certain age and dignity. "Now, white man, unless you are a bigger wizard than either of us you had better clear off, for the fire-fight is about to begin."

I thought this sound advice.

"Good luck go with you, my black uncle," I said. "I hope you don't feel the iniquities of a mis-spent life weighing on you at the last."

"You look after yourself, and think of your own sins, young man," he answered, with a grim smile, and taking a pinch of snuff, while at that very moment a flash of lightning, I don't know from which storm, struck the ground within thirty paces of me. That was enough for me, I took to my heels, and as I went I heard old Indaba-zimbi's dry chuckle of amusement.

I climbed the hill till I came to where the chief was sitting with his indunas, or headmen, and sat down near to him. I looked at the man's face and saw that he was intensely anxious for his son's safety, and by no means confident of the young man's powers to resist the magic of Indaba-zimbi. He was talking in a low voice to the induna next to him. I affected to take no notice and to be concentrating my attention on the novel scene before me; but in those days I had very quick ears, and caught the drift of the conversation.

"Hearken!" the chief was saying, "if the magic of Indaba-zimbi prevails against my son I will endure him no more. Of this I am sure, that when he has slain my son he will slay me, me also, and make himself chief in my place. I fear Indaba-zimbi. *Ou!*"

"Black One," answered the induna, "wizards die as dogs die, and, once dead, dogs bark no more."

"And once dead," said the chief, "wizards work no more spells," and he bent and whispered in the induna's ear, looking at the assegai in his hand as he whispered.

"Good, my father, good!" said the induna, presently. "It shall be done to-night, if the lightning does not do it first."

"A bad look-out for old Indaba-zimbi," I said to myself. "They mean to kill him." Then I thought no more of the matter for a while, the scene before me was too tremendous.

The two storms were rapidly rushing together. Between them was a gulf of blue sky, and from time to time flashes of blinding light passed across this gulf, leaping from cloud to cloud. I remember that they reminded me of the story of the heathen god Jove and his thunderbolts. The storm that was shaped like a giant and ringed with the glory of the sinking sun made an excellent Jove, and I am sure that the bolts which leapt from it could not have been surpassed even in mythological times. Oddly enough, as yet the flashes were not followed by thunder. A deadly stillness lay upon the place, the cattle stood silently on the hillside, even the natives were awed to silence. Dark shadows crept along the bosom of the hills, the river to the right and left was hidden in wreaths of cloud, but before us and beyond the combatants it shone like a line of silver beneath the narrowing space of open sky. Now the western tempest was scrawled all over with lines of intolerable light, while the inky head of the cloud-giant to the east was continually suffused with a white and deadly glow that came and went in pulses, as though a blood of flame was being pumped into it from the heart of the storm.

The silence deepened and deepened, the shadows grew blacker and blacker, then suddenly all nature began to moan beneath the breath of an icy wind. On sped the wind; the smooth surface of the river was ruffled by it into little waves, the tall grass bowed low before it, and in its wake came the hissing sound of furious rain.

Ah! the storms had met. From each there burst an awful blaze of dazzling flame, and now the hill on which we sat rocked at the noise of the following thunder. The light went out of the sky, darkness fell suddenly on the land, but not for long. Presently the whole landscape grew vivid in the flashes, it appeared and disappeared, now everything was visible for miles, now even the men at my side vanished in the blackness. The thunder rolled and cracked and pealed like the trump of doom, whirlwinds tore round, lifting dust and even stones high into the air, and in a low, continuous undertone rose the hiss of the rushing rain.

I put my hand before my eyes to shield them from the terrible glare, and looked beneath it towards the lists of iron-stone. As flash followed flash, from time to time I caught sight of the two wizards. They were slowly advancing towards one another, each pointing at his foe with the assegai in his hand. I could see their every movement, and it seemed to me that the chain lightning was striking the iron-stone all round them.

Suddenly the thunder and lightning ceased for a minute, everything grew black, and, except for the rain, silent.

"It is over one way or the other, chief," I called out into the darkness.

"Wait, white man, wait!" answered the chief, in a voice thick with anxiety and fear.

Hardly were the words out of his mouth when the heavens were lit up again till they literally seemed to flame. There were the men, not ten paces apart. A great flash fell between them, I saw them stagger beneath the shock. Indaba-zimbi recovered himself first – at any rate when the next flash came he was standing bolt upright, pointing with his assegai towards his enemy. The chief's son was still on his legs, but he was staggering like a drunken man, and the assegai had fallen from his hand.

Darkness! then again a flash, more fearful, if possible, than any that had gone before. To me it seemed to come from the east, right over the head of Indaba-zimbi. At that instant I saw the chief's son wrapped, as it were, in the heart of it. Then the thunder pealed, the rain burst over us like a torrent, and I saw no more.

The worst of the storm was done, but for a while the darkness was so dense that we could not move, nor, indeed, was I inclined to leave the safety of the hillside where the lightning was never known to strike, and venture down to the iron-stone. Occasionally there still came flashes, but, search as we would, we could see no trace of either of the wizards. For my part, I believed that they were both dead. Now the clouds slowly rolled away down the course of the river, and with them went the rain; and now the stars shone out in their wake.

"Let us go and see," said the old chief, rising and shaking the water from his hair. "The fire-fight is ended, let us go and see who has conquered."

I rose and followed him, dripping as though I had swum a hundred yards with my clothes on, and after me came all the people of the kraal.

We reached the spot; even in that light I could see where the iron-stone had been split and fused by the thunderbolts. While I was staring about me, I suddenly heard the chief, who was on my right, give a low moan, and saw the people cluster round him. I went up and looked. There, on the ground, lay the body of his son. It was a dreadful sight. The hair was burnt off his head, the copper rings upon his arms were fused, the assegai handle which lay near was literally shivered into threads, and, when I took hold of his arm, it seemed to me that every bone of it was broken.

The men with the chief stood gazing silently, while the women wailed.

"Great is the magic of Indaba-zimbi!" said a man, at length. The chief turned and struck him a heavy blow with the kerrie in his hand.

"Great or not, thou dog, he shall die," he cried, "and so shalt thou if thou singest his praises so loudly."

I said nothing, but thinking it probable that Indaba-zimbi had shared the fate of his enemy, I went to look. But I could see nothing of him, and at length, being thoroughly chilled with the wet, started back to my waggon to change my clothes. On reaching it, I was rather surprised to find a strange Kaffir seated on the driving-box wrapped up in a blanket.

"Hullo! come out of that," I said.

The figure on the box slowly unrolled the blanket, and with great deliberation took a pinch of snuff.

"It was a good fire-fight, white man, was it not?" said Indaba-zimbi, in his high, cracked voice. "But he never had a chance against me, poor boy. He knew nothing about it. See, white man, what comes of presumption in the young. It is sad, very sad, but I made the flashes fly, didn't I?"

"You old humbug," I said, "unless you are careful you will soon learn what comes of presumption in the old, for your chief is after you with an assegai, and it will take all your magic to dodge that."

"Now you don't say so," said Indaba-zimbi, clambering off the waggon with rapidity; "and all because of this wretched upstart. There's gratitude for you, white man. I expose him, and they want to kill me. Well, thank you for the hint. We shall meet again before long," and he was gone like a shot, and not too soon, for just then some of the chief's men came up to the waggon.

On the following morning I started homewards. The first face I saw on arriving at the station was that of Indaba-zimbi.

"How do you do, Macumazahn?" he said, holding his head on one side and nodding his white lock. "I hear you are Christians here, and I wish to try a new religion. Mine must be a bad one seeing that my people wanted to kill me for exposing an impostor."

CHAPTER III
Northwards

I make no apology to myself, or to anybody who may happen to read this narrative in future, for having set out the manner of my meeting with Indaba-zimbi: first, because it was curious, and secondly, because he takes some hand in the subsequent events. If that old man was a humbug, he was a very clever one. What amount of truth there was in his pretensions to supernatural powers it is not for me to determine, though I may have my own opinion on the subject. But there was no mistake as to the extraordinary influence he exercised over his fellow-natives. Also he quite got round my poor father. At first the old gentleman declined to have him at the station, for he had a great horror of these Kaffir wizards or witch-finders. But Indaba-zimbi persuaded him that be was anxious to investigate the truths of Christianity, and challenged him to discussion. The argument lasted for two years – to the time of my father's death, indeed. At the conclusion of each stage Indaba-zimbi would remark, in the words of the Roman Governor, Almost praying white man, "thou persuadest me to become a Christian," but he never quite became one – indeed, I do not think he ever meant to. It was to him that my father addressed his "Letters to a Native Doubter". This work, which, unfortunately, remains in manuscript, is full of wise saws and learned instances. It ought to be published together with a *précis* of the doubter's answers, which were verbal.

So the talk went on. If my father had lived I believe it would be going on now, for both the disputants were quite inexhaustible. Meanwhile Indaba-zimbi was allowed to live in the station on condition that he practised no witchcraft, which my father firmly believed to be a wile of the devil. He said that he would not, but for all that there was never an ox lost, or a sudden death, but he was consulted by those interested.

When he had been with us a year, a deputation came to him from the tribe he had left, asking him to return. Things had not gone well with them since he went away, they said, and now the chief, his enemy, was dead. Old Indaba-zimbi listened to them till they had done, and, as he listened, raked sand into a little heap with his toes. Then he spoke, pointing to the little heap, "There is your tribe to-day," he said. Then he lifted his heel and stamped the heap flat. "There is your tribe before three moons are gone. Nothing is left of it. You drove me away: I will have no more to do with you; but when you are being killed think of my words."

The messengers went. Three months afterwards I heard that the whole community had been wiped out by an Impi of raiding Pondos.

When I was at length ready to start upon my expedition, I went to old Indaba-zimbi to say good-bye to him, and was rather surprised to find him engaged in rolling up medicine, assegais, and other sundries in his blankets.

"Good-bye, Indaba-zimbi," I said, "I am going to trek north."

"Yes, Macumazahn," he answered, with his head on one side; "and so am I – I want to see that country. We will go together."

"Will we!" I said; "wait till you are asked, you old humbug."

"You had better ask me, then, Macumazahn, for if you don't you will never come back alive. Now that the old chief (my father) is gone to where the storms come from," and he nodded to the sky, "I feel myself getting into bad habits again. So last night I just threw up the bones and worked out about your journey, and I can tell you this, that if you don't take me you will die, and, what is more, you will lose one who is dearer to you than life in a strange fashion. So just because you gave me that hint a couple of years ago, I made up my mind to come with you."

"Don't talk stuff to me," I said.

"Ah, very well, Macumazahn, very well; but what happened to my own people six months ago, and what did I tell the messengers would happen? They drove me away, and they are gone. If you drive me away you will soon be gone too," and he nodded his white lock at me and smiled.

Now I was not more superstitious than other people, but somehow old Indaba-zimbi impressed me. Also I knew his extraordinary influence over every class of native, and bethought me that he might be useful in that way.

"All right," I said: "I appoint you witch-finder to the expedition without pay."

"First serve, then ask for wages," he answered. "I am glad to see that you have enough imagination not to be altogether a fool, like most white men, Macumazahn. Yes, yes, it is want of imagination that makes people fools; they won't believe what they can't understand. You can't understand my prophecies any more than the fool at the kraal could understand that I was his master with the lightning. Well, it is time to trek, but if I were you, Macumazahn, I should take one waggon, not two."

"Why?" I said.

"Because you will lose your waggons, and it is better to lose one than two."

"Oh, nonsense!" I said.

"All right, Macumazahn, live and learn." And without another word he walked to the foremost waggon, put his bundle into it, and climbed on to the front seat.

So having bid an affectionate adieu to my white friends, including the old Scotchman who got drunk in honour of the event, and quoted Burns till the tears ran down his face, at length I started, and travelled slowly northwards. For the first three weeks nothing very particular befell me. Such Kaffirs as we came in contact with were friendly, and game literally swarmed. Nobody living in those parts of South Africa nowadays can have the remotest idea of what the veldt was like even thirty years ago.

Often and often I have crept shivering on to my waggon-box just as the sun rose and looked out. At first one would see nothing but a vast field of white mist suffused towards the east by a tremulous golden glow, through which the tops of stony koppies stood up like gigantic beacons. From the dense mist would come strange sounds – snorts, gruntings, bellows, and the thunder of countless hoofs. Presently this great curtain would grow thinner, then it would melt, as the smoke from a pipe melts into the air, and for miles on miles the wide rolling country interspersed with bush opened to the view. But it was not tenantless as it is now, for as far as the eye could reach it would be literally black with game. Here to the right might be a herd of vilderbeeste that could not number less than two thousand. Some were grazing, some gambolled, whisking their white tails into the air, while all round the old bulls stood upon hillocks sniffing suspiciously at the breeze. There, in front, a thousand yards away, though to the unpractised eye they looked much closer, because of the dazzling clearness of the atmosphere, was a great herd of springbok trekking along in single file. Ah, they have come to the waggon-track and do not like the look of it. What will they do? Go back? Not a bit of it. It is nearly thirty feet wide, but that is nothing to a springbok. See, the first of them bounds into the air like a ball. How beautifully the sunshine gleams upon his golden hide! He has cleared it, and the others come after him in numberless succession, all except the fawns, who cannot jump so far, and have to scamper over the doubtful path with a terri-fied *bah*. What is that yonder, moving above the tops of the mimosa, in the little dell at the foot of the koppie? Giraffes, by George! three of them; there will be marrow-bones for supper to-night. Hark! the ground shakes behind us, and over the brow of the rise rush a vast herd of blesbock. On they come at full gallop, their long heads held low, they look like so many bearded goats. I thought so – behind them is a pack of wild dogs, their fur draggled, their tongues lolling. They are in full cry; the giraffes hear them and are away, rolling round the koppie like a ship in a heavy sea. No marrow-bones after all. See! the foremost dogs are close on a buck. He has galloped far and is outworn. One springs at his flank and misses him. The buck gives a kind of groan, looks wildly round and sees the waggon. He seems to hesitate a moment, then in his despair rushes up to it, and falls exhausted among the oxen. The dogs pull up some thirty paces away, panting and snarling. Now, boy, the gun – no, not the rifle, the shot-gun loaded with loopers.

Bang! bang! there, my friends, two of you will never hunt buck again. No, don't touch the buck, for he has come to us for shelter, and he shall have it.

Ah, how beautiful is nature before man comes to spoil it!

Such a sight as this have I seen many a hundred times, and I hope to see it again before I die.

The first real adventure that befell me on this particular journey was with elephants, which I will relate because of its curious termination. Just before we crossed the Orange River we came to a stretch of forest-land some twenty miles broad. The night we entered this forest we camped in a lovely open glade. A few yards ahead tambouki grass was growing to the height of a man, or rather it had been; now, with the exception of a few stalks here and there, it was crushed quite flat. It was already dusk when we camped; but after the moon got up I walked from the fire to see how this had happened. One glance was enough for me; a great herd of elephants had evidently passed over the tall grass not many hours before. The sight of their spoor rejoiced me exceedingly, for though I had seen wild elephants, at that time I had never shot one. Moreover, the sight of elephant spoor to the African hunter is what "colour in the pan" is to the prospector of gold. It is by ivory that he lives, and to shoot it or trade it is his chief aim in life. My resolution was soon taken. I would camp the waggons for a while in the forest, and start on horseback after the elephants.

I communicated my decision to Indaba-zimbi and the other Kaffirs. The latter were not loth, for your Kaffir loves hunting, which means plenty of meat and congenial occupation, but Indaba-zimbi would express no opinion. I saw him retire to a little fire that he had lit for himself, and go through some mysterious performances with bones and clay mixed with ashes, which were watched with the greatest interest by the other Kaffirs. At length he rose, and, coming forward, informed me that it was all right, and that I did well to go and hunt the elephants, as I should get plenty of ivory; but he advised me to go on foot. I said I should do nothing of the sort, but meant to ride. I am wiser now; this was the first and last time that I ever attempted to hunt elephants on horseback.

Accordingly we started at dawn, I, Indaba-zimbi, and three men; the rest I left with the waggons. I was on horseback, and so was my driver, a good rider and a skilful shot for a Kaffir, but Indaba-zimbi and the others walked. From dawn till mid-day we followed the trail of the herd, which was as plain as a high road. Then we off-saddled to let the horses rest and feed, and about three o'clock started on again. Another hour or so passed, and still there was no sign of elephants. Evidently the herd had travelled fast and far, and I began to think that we should have to give it up, when suddenly I caught sight of a brown mass moving through the thorn-trees on the side of a slope about a quarter of a mile away. My heart seemed to jump into my mouth. Where is the hunter who has not felt like this at the sight of his first elephant?

I called a halt, and then the wind being right, we set to work to stalk the bull. Very quietly I rode down the hither side of the slope till we came to the bottom, which was densely covered with bush. Here I saw that the elephants had been feeding, for broken branches and upturned trees lay all about. I did not take much notice, however, for all my thoughts were fixed upon the bull I was stalking, when suddenly my horse gave a violent start that nearly threw me from the saddle, and there came a mighty rush and upheaval of something in front of me. I looked: there was the hinder part of a second bull elephant not four yards off. I could just catch sight of its outstretched ears projecting on either side. I had disturbed it sleeping, and it was running away.

Obviously the best thing to do would have been to let it run, but I was young in those days and foolish, and in the excitement of the moment I lifted my *roer* or elephant gun and fired at the great brute over my horse's head. The recoil of the heavy gun nearly knocked me off the saddle. I recovered myself, however, and, as I did so, saw the bull lurch forward, for the impact of a three-ounce bullet in the flank will quicken the movements even of an elephant. By this time I had realized the folly of the shot and devoutly hoped that the bull would take no further notice of it. But he took a different view of the matter. Pulling himself up in a series of plunges, he spun round and came for me with outstretched ears and uplifted trunk, screaming terribly. I was quite defenceless, for my gun was empty, and my first thought was of escape. I dug my heels into the sides of my horse, but he would not move an inch. The poor animal was paralysed with terror, and he simply stood still, his fore-legs outstretched, and quivering all over like a leaf.

On rushed the elephant, awful to see; I made one more vain effort to stir the horse. Now the trunk of the great bull swung aloft above my head. A thought flashed through my brain. Quick as light I rolled from the saddle. By the side of the horse lay a fallen tree, as thick through as a man's body. This tree was lifted a little off the ground by the broken boughs which took its weight, and with a single movement, so active is one in such necessities, I flung myself beneath it. As I did so, I heard the trunk of the elephant descend with a mighty thud on the back of my poor horse, and the next instant I was almost in darkness, for the horse, whose back was broken, fell over across the tree under which I lay ensconced. But he did not stop there long. In ten seconds more the bull had wound his trunk about my dead nag's neck, and, with a mighty effort, hurled him clear of the bole. I wriggled backwards as far as I could towards the roots of the tree, for I knew what he was after. Presently I saw the red tip of the bull's trunk stretching itself towards me. If he could manage to hook it round any part of me I was lost. But in the position I occupied, that was just what he could not do, although he knelt down to facilitate his operations.

On came the snapping tip like a great open-mouthed snake; it closed upon my hat, which vanished. Again it was thrust down, and a scream of rage was bellowed through it within four inches of my head. Now it seemed to elongate itself. Oh, heavens! now it had me by the hair, which, luckily for myself, was not very long. Then it was my turn to scream, for next instant half a square inch of hair was dragged from my scalp by the roots. I was being plucked alive, as I have seen cruel Kaffir kitchen boys pluck a fowl.

The elephant, however, disappointed with these moderate results, changed his tactics. He wound his trunk round the fallen tree and lifted. The bole stirred, but fortunately the broken branches embedded in the spongy soil, and some roots, which still held, prevented it from being turned over, though he lifted it so much that, had it occurred to him, he could now easily have drawn me out with his trunk. Again he hoisted with all his mighty strength, and I saw that the tree was coming, and roared aloud for help. Some shots were fired close by in answer, but if they hit the bull, their only effect was to stir his energies to more active life. In another few seconds my shelter would be torn away, and I should be done for. A cold perspiration burst out over me as I realized that I was lost. Then of a sudden I remembered that I had a pistol in my belt, which I often used for despatching wounded game. It was loaded and capped. By this time the bole was lifted so much that I could easily get my hand down to my middle and draw the pistol from its case. I drew and cocked it. Now the tree was coming over, and there, within three feet of my head, was the great brown trunk of the elephant. I placed the muzzle of the pistol within an inch of it and fired. The result was instantaneous. Down sunk the tree again, giving one of my legs a considerable squeeze, and next instant I heard a crashing sound. The elephant had bolted.

By this time, what between fright and struggling, I was pretty well tired. I cannot remember how I got from under the fallen tree, or indeed anything, until I found myself sitting on the ground drinking some peach brandy from a flask, and old Indaba-zimbi opposite to me nodding his white lock sagely, while he fired off moral reflections on the narrowness of my escape, and my unwisdom in not having taken his advice to go on foot. That reminded me of my horse – I got up and went to look at it. It was quite dead, the blow of the elephant's trunk had fallen on the saddle, breaking the framework, and rendering it useless. I reflected that in another two seconds it would have fallen on *me*. Then I called to Indaba-zimbi and asked which way the elephants had gone.

"There!" he said, pointing down the gully, "and we had better go after them, Macumazahn. We have had the bad luck, now for the good."

There was philosophy in this, though, to tell the truth, I did not feel particularly sharp set on elephants at the moment. I seemed to have had enough of them. However, it would never do to show the white feather before the boys, so I assented with much outward readiness, and we started, I on the second horse, and the others on foot. When we had travelled for the best part of an hour down the valley, all of a sudden we came upon the whole herd, which numbered a little more than eighty. Just in front of them the bush was so thick that they seemed to hesitate about entering it, and the sides of the valley were so rocky and steep at this point that they could not climb them.

They saw us at the same moment as we saw them, and inwardly I was filled with fears lest they should take it into their heads to charge back up the gully. But they did not; trumpeting aloud, they rushed at the thick bush which went down before them like corn before a sickle. I do not think that in all my experiences I ever heard anything to equal the sound they made as they crashed through and over the shrubs and trees. Before them was a dense forest belt from a hundred to a hundred and fifty feet in width. As they rushed on, it fell, so that behind them was nothing but a level roadway strewed with fallen trunks, crushed branches, and here and there a tree, too strong even for them, left standing amid the wreck. On they went, and, notwithstanding the nature of the ground over which they had to travel, they kept their distance ahead of us. This sort of thing continued for a mile or more, and then I saw that in front of the elephants the valley opened into a space covered with reeds and grass – it might have been five or six acres in extent – beyond which the valley ran on again.

The herd reached the edge of this expanse, and for a moment pulled up, hesitating – evidently they mistrusted it. My men yelled aloud, as only Kaffirs can, and that settled them. Headed by the wounded bull, whose martial ardour, like my own, was somewhat cooled, they spread out and dashed into the treacherous swamp – for such it was, though just then there was no water to be seen. For a few yards all went well with them, though clearly they found it heavy going; then suddenly the great bull sunk up to his belly in the stiff peaty soil, and remained fixed. The others, mad with fear, took no heed of his struggles and trumpetings, but plunged on to meet the same fate. In five minutes the whole herd of them were hopelessly bogged, and the more they struggled to escape, the deeper they sunk. There was one exception, indeed, a cow managed to win back to firm shore, and, lifting her trunk, prepared to charge us as we came up. But at that moment she heard the scream of her calf, and rushed back to its assistance, only to be bogged with the others.

Such a scene I never saw before or since. The swamp was spotted all over with the large forms of the elephants, and the air rang with their screams of rage and terror as they waved their trunks wildly to and fro. Now and then a monster would make a great effort and drag his mass from its peaty bed, only to stick fast again at the next step. It was a most pitiable sight, though one that gladdened the hearts of my men. Even the best natives have little compassion for the sufferings of animals.

Well, the rest was easy. The marsh that would not bear the elephants carried our weight well enough. Before midnight all were dead, for we shot them by moonlight. I would gladly have spared the young ones and some of the cows, but to do so would only have meant leaving them to perish of hunger; it was kinder to kill them at once. The wounded bull I slew with my own hand, and I cannot say that I felt much compunction in so doing. He knew me again, and made a desperate effort to get at me, but I am glad to say that the peat held him fast.

The pan presented a curious sight when the sun rose next morning. Owing to the support given by the soil, few of the dead elephants had fallen: there they stood as though they were asleep.

I sent back for the waggons, and when they arrived on the morrow, formed a camp, about a mile away from the pan. Then began the work of cutting out the elephants' tusks; it took over a week, and for obvious reasons was a disgusting task. Indeed, had it not been for the help of some wandering bushmen, who took their pay in elephant meat, I do not think we could ever have managed it.

At last it was done. The ivory was far too cumbersome for us to carry, so we buried it, having first got rid of our bushmen allies. My boys wanted me to go back to the Cape with it and sell it, but I was too much bent on my journey to do this. The tusks lay buried for five years. Then I came and dug them up; they were but little harmed. Ultimately I sold the ivory for something over twelve hundred pounds – not bad pay for one day's shooting.

This was how I began my career as an elephant hunter. I have shot many hundreds of these animals since, but have never again attempted to do so on horseback.

CHAPTER IV
The Zulu Impi

After burying the elephant tusks, and having taken careful notes of the bearings and peculiarities of the country so that I might be able to find the spot again, we proceeded on our journey. For a month or more I trekked along the line which now divides the Orange Free State from Griqualand West, and the Transvaal from Bechuanaland. The only difficulties met with were such as are still common to African travellers – occasional want of water and troubles about crossing sluits and rivers. I remember that I outspanned on the spot where

Kimberley now stands, and had to press on again in a hurry because there was no water. I little dreamed then that I should live to see Kimberley, a great city producing millions of pounds worth of diamonds annually, and old Indaba-zimbi's magic cannot have been worth so much after all, or he would have told me.

I found the country almost entirely depopulated. Not very long before Mosilikatze the Lion, Chaka's General had swept across it in his progress towards what is now Matabeleland. His footsteps were evident enough. Time upon time I trekked up to what evidently had been the sites of Kaffir kraals. Now the kraals were ashes and piles of tumbled stones, and strewn about among the rank grass lay the bones of hundreds of men, women, and children, all of whom had kissed the Zulu assegai. I remember that in one of these desolate places I found the skull of a child in which a ground-lark had built its nest. It was the twittering of the young birds inside that first called my attention to it. Shortly after this we met with our second great adventure, a much more serious and tragic one than the first.

We were trekking parallel with the Kolong river when a herd of blesbock crossed the track. I fired at one of them and hit it behind. It galloped about a thousand yards with the rest of the herd, then lay down. As we were in want of meat, not having met with any game for a few days past, I jumped on to my horse, and, telling Indaba-zimbi that I would overtake the waggons or meet them on the further side of a rise about an hour's trek away, I started after the wounded buck. As soon as I came within a hundred yards of it, however, it sprang up and ran away as fast as though it were untouched, only to lie down again at a distance. I followed, thinking that strength would soon fail it. This happened three times. On the third occasion it vanished behind a ridge, and, though by now I was out of both temper and patience, I thought I might as well ride to the crest and see if I could get a shot at it on the further side.

I reached the ridge, which was strewn with stones, looked over it; and saw – a Zulu Impi!

I rubbed my eyes and looked again. Yes, there was no doubt of it.

They were halted about a thousand yards away, by the water; some were lying down, some were cooking at fires, others were stalking about with spears and shields in their hands; there might have been two thousand or more of them in all. While I was wondering – and that with no little uneasiness – what on earth they could be doing there, suddenly I heard a wild cry to the right and left of me. I glanced first one way, then the other. From either side a great Zulu was bearing down on me, their broad stabbing assegais aloft, and black shields in their left hands. The man to the right was about fifteen yards away, he to the left was not more than ten. On they came, their fierce eyes almost starting out of their heads, and I felt, with a cold thrill of fear, that in another three seconds those broad "bangwans" might be buried in my vitals. On such occasions we act, I suppose, more from instinct than anything else – there is no time for thought. At any rate, I dropped the reins and, raising my gun, fired point blank at the left-hand man. The bullet struck full in the middle of his shield, pierced it and passed through him, and over he rolled upon the veldt. I swung round in the saddle; most happily my horse was accustomed to standing still when I fired from his back, also he was so surprised that he did not know which way to shy. The other savage was almost on me; his outstretched shield touched the muzzle of my gun as I pulled the trigger of the left barrel. It exploded, the warrior sprung high into the air, and fell against my horse dead, his spear passing just in front of my face.

Without waiting to reload, or even to look if the main body of the Zulus had seen the death of their two scouts, I turned my horse and drove my heels into his sides. As soon as I was down the slope of the rise I pulled a little to the right in order to intercept the waggons before the Zulus saw them. I had not gone three hundred yards in this new direction when, to my utter astonishment, I struck a trail marked with waggon-wheels and the hoofs of oxen. Of waggons there must have been at least eight, and several hundred cattle. Moreover, they had passed within twelve hours; I could tell that by the spoor. Then I understood; the Impi was following the track of the waggons, which, in all probability, belonged to a party of emigrant Boers.

The spoor of the waggons ran in the direction I wished to go, so I followed it. About a mile further on I came to the crest of a rise, and there, about five furlongs away, I saw the waggons drawn up in a rough laager upon the banks of the river. There, too, were my own waggons trekking down the slope towards them.

In another five minutes I was there. The Boers – for Boers they were – were standing about outside the little laager watching the approach of my two waggons. I called to them, and they turned and saw me. The very first man my eyes fell on was a Boer named Hans Botha, whom I had known well years ago in the Cape. He was not a bad specimen of his class, but a very restless person, with a great objection to authority, or, as he expressed it, "a love of freedom". He had joined a party of the emigrant Boers some years before, but, as I learned presently, had quarrelled with its leader, and was now trekking away into the wilderness to found a little colony of his own. Poor fellow! It was his last trek.

"How do you do, Meinheer Botha?" I said to him in Dutch.

The man looked at me, looked again, then, startled out of his Dutch stolidity, cried to his wife, who was seated on the box of the waggon:

"Come here, Frau, come. Here is Allan Quatermain, the English-man, the son of the 'Predicant'. How goes it, Heer Quartermain, and what is the news down in the Cape yonder?"

"I don't know what the news is in the Cape, Hans," I answered, solemnly; "but the news here is that there is a Zulu Impi upon your spoor and within two miles of the waggons. That I know, for I have just shot two of their sentries," and I showed him my empty gun.

For a moment there was a silence of astonishment, and I saw the bronzed faces of the men turn pale beneath their tan, while one or two of the women gave a little scream, and the children crept to their sides.

"Almighty!" cried Hans, "that must be the Umtetwa regiment that Dingaan sent against the Basutus, but who could not come at them because of the marshes, and so were afraid to return to Zululand, and struck north to join Mosilikatze."

"Laager up, Carles! Laager up for your lives, and one of you jump on a horse and drive in the cattle."

At that moment my own waggons came up. Indaba-zimbi was sitting on the box of the first, wrapped in a blanket. I called him and told him the news.

"Ill tidings, Macumazahn," he said; "there will be dead Boers about to-morrow morning, but they will not attack till dawn, then they will wipe out the laager *so!*" and he passed his hand before his mouth.

"Stop that croaking, you white-headed crow," I said, though I knew that his words were true. What chance had a laager of ten waggons all told against at least two thousand of the bravest savages in the world?

"Macumazahn, will you take my advice this time?" Indaba-zimbi said, presently.

"What is it?" I asked.

"This. Leave your waggons here, jump on that horse, and let us two run for it as hard as we can go. The Zulus won't follow us, they will be looking after the Boers."

"I won't leave the other white men," I said; "it would be the act of a coward. If I die, I die."

"Very well, Macumazahn, then stay and be killed," he answered, taking a pinch of snuff. "Come, let us see about the waggons," and we walked towards the laager.

Here everything was in confusion. However, I got hold of Hans Botha and put it to him if it would not be best to desert the waggons and make a run for life.

"How can we do it?" he answered; "two of the women are too fat to go a mile, one is sick in childbed, and we have only six horses among us. Besides, if we did we should starve in the desert. No, Heer Allan, we must fight it out with the savages, and God help us!"

"God help us, indeed. Think of the children, Hans!"

"I can't bear to think," he answered, in a broken voice, looking at his own little girl, a sweet, curly-haired, blue-eyed child of six, named Tota, whom I had often nursed as a baby. "Oh, Heer Allan, your father, the Predicant, always warned me against trekking north, and I never would listen to him because I thought him a cursed Englishman; now I see my folly. Heer Allan, if you can, try to save my child from those black devils; if you live longer than I do, or if you can't save her, kill her," and he clasped my hand.

"It hasn't come to that yet, Hans," I said.

Then we set to work on the laager. The waggons, of which, including my two, there were ten, were drawn into the form of a square, and the disselboom of each securely lashed with reims to the underworks of that in front of it. The wheels also were locked, and the space between the ground and the bed-planks of the waggons was stuffed with branches of the "wait-a-bit" thorn that fortunately grew near in considerable quantities. In this way a barrier was formed of no mean strength as against a foe unprovided with firearms, places being left for the men to fire from. In a little over an hour everything was done that could be done, and a discussion arose as to the disposal of the cattle, which had been driven up close to the camp. Some of the Boers were anxious to get them into the laager, small as it was, or at least as many of them as it would hold. I argued strongly against this, pointing out that the brutes would probably be seized with panic as soon as the firing began, and trample the defenders of the laager under foot. As an alternative plan I suggested that some of the native servants should drive the herd along the valley of the river till they reached a friendly tribe or some other place of safety. Of course, if the Zulus saw them they would be taken, but the nature of the ground was favourable, and it was possible that they might escape if they started at once. The proposition was promptly agreed to, and, what is more, it was settled that one Dutchman and such of the women and children as could travel should go with them. In half an hour's time twelve of them started with the natives, the Boer in charge, and the cattle. Three of my own men went with the latter, the three others and Indaba-Zimbi stopped with me in the laager.

The parting was a heart-breaking scene, upon which I do not care to dwell. The women wept, the men groaned, and the children looked on with scared white faces. At length they were gone, and I for one was thankful of it. There remained in the laager seventeen white men, four natives, the two Boer fraus who were too stout to travel, the woman in childbed and her baby, and Hans Botha's little daughter Tota, whom he could not make up his mind to part with. Happily her mother was already dead. And here I may state that ten of the women and children, together with about half of the cattle, escaped. The Zulu Impi never saw them, and on the third day of travel they came to the fortified place of a Griqua chief, who sheltered them on receiving half the cattle in payment. Thence by slow degrees they journeyed down to the Cape Colony, reaching a civilized region within a little more than a year from the date of the attack on the laager.

The afternoon was now drawing towards evening, but still there were no signs of the Impi. A wild hope struck us that they might have gone on about their business. Ever since Indaba-zimbi had heard that the regiment was supposed to belong to the Umtetwa tribe, he had, I noticed, been plunged in deep thought. Presently he came to me and volunteered to go out and spy upon their movements. At first Hans Botha was against this idea saying that he was a "verdomde swartzel" – an accursed black creature – and would betray us. I pointed out that there was nothing to betray. The Zulus must know where the waggons were, but it was important for us to gain information of their movements. So it was agreed that Indaba-zimbi should go. I told him this. He nodded his white lock, said "All right, Macumazahn," and started. I noticed with some surprise, however, that before he did so he went to the waggaon and fetched his "mouti", or medicine, which, together with his other magical apparatus, he always carried in a skin bag. I asked him why he did this. He answered that it was to make himself invulnerable against the spears of the Zulus. I did not in the least believe his explanation, for in my heart I was sure that he meant to take the opportunity to make a bolt of it, leaving me to my fate. I did not, however, interfere to prevent this, for I had an affection for the old fellow, and sincerely hoped that he might escape the doom which overshadowed us.

So Indaba-zimbi sauntered off, and as I looked at his retreating form I thought that I should never see it again. But I was mistaken, and little knew that he was risking his life, not for the Boers whom he hated one and all, but for me whom in his queer way he loved.

When he had gone we completed our preparations for defence, strengthening the waggons and the thorns beneath with earth and stones. Then at sunset we ate and drank as heartily as we could under the circumstances, and when we had done, Hans Botha, as head of the party, offered up prayer to God for our preservation. It was a touching sight to see the burly Dutchman, his hat off, his broad face lit up by the last rays of the setting sun, praying aloud in homely, simple language to Him who alone could save us from the spears of a cruel foe. I remember that the last sentence of his prayer was, "Almighty, if we must be killed, save the women and children and my little girl Tota from the accursed Zulus, and do not let us be tortured."

I echoed the request very earnestly in my own heart, that I know, for in common with the others I was dreadfully afraid, and it must be admitted not without reason.

Then the darkness came on, and we took up our appointed places each with a rifle in his hands and peered out into the gloom in silence. Occasionally one of the Boers lit his pipe with a brand from the smouldering fire, and the glow of it would shine for a few moments on his pale, anxious face.

Behind me one of the stout "fraus" lay upon the ground. Even the terror of our position could not keep her heavy eyes from their accustomed sleep, and she snored loudly. On the further side of her, just by the fire, lay little Tota, wrapped in a kaross. She was asleep also, her thumb in her mouth, and from time to time her father would come to look at her.

So the hours wore on while we waited for the Zulus. But from my intimate knowledge of the habits of natives I had little fear that they would attack us at night, though, had they done so, they could have compassed our destruction with but small loss to themselves. It is not the habit of this people, they like to fight in the light of day – at dawn for preference.

About eleven o'clock, just as I was nodding a little at my post, I heard a low whistle outside the laager. Instantly I was wide awake, and all along the line I heard the clicking of locks as the Boers cocked their guns.

"Macumazahn," said a voice, the voice of Indaba-zimbi, "are you there?"

"Yes," I answered.

"Then hold a light so that I can see how to climb into the laager," he said.

"Yah! yah! hold a light," put in one of the Boers. "I don't trust that black schepsel of yours, Heer Quatermain; he may have some of his countrymen with him." Accordingly a lantern was produced and held towards the voice. There was Indaba-zimbi alone. We let him into the laager and asked him the news.

"This is the news, white men," he said. "I waited till dark, and creeping up to the place where the Zulus are encamped, hid myself behind a stone and listened. They are a great regiment of Umtetwas as Baas Botha yonder thought. They struck the spoor of the waggons three days ago and followed it. To-night they sleep upon their spears, to-morrow at daybreak they will attack the laager and kill everybody. They are very bitter against the Boers, because of the battle at Blood River and the other fights, and that is why they followed the waggons instead of going straight north after Mosilikatze."

A kind of groan went up from the group of listening Dutchmen.

"I tell you what it is, Heeren," I said, "instead of waiting to be butchered here like buck in a pitfall, let us go out now and fall upon the Impi while it sleeps."

This proposition excited some discussion, but in the end only one man could be found to vote for it. Boers as a rule lack that dash which makes great soldiers; such forlorn hopes are not in their line, and rather than embark upon them they prefer to take their chance in a laager, however poor that chance may be. For my own part I firmly believe that had my advice been taken we should have routed the Zulus. Seventeen desperate white men, armed with guns, would have produced no small effect upon a camp of sleeping savages. But it was not taken, so it is no use talking about it.

After that we went back to our posts, and slowly the weary night wore on towards the dawn. Only those who have watched under similar circumstances while they waited the advent of almost certain and cruel death, can know the torturing suspense of those heavy hours. But they went somehow, and at last in the far east the sky began to lighten, while the cold breath of dawn stirred the tilts of the waggons and chilled me to the bone. The fat Dutchwoman behind me woke with a yawn, then, remembering all, moaned aloud, while her teeth chattered with cold and fear. Hans Botha went to his waggon and got a bottle of peach brandy, from which he poured into a tin pannikin, giving us each a stiff dram, and making attempts to be cheerful as he did so. But his affected jocularity only seemed to depress his comrades the more. Certainly it depressed me.

Now the light was growing, and we could see some way into the mist which still hung densely over the river, and now – ah! there it was. From the other side of the hill, a thousand yards or more from the laager, came a faint humming sound. It grew and grew till it gathered to a chant – the awful war chant of the Zulus. Soon I could catch the words. They were simple enough:

> We shall slay, we shall slay! Is it not so, my brothers?
> Our spears shall blush blood-red. Is it not so, my brothers?
> For we are the sucklings of Chaka, blood is our milk, my brothers.
> Awake, children of the Umtetwa, awake!
> The vulture wheels, the jackal sniffs the air;
> Awake, children of the Umtetwa – cry aloud, ye ringed men:
> There is the foe, we shall slay them. Is it not so, my brothers?
> *S'gee! S'gee! S'gee!*

Such is a rough translation of that hateful chant which to this very day I often seem to hear. It does not look particularly imposing on paper, but if, while he waited to be killed, the reader could have heard it as it rolled through the still air from the throats of nearly three thousand warriors singing all to time, he would have found it impressive enough.

Now the shields began to appear over the brow of the rise. They came by companies, each company about ninety strong. Altogether there were thirty-one companies. I counted them. When all were over they formed themselves into a triple line, then trotted down the slope towards us. At a distance of a hundred and fifty yards, or just out of shot of such guns as we had in those days, they halted and began singing again:

> "Yonder is the kraal of the white man – a little kraal, my brothers;
> We shall eat it up, we shall trample it flat, my brothers.
> But where are the white man's cattle – where are his oxen, my
>   brothers?"

This question seemed to puzzle them a good deal, for they sang the song again and again. At last a herald came forward, a great man with ivory rings on his arm, and, putting his hands to his mouth, called out to us asking where our cattle were.

Hans Botha climbed on to the top of a waggon and roared out that they might answer that question themselves.

Then the herald called again, saying that he saw that the cattle had been sent away.

"We shall go and find the cattle," he said, "then we shall come and kill you, because without cattle you must stop where you are, but if we wait to kill you before we get the cattle, they may have trekked too far for us to follow. And if you try to run away we shall easily catch you white men!"

This struck me as a very odd speech, for the Zulus generally attack an enemy first and take his cattle afterwards; still, there was a certain amount of plausibility about it. While I was still wondering what it all might mean, the Zulus began to run past us in companies towards the river. Suddenly a shout announced that they had found the spoor of the cattle, and the whole Impi of them started down it at a run till they vanished over a rise about a quarter of a mile away.

We waited for half an hour or more, but nothing could we see of them.

"Now I wonder if the devils have really gone," said Hans Botha to me. "It is very strange."

"I will go and see," said Indaba-zimbi, "if you will come with me, Macumazahn. We can creep to the top of the ridge and look over."

At first I hesitated, but curiosity overcame me. I was young in those days and weary with suspense.

"Very well," I said, "we will go."

So we started. I had my elephant gun and ammunition. Indaba-zimbi had his medicine bag and an assegai. We crept to the top of the rise like sportsmen stalking a buck. The slope on the other side was strewn with rocks, among which grew bushes and tall grass.

"They must have gone down the Donga," I said to Indaba-zimbi, "I can't see one of them."

As I spoke there came a roar of men all round me. From every rock, from every tuft of grass rose a Zulu warrior. Before I could turn, before I could lift a gun, I was seized and thrown.

"Hold him! Hold the White Spirit fast!" cried a voice. "Hold him, or he will slip away like a snake. Don't hurt him, but hold him fast. Let Indaba-zimbi walk by his side."

I turned on Indaba-zimbi. "You black devil, you have betrayed me!" I cried.

"Wait and see, Macumazahn," he answered, coolly. "Now the fight is going to begin."

CHAPTER V

The End of the Laager

I gasped with wonder and rage. What did that scoundrel Indaba-zimbi mean? Why had I been drawn out of the laager and seized, and why, being seized, was I not instantly killed? They called me the "White Spirit". Could it be that they were keeping me to make me into medicine? I had heard of such things being done by Zulus and kindred tribes, and my blood ran cold at the thought. What an end! To be pounded up, made medicine of, and eaten!

However, I had little time for further reflection, for now the whole Impi was pouring back from the donga and river-banks where it had hidden while their ruse was carried out, and once more formed up on the side of the slope. I was taken to the crest of the slope and placed in the centre of the reserve line in the especial charge of a huge Zulu named Bombyane, the same man who had come forward as a herald. This brute seemed to regard me with an affectionate curiosity. Now and again he poked me in the ribs with the handle of his assegai, as though to assure himself that I was solid, and several times he asked me to be so good as to prophesy how many Zulus would be killed before the "Amaboona", as they called the Boers, were "eaten up".

At first I took no notice of him beyond scowling, but presently, goaded into anger, I prophesied that he would be dead in an hour!

He only laughed aloud. "Oh! White Spirit," he said, "is it so? Well, I've walked a long way from Zululand, and shall be glad of a rest."

And he got it shortly, as will be seen.

Now the Zulus began to sing again:

> We have caught the White Spirit, my brother! my brother!
> Iron-Tongue whispered of him, he smelt him out, my brother.
> Now the Maboona are ours – they are already dead, my brother."

So that treacherous villain Indaba-zimbi *had* betrayed me. Suddenly the chief of the Impi, a grey-haired man named Sususa, held up his assegai, and instantly there was silence. Then he spoke to some indunas who stood near him. Instantly they ran to the right and left down the first line, saying a word to the captain of each company as they passed him. Presently they were at the respective ends of the line, and simultaneously held up their spears. As they did so, with an awful roar of "Bulala Amaboona" – "Slay the Boers", the entire line, numbering nearly a thousand men, bounded forward like a buck startled from its form, and rushed down upon the little laager. It was a splendid sight to see them, their assegais glittering in the sunlight as they rose and fell above their black shields, their war-plumes bending back upon the wind, and their fierce faces set intently on the foe, while the solid earth shook beneath the thunder of their rushing feet. I thought of my poor friends the Dutchmen, and trembled. What chance had they against so many?

Now the Zulus, running in the shape of a bow so as to wrap the laager round on three sides, were within seventy yards, and now from every waggon broke tongues of fire. Over rolled a number of the Umtetwa, but the rest cared little. Forward they sped straight to the laager, striving to force a way in. But the Boers plied them with volley after volley, and, packed as the Zulus were, the elephant guns loaded with slugs and small shot did frightful execution. Only one man even got on to a waggon, and as he did so I saw a Boer woman strike him on the head with an axe. He fell down, and slowly, amid howls of derision from the two lines on the hill-side, the Zulus drew back.

"Let us go, father!" shouted the soldiers on the slope, among whom I was, to their chief, who had come up. "You have sent out the little girls to fight, and they are frightened. Let us show them the way."

"No, no!" the chief Sususa answered, laughing. "Wait a minute and the little girls will grow to women, and women are good enough to fight against Boers!"

The attacking Zulus heard the mockery of their fellows, and rushed forward again with a roar. But the Boers in the laager had found time to load, and they met with a warm reception. Reserving their fire till the Zulus were packed like sheep in a kraal, they loosed into them with the *roers*, and the warriors fell in little heaps. But I saw that the blood of the Umtetwas was up; they did not mean to be beaten back this time, and the end was near. See! six men had leapt on to a waggon, slain the man behind it, and sprung into the laager. They were killed there, but others followed, and then I turned my head. But I could not shut my ears to the cries of rage and death, and the terrible *S'gee! S'gee!* of the savages as they did their work of murder. Once only I looked up and saw poor Hans Botha standing on a waggon smiting down men with the butt of his rifle. Then assegais shot up towards him like tongues of steel, and when I looked again he was gone.

I turned sick with fear and rage. But alas! what could I do? They were all dead now, and probably my own turn was coming, only my death would not be so swift.

The fight was ended, and the two lines on the slope broke their order, and moved down to the laager. Presently we were there, and a dreadful sight it was. Many of the attacking Zulus were dead – quite fifty I should say, and at least a hundred and fifty were wounded, some of them mortally. The chief Sususa gave an order, the dead men were picked up and piled in a heap, while those who were slightly hurt walked off to find some one to tie up their wounds. But the more serious cases met with a different treatment. The chief or one of his indunas considered each case, and if it was in any way bad, the man was taken up and thrown into the river which ran near. None of them offered any objection, though one poor fellow swam to shore again. He did not stop there long, however, for they pushed him back and drowned him by force.

The strangest case of all was that of the chief's own brother. He had been captain of the line, and his ankle was smashed by a bullet. Sususa came up to him, and, having examined the wound, rated him soundly for failing in the first onslaught.

The poor fellow made the excuse that it was not his fault, as the Boers had hit him in the first rush. His brother admitted the truth of this, and talked to him amicably.

"Well," he said at length, offering him a pinch of snuff, "you cannot walk again."

"No, chief," said the wounded man, looking at his ankle.

"And to-morrow we must walk far," went on Sususa.

"Yes, chief."

"Say, then, will you sit here on the veldt, or –" and he nodded towards the river.

The man dropped his head on his breast for a minute as though in thought. Presently he lifted it and looked Sususa straight in the face.

"My ankle pains me, my brother," he said; "I think I will go back to Zululand, for there is the only kraal I wish to see again, even if I creep about it like a snake."*

"It is well, my brother," said the chief. "Rest softly," and having shaken hands with him, he gave an order to one of the indunas, and turned away.

Then men came, and, supporting the wounded man, led him down to the banks of the stream. Here, at his request, they tied a heavy stone round his neck, and then threw him into a deep pool. I saw the whole sad scene, and the victim never even winced. It was impossible not to admire the extraordinary courage of the man, or to avoid being struck with the cold-blooded cruelty of his brother the chief. And yet the act was necessary from his point of view. The man must either die swiftly, or be left to perish of starvation, for no Zulu force will encumber itself with wounded men. Years of merciless warfare had so hardened these people that they looked on death as nothing, and were, to do them justice, as willing to meet it themselves as to inflict it on others. When this very Impi had been sent out by the Zulu King Dingaan, it consisted of some nine thousand men. Now it numbered less than three; all the rest were dead. They, too, would probably soon be dead. What did it matter? They lived by war to die in blood. It was their natural end. "Kill till you are killed." That is the motto of the Zulu soldier. It has the merit of simplicity.

---

* The Zulus believe that after death their spirits enter into the bodies of large green snakes, which glide about the kraals. To kill these snakes is sacrilege. – Editor

Meanwhile the warriors were looting the waggons, including my own, having first thrown all the dead Boers into a heap. I looked at the heap; all of them were there, including the two stout fraus, poor things. But I missed one body, that of Hans Botha's daughter, little Tota. A wild hope came into my heart that she might have escaped; but no, it was not possible. I could only pray that she was already at rest.

Just then the great Zulu, Bombyane, who had left my side to indulge in the congenial occupation of looting, came out of a waggon crying that he had got the "little white one". I looked; he was carrying the child Tota, gripping her frock in one of his huge black hands. He stalked up to where we were, and held the child before the chief. "Is it dead, father?" he said, with a laugh.

Now, as I could well see, the child was not dead, but had been hidden away, and fainted with fear.

The chief glanced at it carelessly, and said:

"Find out with your kerrie."

Acting on this hint the black devil held up the child, and was about to kill it with his knobstick. This was more than I could bear. I sprang at him and struck him with all my force in the face, little caring if I was speared or not. He dropped Tota on the ground.

"Ou!" he said, putting his hand to his nose, "the White Spirit has a hard fist. Come, Spirit, I will fight you for the child."

The soldiers cheered and laughed. "Yes! yes!" they said, "let Bombyane fight the White Spirit for the child. Let them fight with assegais."

For a moment I hesitated. What chance had I against this black giant? But I had promised poor Hans to save the child if I could, and what did it matter? As well die now as later. However, I had wit enough left to make a favour of it, and intimated to the chief through Indaba-zimbi that I was quite willing to condescend to kill Bombyane, on condition that if I did so the child's life should be given to me. Indaba-zimbi interpreted my words, but I noticed that he would not look on me as he spoke, but covered his face with his hands and spoke of me as "the ghost" or the "son of the spirit". For some reason that I have never quite understood, the chief consented to the duel. I fancy it was because he believed me to be more than mortal and was anxious to see the last of Bombyane.

"Let them fight," he said. "Give them assegais and no shields; the child shall be to him who conquers."

"Yes! yes!" cried the soldiers. "Let them fight. Don't be afraid, Bombyane; if he is a spirit, he's a very small one."

"I never was frightened of man or beast, and I am not going to run away from a White Ghost," answered the redoubtable Bombyane, as he examined the blade of his great bangwan or stabbing assegai.

Then they made a ring round us, gave me a similar assegai, and set us some ten paces apart. I kept my face as calm as I could, and tried to show no signs of fear, though in my heart I was terribly afraid. Humanly speaking, my doom was on me. The giant warrior before me had used the assegai from a child – I had no experience of that weapon. Moreover, though I was quick and active, he must have been at least twice as strong as I am. However, there was no help for it, so, setting my teeth, I grasped the great spear, breathed a prayer, and waited.

The giant stood awhile looking at me, and, as he stood, Indaba-zimbi walked across the ring behind me, muttering as he passed, "Keep cool, Macumazahn, and wait for him. I will make it all right."

As I had not the slightest intention of commencing the fray, I thought this good advice, though how Indaba-zimbi could "make it all right" I failed to see.

Heavens! how long that half-minute seemed! It happened many years ago, but the whole scene rises up before my eyes as I write. There behind us was the blood-stained laager, and near it lay the piles of dead; round us was rank upon rank of plumed savages, standing in silence to wait the issue of the duel, and in the centre stood the grey-haired chief and general, Sususa, in all his war finery, a cloak of leopard skin upon his shoulders. At his feet lay the senseless form of little Tota, to my left squatted Indaba-zimbi, nodding his white lock and muttering something – probably spells; while in front was my giant antagonist, his spear aloft and his plumes wavering in the gentle wind. Then over all, over grassy slope, river, and koppie, over the waggons of the laager, the piles of dead, the dense masses of the living, the swooning child, over all shone the bright impartial sun, looking down like the indifferent eye of Heaven upon the loveliness of nature and the cruelty of man. Down by the river grew thorn-trees, and from them floated the sweet scent of the mimosa flower, and came the sound of cooing turtle-doves. I never smell the one or hear the other without the scene flashing into my mind again, complete in its every detail.

Suddenly, without a sound, Bombyane shook his assegai and rushed straight at me. I saw his huge form come; like a man in a dream, I saw the broad spear flash on high; now he was on me! Then, prompted to it by some providential impulse – or had the spells of Indaba-zimbi anything to do with the matter? – I dropped to my knee, and quick as light stretched out my spear. He drove at me: the blade passed over my head. I felt a weight on my assegai; it was wrenched from my hand, his great limbs knocked against me. I glanced round. Bombyane was staggering along with head thrown back and outstretched arms from which his spear had fallen. His spear had fallen, but the blade of mine stood out between his shoulders – I had transfixed him. He stopped, swung round slowly as though to look at me: then with a sigh the giant sank down – *dead*.

For a moment there was silence; then a great cry rose – a cry of "Bombyane is dead. The White Spirit has slain Bombyane. Kill the wizard, kill the ghost who has slain Bombyane by witchcraft."

Instantly I was surrounded by fierce faces, and spears flashed before my eyes. I folded my arms and stood calmly waiting the end. In a moment it would have come, for the warriors were mad at seeing their champion overthrown thus easily. But presently through the tumult I heard the high, cracked voice of Indaba-zimbi.

"Stand back, you fools!" it cried; "can a spirit then be killed?"

"Spear him! spear him!" they roared in fury. "Let us see if he is a spirit. How did a spirit slay Bombyane with an assegai? Spear him, rain-maker, and we shall see."

"Stand back," cried Indaba-zimbi again, "and I will show you if he can be killed. I will kill him myself, and call him back to life again before your eyes."

"Macumazahn, trust me," he whispered in my ear in the Sisutu tongue, which the Zulus did not understand. "Trust me; kneel on the grass before me, and when I strike at you with the spear, roll over like one dead; then, when you hear my voice again, get up. Trust me – it is your only hope."

"Having no choice I nodded my head in assent, though I had not the faintest idea of what he was about to do. The tumult lessened somewhat, and once more the warriors drew back.

"Great White Spirit – Spirit of victory," said Indaba-zimbi, addressing me aloud, and covering his eyes with his hand, "hear me and forgive me. These children are blind with folly, and think thee mortal because thou hast dealt death upon a mortal who dared to stand against thee. Deign to kneel down before me and let me pierce thy heart with this spear, then when I call upon thee, arise unhurt."

I knelt down, not because I wished to, but because I must. I had not overmuch faith in Indaba-zimbi, and thought it probable that he was in truth about to make an end of me. But really I was so worn with fears, and the horrors of the night and day had so shaken my nerves, that I did not greatly care what befell me. When I had been kneeling thus for about half a minute Indaba-zimbi spoke.

"People of the Umtetwa, children of T'Chaka;" he said, "draw back a little way, lest an evil fall on you, for now the air is thick with ghosts."

They drew back a space, leaving us in a circle about twelve yards in diameter.

"Look on him who kneels before you," went on Indaba-zimbi, "and listen to my words, to the words of the witch-finder, the words of the rain-maker, Indaba-zimbi, whose fame is known to you. He seems to be a young man, does he not? I tell you, children of the

Umtetwa, he is no man. He is the Spirit who gives victory to the white men, he it is who gave them assegais that thunder and taught them how to slay. Why were the Impis of Dingaan rolled back at the Blood River? Because *he* was there. Why did the Amaboona slay the people of Mosilikatze by the thousand? Because *he* was there. And so I say to you that had I not drawn him from the laager by my magic but three hours ago, you would have been conquered – yes, you would have been blown away like the dust before the wind; you would have been burnt up like the dry grass in the winter when the fire is awake among it. Ay, because he had but been there many of your bravest were slain in overcoming a few – a pinch of men who could be counted on the fingers. But because I loved you, because your chief Sususa is my half-brother – for had we not one father? – I came to you, I warned you. Then you prayed me and I drew the Spirit forth. But you were not satisfied when the victory was yours, when the Spirit, of all you had taken asked but one little thing – a white child to take away and sacrifice to himself, to make the medicine of his magic of –"

Here I could hardly restrain myself from interrupting, but thought better of it.

"You said him nay; you said, 'Let him fight with our bravest man, let him fight with Bombyane the giant for the child.' And he deigned to slay Bombyane as you have seen, and now you say, 'Slay him; he is no spirit.' Now I will show you if he is a spirit, for I will slay him before your eyes, and call him to life again. But you have brought this upon yourselves. Had you believed, had you offered no insult to the Spirit, he would have stayed with you, and you should have become unconquerable. Now he will arise and leave you, and woe be on you if you try to stay him.

"Now all men," he went on, "look for a space upon this assegai that I hold up," and he lifted the bangwan of the deceased Bombyane high above his head so that all the multitude could see it. Every eye was fixed upon the broad bright spear. For a while he held it still, then he moved it round and round in a circle, muttering as he did so, and still their gaze followed it. For my part, I watched his movements with the greatest anxiety. That assegai had already been nearer my person than I found at all pleasant, and I had no desire to make a further acquaintance with it. Nor, indeed, was I sure that Indaba-zimbi was not really going to kill me. I could not understand his proceedings at all, and at the best I did not relish playing the *corpus vile* to his magical experiments.

"*Look! look! look!*" he screamed.

Then suddenly the great spear flashed down towards my breast. I felt nothing, but, to my sight, it seemed as though it had passed through me.

"See!" roared the Zulus. "Indaba-zimbi has speared him; the red assegai stands out behind his back."

"Roll over, Macumazahn," Indaba-zimbi hissed in my ear, "roll over and pretend to die – quick! quick!"

I lost no time in following these strange instructions, but falling on to my side, threw my arms wide, kicked my legs about, and died as artistically as I could. Presently I gave a stage shiver and lay still.

"See!" said the Zulus, "he is dead, the Spirit is dead. Look at the blood upon the assegai!"

"Stand back! stand back!" cried Indaba-zimbi, or the ghost will haunt you. "Yes, he is dead, and now I will call him back to life again. Look!" and putting down his hand, he plucked the spear from wherever it was fixed, and held it aloft. The spear is red, is it not? Watch, men, watch! *it grows white!*"

"Yes, it grows white," they said. "Ou! it grows white."

"It grows white because the blood returns to whence it came," said Indaba-zimbi. "Now, great Spirit, hear me. Thou art dead, the breath has gone out of thy mouth. Yet hear me and arise. Awake, White Spirit, awake and show thy power. Awake! arise unhurt!"

I began to respond cheerfully to this imposing invocation.

"Not so fast, Macumazahn," whispered Indaba-zimbi.

I took the hint, and first held up my arm, then lifted my head and let it fall again.

"He lives! by the head of T'Chaka he lives!" roared the soldiers, stricken with mortal fear.

Then slowly and with the greatest dignity I gradually arose, stretched my arms, yawned like one awaking from heavy sleep, turned and looked upon them unconcernedly. While I did so, I noticed that old Indaba-zimbi was almost fainting from exhaustion. Beads of perspiration stood upon his brow, his limbs trembled, and his breast heaved.

As for the Zulus, they waited for no more. With a howl of terror the whole regiment turned and fled across the rise, so that presently we were left alone with the dead, and the swooning child.

"How on earth did you do that, Indaba-zimbi?" I asked in amaze.

"Do not ask me, Macumazahn," he gasped. "You white men are very clever, but you don't quite know everything. There are men in the world who can make people believe they see things which they do not see. Let us be going while we may, for when those Umtetwas have got over their fright, they will come back to loot the waggons, and then perhaps *they* will begin asking questions that I can't answer."

And here I may as well state that I never got any further information on this matter from old Indaba-zimbi. But I have my theory, and here it is for whatever it may be worth. I believe that Indaba-zimbi *mesmerized* the whole crowd of onlookers, myself included, making them believe that they saw the assegai in my heart, and the blood upon the blade. The reader may smile and say, "Impossible", but I would ask him how the Indian jugglers do their tricks unless it is by mesmerism. The spectators *seem* to see the boy go under the basket and there pierced with daggers, they *seem* to see women in a trance supported in mid air upon the point of a single sword. In themselves these things are not possible, they violate the laws of nature, as those laws are known to us, and therefore must surely be illusion. And so through the glamour thrown upon them by Indaba-zimbi's will, that Zulu Impi seemed to see me transfixed with an assegai which never touched me. At least, that is my theory; if any one has a better, let him adopt it. The explanation lies between illusion and magic of a most imposing character, and I prefer to accept the first alternative.

CHAPTER VI

Stella

I was not slow to take Indaba-zimbi's hint. About a hundred and fifty yards to the left of the laager was a little dell where I had hidden my horse, together with one belonging to the Boers, and my saddle and bridle. Thither we went, I carrying the swooning Tota in my arms. To our joy we found the horses safe, for the Zulus had not seen them. Now, of course, they were our only means of locomotion, for the oxen had been sent away, and even had they been there we could not have found time to inspan them. I laid Tota down, caught my horse, undid his knee halter, and saddled up. As I was doing so a thought struck me, and I told Indaba-zimbi to run to the laager and see if he could find my double-barrelled gun and some powder and shot, for I had only my elephant *roer* and a few charges of powder and ball with me.

He went, and while he was away, poor little Tota came to herself and began to cry, till she saw my face.

"Ah, I have had such a bad dream," she said, in Dutch.

"I dreamed that the black Kaffirs were going to kill me. Where is my papa?"

I winced at the question. "Your papa has gone on a journey, dear," I said, "and left me to look after you. We shall find him one day. You don't mind going with Heer Allan, do you?"

"No," she said, a little doubtfully, and began to cry again. Presently she remembered that she was thirsty, and asked for water. I led her to the river and she drank. "Why is my hand red, Heer Allan?" she asked, pointing to the smear of Bombyane's blood-stained fingers.

At this moment I felt very glad that I had killed Bombyane.

"It is only paint, dear," I said; "see, we will wash it and your face."

As I was doing this, Indaba-zimbi returned. The guns were all gone; he said the Zulus had taken them and the powder. But he had found some things and brought them in a sack. There was a thick blanket, about twenty pounds weight of biltong or sun-dried meat, a few double-handfuls of biscuits, two water-bottles, a tin pannikin, some matches and sundries.

"And now, Macumazahn," he said, "we had best be going, for those Umtetwas are coming back. I saw one of them on the brow of the rise."

That was enough for me. I lifted little Tota on to the bow of my saddle, climbed into it and rode off, holding her in front of me. Indaba-zimbi slipped a reim into the mouth of the best of the Boer horses, threw the sack of sundries on to its back and mounted also, holding the elephant gun in his hand. We went eight or nine hundred yards in silence till we were quite out of range of sight from the waggons, which were in a hollow. Then I pulled up, with such a feeling of thankfulness in my heart as cannot be told in words; for now I knew that, mounted as we were, those black demons could never catch us. But where were we to steer for? I put the question to Indaba-zimbi, asking him if he thought that we had better try and follow the oxen which we had sent away with the Kaffirs and women on the preceding night. He shook his head.

"The Umtetwas will go after the oxen presently," he answered, "and we have seen enough of them."

"Quite enough," I answered, with enthusiasm; "I never want to see another; but where are we to go? Here we are alone with one gun and a little girl in the vast and lonely veldt. Which way shall we turn?"

"Our faces were towards the north before we met the Zulus," answered Indaba-zimbi; "let us still keep them to the north. Ride on, Macumazahn; to-night when we off-saddle I will look into the matter."

So all that long afternoon we rode on, following the course of the river. From the nature of the ground we could only go slowly, but before sunset I had the satisfaction of knowing that there must be at least twenty-five miles between us and those accursed Zulus. Little Tota slept most of the way, the motion of the horse was easy, and she was worn out.

At last the sunset came, and we off-saddled in a dell by the river. There was not much to eat, but I soaked some biscuit in water for Tota, and Indaba-zimbi and I made a scanty meal of biltong. When we had done I took off Tota's frock, wrapped her up in the blanket near the fire we had made, and lit a pipe. I sat there by the side of the sleeping orphaned child, and from my heart thanked Providence for saving her life and mine from the slaughter of that day. What a horrible experience it had been! It seemed like a nightmare to look back upon. And yet it was sober fact, one among those many tragedies which dotted the paths of the emigrant Boers with the bones of men, women, and children. These horrors are almost forgotten now; people living in Natal, for instance, can scarcely realize that some forty years ago six hundred white people, many of them women and children, were thus massacred by the Impis of Dingaan. But it was so, and the name of the district, *Weenen*, or the Place of Weeping, will commemorate them for ever.

Then I fell to reflecting on the extraordinary adroitness old Indaba-zimbi had shown in saving my life. It appeared that he himself had lived among the Umtetwa Zulus in his earlier manhood, and was a noted rain-doctor and witch-finder. But when T'Chaka, Dingaan's brother, ordered a general massacre of the witch-finders, he alone had saved his life by his skill in magic, and ultimately fled south for reasons too long to set out here. When he heard, therefore, that the regiment was an Umtetwa regiment, which, leaving their wives and children, had broken away from Zululand to escape the cruelties of Dingaan; under pretence of spying on them, he took the bold course of going straight up to the chief, Sususa, and addressing him as his brother, which he was. The chief knew him at once, and so did the soldiers, for his fame was still great among them. Then he told them his cock and bull story about my being a white spirit, whose presence in the laager would render it invincible, and with the object of saving my life in the slaughter which he knew must ensue, agreed to charm me out of the laager and deliver me into their keeping. How the plan worked has already been told; it was a risky one; still, but for it my troubles would have been done with these many days.

So I lay and thought with a heart full of gratitude, and as I did so saw old Indaba-zimbi sitting by the fire and going through some mysterious performances with bones, which he produced from his bag, and ashes mixed with water. I spoke to him and asked what he was about. He replied that he was tracing out the route that we should follow. I felt inclined to answer "bosh!" but remembering the very remarkable instances which he had given of his prowess in occult matters I held my tongue, and taking little Tota into my arms, worn out with toil and danger and emotion, I went to sleep.

I awoke just as the dawn was beginning to flame across the sky in sheets of primrose and of gold, or rather it was little Tota who woke me by kissing me as she lay between sleep and waking, and calling me "papa". It wrung my heart to hear her, poor orphaned child. I got up, washed and dressed her as best I could, and we breakfasted as we had supped, on biltong and biscuit. Tota asked for milk, but I had none to give her. Then we caught the horses, and I saddled mine.

"Well, Indaba-zimbi," I said, "now what path do your bones point to?"

"Straight north," he said. "The journey will be hard, but in about four days we shall come to the kraal of a white man, an Englishman, not a Boer. His kraal is in a beautiful place, and there is a great peak behind it where there are many baboons."

I looked at him. "This is all nonsense, Indaba-zimbi," I said. "Whoever heard of an Englishman building a house in these wilds, and how do you know anything about it? I think that we had better strike east towards Port Natal."

"As you like, Macumazahn," he answered, "but it will take us three months' journey to get to Port Natal, if we ever get there, and the child will die on the road. Say, Macumazahn, have my words come true heretofore, or have they not? Did I not tell you not to hunt the elephants on horseback? Did I not tell you to take one waggon with you instead of two, as it is better to lose one than two?"

"You told me all these things," I answered.

"And so I tell you now to ride north, Macumazahn, for there you will find great happiness – yes, and great sorrow. But no man should run away from happiness because of the sorrow. As you will, as you will!"

Again I looked at him. In his divinations I did not believe, yet I came to the conclusion that he was speaking what he knew to be the truth. It struck me as possible that he might have heard of some white man living like a hermit in the wilds, but preferring to keep up his prophetic character would not say so.

"Very well, Indaba-zimbi," I said, "let us ride north."

Shortly after we started, the river we had followed hitherto turned off in a westerly direction, so we left it. All that day we rode across rolling uplands, and about an hour before sunset halted at a little stream which ran down from a range of hills in front of us. By this time I was heartily tired of the biltong, so taking my elephant rifle – for I had nothing else – I left Tota with Indaba-zimbi, and started to try if I could shoot something. Oddly enough we had seen no buck all the day, nor did we see any on the subsequent days. For some mysterious reason they had temporarily left the district. I crossed the little streamlet in order to enter the belt of thorns which grew upon the hill-side beyond, for there I hoped to find game. As I did so I was rather disturbed to see the spoor of two lions in the soft sandy edge of a pool. Breathing a hope that they might not still be in the neighbourhood, I went on into the belt of scattered thorns. For a long while I hunted about without seeing anything, except one duiker antelope, which bounded off with a crash from the other side of a stone without giving me a chance. At length, just as it grew dusk, I spied a Petie buck, a graceful little creature, scarcely bigger than a large hare, standing on a stone, about forty yards from me. Under ordinary circumstances I should never have dreamed of firing at such a thing, especially with an elephant gun, but we were hungry. So I sat down with my back against a rock, and aimed steadily at its head. I did this because if I struck it in the body the three-ounce ball would have knocked it to bits. At last I pulled the trigger, the gun went off with the report of a small cannon, and the buck disappeared. I ran to the spot with more anxiety than I should have felt in an ordinary way over a koodoo or an eland. To my delight there the little creature lay – the huge bullet had decapitated it. Considering all the circumstances I do not think I have often made a better shot than this, but if any one doubts, let him try his hand at a rabbit's head fifty yards away with an elephant gun and a three-ounce ball.

I picked up the Petie in triumph and returned to the camp. There we skinned him and toasted his flesh over the fire. He just made a good meal for us, though we kept the hind legs for breakfast.

There was no moon this night, and so it chanced that when I suddenly remembered about the lion spoor, and suggested that we had better tie up the horses quite close to us, we could not find them, though we knew they were grazing within fifty yards. This being so we could only make up the fire and take our chance. Shortly afterwards I went to sleep with little Tota in my arms. Suddenly I was awakened by hearing that peculiarly painful sound, the scream of a horse, quite close to the fire, which was still burning brightly. Next second there came a noise of galloping hoofs, and before I could even rise my poor horse appeared in the ring of firelight. As in a flash of lightning I saw his staring eyes and wide-stretched nostrils, and the broken reim with which he had been knee-haltered, flying in the air. Also I saw something else, for on his back was a great dark form with glowing eyes, and from the form came a growling sound. It was a lion.

The horse dashed on. He galloped right through the fire, for which he had run in his terror, fortunately, however, without treading on us, and vanished into the night. We heard his hoofs for a hundred yards or more, then there was silence, broken now and again by distant growls. As may be imagined, we did not sleep any more that night, but waited anxiously till the dawn broke, two hours later.

As soon as there was sufficient light we rose, and, leaving Tota still asleep, crept cautiously in the direction in which the horse had vanished. When we had gone fifty yards or so, we made out its remains lying on the veldt, and caught sight of two great cat-like forms slinking away in the grey light.

To go any further was useless; we knew all about it now, so we turned to look for the other horse. But our cup of misfortune was not yet full; the horse was nowhere to be found. Soon we came upon its spoor, and then we saw what had happened. Terrified by the sight and smell of the lions, it had with a desperate effort also burst the reim with which it had been knee-haltered, and galloped far away. I sat down, feeling as though I could cry like a woman. For now we were left alone in these vast solitudes without a horse to carry us, and with a child who was not old enough to walk for more than a little way at a time.

Well, it was no use giving in, so with few words we went back to our camp, where I found Tota crying because she had woke to find herself alone. Then we ate a little food and prepared to start. First we divided such articles as we must take with us into two equal parts, rejecting everything that we could possibly do without. Then, by an afterthought, we filled our water-bottles, though at the time I was rather against doing so, because of the extra weight. But Indaba-zimbi overruled me in the matter, fortunately for all three of us. I settled to look after Tota for the first march, and to give the elephant gun to Indaba-zimbi. At length all was ready, and we set out on foot. By the help of occasional lifts over rough places, Tota managed to walk up the slope of the hill-side where I had shot the Petie buck. At length we reached it, and, looking at the country beyond, I gave an exclamation of dismay. To say that it was desert would be saying too much; it was more like the Karroo in the Cape – a vast sandy waste, studded here and there with low shrubs and scattered rocks. But it was a great expanse of desolate land, stretching further than the eye could reach, and bordered far away by a line of purple hills, in the centre of which a great solitary peak soared high into the air.

"Indaba-zimbi," I said, "we can never cross this if we take six days."

"As you will, Macumazahn," he answered; "but I tell you that there" – and he pointed to the peak – "there the white man lives. Turn which way you like, but if you turn you will perish."

I reflected for a moment. Our case was, humanly speaking, almost hopeless. It mattered little which way we went. We were alone, almost without food, with no means of transport, and a child to carry. As well perish in the sandy waste as on the rolling veldt or among the trees of the hill-side. Providence alone could save us, and we must trust to Providence.

"Come on," I said, lifting Tota on to my back, for she was already tired. "All roads lead to rest."

How am I to describe the misery of the next four days? How am I to tell how we stumbled on through that awful desert, almost without food, and quite without water, for there were no streams, and we saw no springs? We soon found how the case was, and saved almost all the water in our bottles for the child. To look back on it is like a nightmare. I can scarcely bear to dwell on it. Day after day, by turns carrying the child through the heavy sand; night after night lying down in the scrub, chewing the leaves, and licking such dew as there was from the scanty grass! Not a spring, not a pool, not a head of game! It was the third night; we were nearly mad with thirst. Tota was in a comatose condition. Indaba-zimbi still had a little water in his bottle – perhaps a wine-glassful. With it we moistened our lips and blackened tongues. Then we gave the rest to the child. It revived her. She awoke from her swoon to sink into sleep.

See, the dawn was breaking. The hills were not more than eight miles or so away now, and they were green. There must be water there.

"Come," I said.

Indaba-zimbi lifted Tota into the kind of sling that we had made out of the blanket in which to carry her on our backs, and we staggered on for an hour through the sand. She woke crying for water, and alas! we had none to give her; our tongues were hanging from our lips, we could scarcely speak.

We rested awhile, and Tota mercifully swooned away again. Then Indaba-zimbi took her. Though he was so thin the old man's strength was wonderful.

Another hour; the slope of the great peak could not be more than two miles away now. A couple of hundred yards off grew a large baobab tree. Could we reach its shade? We had done half the distance when Indaba-zimbi fell from exhaustion. We were now so weak that neither of as could lift the child on to our backs. He rose again, and we each took one of her hands and dragged her along the road. Fifty yards – they seemed to be fifty miles. Ah, the tree was reached at last; compared with the heat outside, the shade of its dense foliage seemed like the dusk and cool of a vault. I remember thinking that it was a good place to die in. Then I remember no more.

I woke with a feeling as though the blessed rain were falling on my face and head. Slowly, and with great difficulty, I opened my eyes, then shut them again, having seen a vision. For a space I lay thus, while the rain continued to fall; I saw now that I must be asleep, or off my head with thirst and fever. If I were not off my head how came I to imagine that a lovely dark-eyed girl was bending over me sprinkling water on my face? A white girl, too, not a Kaffir woman. However, the dream went on.

"Hendrika," said a voice in English, the sweetest voice that I had ever heard; somehow it reminded me of wind whispering in the trees at night. "Hendrika, I fear he dies; there is a flask of brandy in my saddle-bag; get it."

"Ah! ah!" grunted a harsh voice in answer; "let him die, Miss Stella. He will bring you bad luck – let him die, I say. I felt a movement of air above me as though the woman of my vision turned swiftly, and once again I opened my eyes. She had risen, this dream woman. Now I saw that she was tall and graceful as a reed. She was angry, too; her dark eyes flashed, and she pointed with her hand at a female who stood before her, dressed in nondescript kind of clothes such as might be worn by either a man or a woman. The woman was young, of white blood, very short, with bowed legs and enormous shoulders. In face she was not bad-looking, but the brow receded, the chin and ears were prominent – in short, she reminded me of nothing so much as a very handsome monkey. She might have been the missing link.

The lady was pointing at her with her hand. "How dare you?" she said. "Are you going to disobey me again? Have you forgotten what I told you, Babyan?"*

"Ah! ah!" grunted the woman, who seemed literally to curl and shrivel up beneath her anger. "Don't be angry with me, Miss Stella, because I can't bear it. I only said it because it was true. I will fetch the brandy."

Then, dream or no dream, I determined to speak.

"Not brandy," I gasped in English as well as my swollen tongue would allow; "give me water."

"Ah, he lives!" cried the beautiful girl, "and he talks English. See, sir, here is water in your own bottle; you were quite close to a spring, it is on the other side of the tree."

I struggled to a sitting position, lifted the bottle to my lips, and drank from it. Oh! that drink of cool, pure water! never had I tasted anything so delicious. With the first gulp I felt life flow back into me. But wisely enough she would not let me have much. "No more! no more!" she said, and dragged the bottle from me almost by force.

"The child," I said – "is the child dead?"

"I do not know yet," she answered. "We have only just found you, and I tried to revive you first."

I turned and crept to where Tota lay by the side of Indaba-zimbi. It was impossible to say if they were dead or swooning. The lady sprinkled Tota's face with the water, which I watched greedily, for my thirst was still awful, while the woman Hendrika did the same office for Indaba-zimbi. Presently, to my vast delight, Tota opened her eyes and tried to cry, but could not, poor little thing, because her tongue

---

*Baboon. – Editor

and lips were so swollen. But the lady got some water into her mouth, and, as in my case, the effect was magical. We allowed her to drink about a quarter of a pint, and no more, though she cried bitterly for it. Just then old Indaba-zimbi came to with a groan. He opened his eyes, glanced round, and took in the situation.

"What did I tell you, Macumazahn?" he gasped, and, seizing the bottle, he took a long pull at it.

Meanwhile I sat with my back against the trunk of the great tree and tried to think. Looking to my left I saw two good horses – one bare-backed, and one with a rudely made lady's saddle on it. By the side of the horses were two dogs, of a stout greyhound breed, that sat watching us, and near the dogs lay a dead oribé buck, which they had evidently been coursing.

"Hendrika," said the lady presently, "they must not eat meat just yet. Go look up the tree and see if there is any ripe fruit on it."

The woman ran swiftly into the plain and obeyed. Presently she returned. "I see some ripe fruit," she said, "but it is high, quite at the top."

"Fetch it," said the lady.

"Easier said than done," I thought to myself; but I was much mistaken. Suddenly the woman bounded at least three feet into the air and caught one of the spreading boughs in her large flat hands; then came a swing that would have filled an acrobat with envy – and she was on it.

"Now there is an end," I thought again, for the next bough was beyond her reach. But again I was mistaken. She stood up on the bough, gripping it with her bare feet, and once more sprang at the one above, caught it and swung herself into it.

I suppose that the lady saw my expression of astonishment. "Do not wonder, sir," she said, "Hendrika is not like other people. She will not fall."

I made no answer, but watched the progress of this extraordinary person with the most breathless interest. On she went, swinging herself from bough to bough, and running along them like a monkey. At last she reached the top and began to swarm up a thin branch towards the ripe fruit. When she was near enough she shook the branch violently. There was a crack – a crash – it broke. I shut my eyes, expecting to see her crushed on the ground before me.

"Don't be afraid," said the lady again, laughing gently. "Look, she is quite safe."

I looked, and so she was. She had caught a bough as she fell, clung to it, and was now calmly dropping to another. Old Indaba-zimbi had also watched this performance with interest, but it did not seem to astonish him over-much. "Baboon-woman?" he said, as though such people were common, and then turned his attention to soothing Tota, who was moaning for more water. Meanwhile Hendrika came down the tree with extraordinary rapidity, and swinging by one hand from a bough, dropped about eight feet to the ground.

In another two minutes we were all three sucking the pulpy fruit. In an ordinary way we should have found it tasteless enough: as it was I thought it the most delicious thing I had ever tasted. After three days spent without food or water, in the desert, one is not particular. While we were still eating the fruit, the lady of my vision set her companion to work to partially flay the oribé which her dogs had killed, and busied herself in making a fire of fallen boughs. As soon as it burned brightly she took strips of the oribé flesh, toasted them, and gave them to us on leaves. We ate, and now were allowed a little more water. After that she took Tota to the spring and washed her, which she sadly needed, poor child! Next came our turn to wash, and oh, the joy of it!

I came back to the tree, walking painfully, indeed, but a changed man. There sat the beautiful girl with Tota on her knees. She was lulling her to sleep, and held up her finger to me enjoining silence. At last the child went off into a sound natural slumber – an example that I should have been glad to follow had it not been for my burning curiosity. Then I spoke.

"May I ask what your name is?" I said.

"Stella," she answered.

"Stella what?" I said.

"Stella nothing," she answered, in some pique; "Stella is my name; it is short and easy to remember at any rate. My father's name is Thomas, and we live up there," and she pointed round the base of the great peak. I looked at her astonished. "Have you lived there long?" I asked.

"Ever since I was seven years old. We came there in a waggon. Before that we came from England – from Oxfordshire; I can show you the place on the big map. It is called Garsingham."

Again I thought I must be dreaming. "Do you know, Miss Stella," I said, "it is very strange – so strange that it almost seems as though it could not be true – but I also came from Garsingham in Oxfordshire many years ago."

She started up. "Are you an English gentleman?" she said. "Ah, I have always longed to see an English gentleman. I have never seen but one Englishman since we lived here, and he certainly was not a gentleman – no white people at all, indeed, except a few wandering Boers. We live among black people and baboons – only I have read about English people – lots of books – poetry and novels. But tell me what is your name? Macumazahn, the black man called you, but you must have a white name, too."

"My name is Allan Quatermain," I said.

Her face turned quite white, her rosy lips parted, and she looked at me wildly with her beautiful dark eyes.

"It is wonderful," she said, "but I have often heard that name. My father has told me how a little boy called Allan Quatermain once saved my life by putting out my dress when it was on fire – see!" – and she pointed to a faint red mark upon her neck – "here is the scar of the burn."

"I remember it," I said. "You were dressed up as Father Christmas. It was I who put out the fire; my wrists were burnt in doing so."

Then for a space we sat silent, looking at each other, while Stella slowly fanned herself with her wide felt hat, in which some white ostrich plumes were fixed.

"This is God's doing," she said at last. "You saved my life when I was a child; now I have saved yours and the little girl's. Is she your own daughter?" she added, quickly.

"No," I answered; "I will tell you the tale presently."

"Yes," she said, "you shall tell me as we go home. It is time to be starting home, it will take us three hours to get there. Hendrika, Hendrika, bring the horses here!"

CHAPTER VII

The Baboon-Woman

Hendrika obeyed, leading the horses to the side of the tree.

"Now, Mr. Allan," said Stella, "you must ride on my horse, and the old black man must ride on the other. I will walk, and Hendrika will carry the little child. Oh, do not be afraid, she is very strong, she could carry you or me."

Hendrika grunted assent. I am sorry that I cannot express her method of speech by any more polite term. Sometimes she grunted like a monkey, sometimes she clicked like a Bushman, and sometimes she did both together, when she became quite unintelligible.

I expostulated against this proposed arrangement, saying that we could walk, which was a fib, for I do not think that I could have done a mile; but Stella would not listen, she would not even let me carry my elephant gun, but took it herself. So we mounted with some difficulty, and Hendrika took up the sleeping Tota in her long, sinewy arms.

"See that the 'Baboon-woman' does not run away into the mountains with the little white one," said Indaba-zimbi to me in Kaffir, as he climbed slowly on to the horse.

Unforunately Hendrika understood his speech. Her face twisted and grew livid with fury. She put down Tota and literally sprang at Indaba-zimbi as a monkey springs. But weary and worn as he was, the old gentleman was too quick for her. With an exclamation of genuine fright he threw himself from the horse on the further side, with the somewhat ludicrous result that all in a moment Hendrika was occupying the seat which he had vacated. Just then Stella realized the position.

"Come down, you savage, come down!" she said, stamping her foot.

The extraordinary creature flung herself from the horse and literally grovelled on the ground before her mistress and burst into tears.

"Pardon, Miss Stella," she clicked and grunted in villainous English, "but he called me 'Babyan-frau' (Baboon-woman)."

"Tell your servant that he must not use such words to Hendrika, Mr. Allan," Stella said to me. "If he does," she added, in a whisper, "Hendrika will certainly kill him."

I explained this to Indaba-zimbi, who, being considerably frightened, deigned to apologize. But from that hour there was hate and war between these two.

Harmony having been thus restored, we started, the dogs following us. A small strip of desert intervened between us and the slope of the peak – perhaps it was two miles wide. We crossed it and reached rich grass lands, for here a considerable stream gathered from the hills; but it did not flow across the barren lands, it passed to the east along the foot of the hills. This stream we had to cross by a ford. Hendrika walked boldly through it, holding Tota in her arms. Stella leapt across from stone to stone like a roebuck; I thought to myself that she was the most graceful creature that I had ever seen. After this the track passed round a pleasantly-wooded shoulder of the peak, which was, I found, known as Babyan Kap or Baboon Head. Of course we could only go at a foot pace, so our progress was slow. Stella walked for some way in silence, then she spoke.

"Tell me, Mr. Allan," she said, "how it was that I came to find you dying in the desert?"

So I began and told her all. It took an hour or more to do so, and she listened intently, now and again asking a question.

"It is all very wonderful," she said when I had done, "very

wonderful indeed. Do you know I went out this morning with Hendrika and the dogs for a ride, meaning to get back home by mid-day, for my father is ill, and I do not like to leave him for long. But just as I was going to turn, when we were about where we are now – yes, that was the very bush – an oribé got up, and the dogs chased it. I followed them for the gallop, and when we came to the river, instead of turning to the left as bucks generally do, the oribé swam the stream and took to the Bad Lands beyond. I followed it, and within a hundred yards of the big tree the dogs killed it. Hendrika wanted to turn back at once, but I said that we would rest under the shade of the tree, for I knew that there was a spring of water near. Well, we went; and there I saw you all lying like dead; but Hendrika, who is very clever in some ways, said no – and you know the rest. Yes, it is very wonderful."

"It is indeed," I said. "Now tell me, Miss Stella, who is Hendrika?"

She looked round before answering to see that the woman was not near.

"Hers is a strange story, Mr. Allan. I will tell you. You must know that all these mountains and the country beyond are full of baboons. When I was a girl of about ten I used to wander a great deal alone in the hills and valleys, and watch the baboons as they played among the rocks. There was one family of baboons that I watched especially – they used to live in a kloof about a mile from the house. The old man baboon was very large, and one of the females had a grey face. But the reason why I watched them so much was because I saw that they had with them a creature that looked like a girl, for her skin was quite white, and, what was more, that she was protected from the weather when it happened to be cold by a fur belt of some sort, which was tied round her throat. The old baboons seemed to be especially fond of her, and would sit with their arms round her neck. For nearly a whole summer I watched this particular white-skinned baboon till at last my curiosity quite overmastered me. I noticed that, though she climbed about the cliffs with the other monkeys, at a certain hour a little before sundown they used to put her with one or two other

much smaller ones into a little cave, while the family went off somewhere to get food, to the mealie fields, I suppose. Then I got an idea
that I would catch this white baboon and bring it home. But of course
I could not do this by myself, so I took a Hottentot – a very clever man
when he was not drunk – who lived on the stead, into my confidence.
He was called Hendrik, and was very fond of me; but for a long while
he would not listen to my plan, because he said that the babyans
would kill us. At last I bribed him with a knife that had four blades,
and one afternoon we started, Hendrik carrying a stout sack made of
hide, with a rope running through it so that the mouth could be
drawn tight

"Well, we got to the place, and, hiding ourselves carefully in the
trees at the foot of the kloof, watched the baboons playing about and
grunting to each other, till at length, according to custom, they took
the white one and three other little babies and put them in the cave.
Then the old man came out, looked carefully round, called to his
family, and went off with them over the brow of the kloof. Now very
slowly and cautiously we crept up over the rocks till we came to the
mouth of the cave and looked in. All the four little baboons were fast
asleep, with their backs towards us, and their arms round each
other's necks, the white one being in the middle. Nothing could
have been better for our plans. Hendrik, who by this time had quite
entered into the spirit of the thing, crept along the cave like a snake,
and suddenly dropped the mouth of the hide bag over the head of the
white baboon. The poor little thing woke up and gave a violent jump
which caused it to vanish right into the bag. Then Hendrik pulled
the string tight, and together we knotted it so that it was impossible
for our captive to escape. Meanwhile the other baby baboons had
rushed from the cave screaming, and when we got outside they were
nowhere to be seen.

"'Come on, Missie,' said Hendrik; 'the babyans will soon be back.'
He had shouldered the sack, inside of which the white baboon was
kicking violently, and screaming like a child. It was dreadful to hear
its shrieks.

"We scrambled down the sides of the kloof and ran for home as fast as we could manage. When we were near the waterfall, and within about three hundred yards of the garden wall, we heard a noise behind us, and there, leaping from rock to rock, and running over the grass, was the whole family of baboons headed by the old man.

"'Run, Missie, run!' gasped Hendrik, and I did, like the wind, leaving him far behind. I dashed into the garden, where some Kaffirs were working, crying, 'The babyans! the babyans!' Luckily the men had their sticks and spears by them and ran out just in time to save Hendrik, who was almost overtaken. The baboons made a good fight for it, however, and it was not till the old man was killed with an assegai that they ran away.

"Well, there is a stone hut in the kraal at the stead where my father sometimes shuts up natives who have misbehaved. It is very strong, and has a barred window. To this hut Hendrik carried the sack, and, having untied the mouth, put it down on the floor, and ran from the place, shutting the door behind him. In another moment the poor little thing was out and dashing round the stone hut as though it were mad. It sprung at the bars of the window, clung there, and beat its head against them till the blood came. Then it fell to the floor, and sat upon it crying like a child, and rocking itself backwards and forwards. It was so sad to see it that I began to cry too.

"Just then my father came in and asked what all the fuss was about. I told him that we had caught a young white baboon, and he was angry, and said that it must be let go. But when he looked at it through the bars of the window he nearly fell down with astonishment.

"'Why!' he said, 'this is not a baboon; it is a white child that the baboons have stolen and brought up!'

"Now, Mr. Allan, whether my father is right or wrong, you can judge for yourself. You see Hendrika — we named her that after Hendrik, who caught her — she is a woman, not a monkey, and yet she has many of the ways of monkeys, and looks like one too. You saw how she can climb, for instance, and you hear how she talks. Also she is very savage, and when she is angry or jealous she seems to go mad, though she is as clever as anybody. I think that she must have been stolen by the baboons when she was quite tiny and nurtured by them, and that is why she is so like them.

"But to go on. My father said that it was our duty to keep Hendrika at any cost. The worst of it was, that for three days she would eat nothing, and I thought that she would die, for all the while she sat and wailed. On the third day, however, I went to the bars of the window place, and held out a cup of milk and some fruit to her. She looked at it for a long while, then crept up moaning, took the milk from my hand, drank it greedily, and afterwards ate the fruit. From that time forward she took food readily enough, but only if I would feed her.

"But I must tell you of the dreadful end of Hendrik. From the day that we captured Hendrika the whole place began to swarm with baboons which were evidently employed in watching the kraals. One day Hendrik went out towards the hills alone to gather some medicine. He did not come back again, so next day search was made. By a big rock which I can show you, they found his scattered and broken bones, the fragments of his assegai, and four dead baboons. They had set upon him and torn him to pieces.

"My father was very much frightened at this, but still he would not let Hendrika go, because he said that she was human, and that it was our duty to reclaim her. And so we did – to a certain extent, at least. After the murder of Hendrik the baboons vanished from the neighbourhood, and have only returned quite recently, so at length we ventured to let Hendrika out. By this time she had grown very fond of me; still, on the first opportunity she ran away. But in the evening she returned again. She had been seeking the baboons, and could not find them. Shortly afterwards she began to speak – I taught her – and from that time she has loved me so that she will not leave me. I think it would kill her if I went away from her. She watches me all day, and at night sleeps on the floor of my hut. Once, too, she saved

198 | HUNTER QUATERMAIN'S STORY

my life when I was swept down the river in flood; but she is jealous, and hates everybody else. Look, how she is glaring at you now because I am talking to you!"

I looked. Hendrika was tramping along with the child in her arms and staring at me in a most sinister fashion out of the corners of her eyes.

While I was reflecting on the Baboon-woman's strange story, and thinking that she was an exceedingly awkward customer, the path took a sudden turn.

"Look!" said Stella, "there is our home. Is it not beautiful?"

It was beautiful indeed. Here on the western side of the great peak a bay had been formed in the mountain, which might have measured eight hundred or a thousand yards across by three-quarters of a mile in depth. At the back of this indentation the sheer cliff rose to the height of several hundred feet, and behind it and above it the great Babyan Peak towered up towards the heavens. The space of ground, embraced thus in the arms of the mountain, as it were, was laid out, as though by the cunning hand of man, in three terraces that rose one above the other. To the right and left of the topmost terrace were chasms in the cliff, and down each chasm fell a waterfall, from no great height, indeed, but of considerable volume. These two streams flowed away on either side of the enclosed space, one towards the north, and the other, the course of which we had been following, round the base of the mountain. At each terrace they made a cascade, so that the traveller approaching had a view of eight waterfalls at once. Along the edge of the stream to our left were placed Kaffir kraals, built in orderly groups with verandahs, after the Basutu fashion, and a very large part of the entire space of land was under cultivation. All of this I noted at once, as well as the extraordinary richness and depth of the soil, which for many ages past had been washed down from the mountain heights. Then following the line of an excellent waggon road, on which we now found ourselves, that wound up from terrace to terrace, my eye lit upon the crowning wonder of the scene. For in the centre of the topmost platform or terrace, which may have enclosed eight or ten acres of ground, and almost surrounded by groves of orange trees, gleamed buildings of which I had never seen the like. There were three groups of them, one in the middle, and one on either side, and a little to the rear, but, as I afterwards discovered, the plan of all was the same. In the centre was an edifice constructed like an ordinary Zulu hut – that is to say, in the shape of a beehive, only it was five times the size of any hut I ever saw, and built of blocks of hewn white marble, fitted together with extraordinary knowledge of the principles and properties of arch building, and with so much accuracy and finish that it was often difficult to find the joints of the massive blocks. From this centre hut ran three covered passages, leading to other buildings of an exactly similar character, only smaller, and each whole block was enclosed by a marble wall about four feet in height.

Of course we were as yet too far off to see all these details, but the general outline I saw at once, and it astonished me considerably. Even old Indaba-zimbi, whom the Baboon-woman had been unable to move, deigned to show wonder.

"Ou!" he said; "this is a place of marvels. Who ever saw kraals built of white stone?"

Stella watched our faces with an expression of intense amusement, but said nothing.

"Did your father build those kraals?" I gasped at length.

"My father! no, of course not," she answered. "How would it have been possible for one white man to do so, or to have made this road? He found them as you see."

"Who built them, then?" I said again.

"I do not know. My father thinks that they are very ancient, for the people who live here now do not know how to lay one stone upon another, and these huts are so wonderfully constructed that, though they must have stood for ages, not a stone of them had fallen. But I can show you the quarry where the marble was cut; it is close by, and behind it is the entrance to an ancient mine, which my father thinks was a silver mine. Perhaps the people who worked the mine built the marble huts. The world is old, and no doubt plenty of people have lived in it and been forgotten."*

Then we rode on in silence. I have seen many beautiful sights in Africa, and in such matters, as in others, comparisons are odious and worthless, but I do not think that I ever saw a lovelier scene. It was no one thing – it was the combination of the mighty peak looking forth on to the everlasting plains, the great cliffs, the waterfalls that sparkled in rainbow hues, the rivers girdling the rich cultivated lands, the gold-specked green of the orange trees, the flashing domes of the marble huts and a thousand other details. Then over all brooded the peace of evening, and the infinite glory of the sunset that filled heaven with changing hues of splendour, that wrapped the mountain and cliffs in cloaks of purple and of gold, and lay upon the quiet face of the water like the smile of a god.

Perhaps also the contrast, and the memory of those three awful days and nights in the hopeless desert, enhanced the charm, and perhaps the beauty of the girl who walked beside me completed it. For of this I am sure, that of all sweet and lovely things that I looked on then, she was the sweetest and the loveliest.

Ah, it did not take me long to find my fate. How long will it be before I find her once again?

---

*Kraals of a somewhat similar nature to those described by Mr. Quatermain have been discovered in the Marico district of the Transvaal, and an illustration of them is to be found in Mr. Anderson's *Twenty-five Years in a Waggon*, vol. ii, p. 55. Mr. Anderson says, "In this district are the ancient stone kraals mentioned in an early chapter; but it requires a fuller description to show that these extensive kraals must have been erected by a white race who understood building in stone and at right angles, with door-posts, lintels and sills, and it required more than Kaffir skill to erect stone huts, with stone circular roofs, beautifully formed and most substantially erected; strong enough, if not disturbed, to last a thousand years." – Editor

CHAPTER VIII
The Marble Kraals

At length the last platform, or terrace, was reached, and we pulled up outside the wall surrounding the central group of marble huts – for so I must call them, for want of a better name. Our approach had been observed by a crowd of natives, whose race I have never been able to determine accurately; they belonged to the Basutu and peaceful section of the Bantu peoples rather than to the Zulu and warlike. Several of these ran up to take the horses, gazing on us with astonishment, not unmixed with awe. We dismounted – speaking for myself, not without difficulty – indeed, had it not been for Stella's support I should have fallen.

"Now you must come and see my father," she said. "I wonder what he will think of it, it is all so strange. Hendrika, take the child to my hut and give her milk, then put her into my bed; I will come presently."

Hendrika went off with a somewhat ugly grin to do her mistress's bidding, and Stella led the way through the narrow gateway in the marble wall, which may have enclosed nearly half an "erf", or three-quarters of an acre of ground in all. It was beautifully planted as a garden, many European vegetables and flowers were growing in it, besides others with which I was not acquainted. Presently we came to the centre hut, and it was then that I noticed the extraordinary beauty and finish of the marble masonry. In the hut, and facing the gateway, was a modern door, rather rudely fashioned of Buckenhout, a beautiful reddish wood that has the appearance of having been sedulously pricked with a pin. Stella opened it, and we entered. The interior of the hut was the size of a large and lofty room, the walls being formed of plain polished marble. It was lighted somewhat dimly, but quite effectively, by peculiar openings in the roof, from which the rain was excluded by overhanging eaves. The marble floor was strewn with native mats and skins of animals. Bookcases filled with books were placed against the walls, there was a table in the centre, chairs seated with rimpi or strips of hide stood about, and beyond the table was a couch on which a man was lying reading.

"Is that you, Stella?" said a voice, that even after so many years seemed familiar to me. "Where have you been, my love? I began to think that you had lost yourself again."

"No, father, dear, I have not lost myself, but I have found somebody else."

At that moment. I stepped forward so that the light fell on me. The old gentleman on the couch rose with some difficulty and bowed with much courtesy. He was a fine-looking old man, with deep-set dark eyes, a pale face that bore many traces of physical and mental suffering, and a long white beard.

"Be welcome, sir," he said. "It is long since we have seen a white face in these wilds, and yours, if I am not mistaken, is that of an Englishman. There has been but one Englishman here for twelve years, and he, I grieve to say, was an outcast flying from justice," and he bowed again and stretched out his hand.

I looked at him, and then of a sudden his name flashed back into my mind. I took his hand.

"How do you do, Mr. Carson?" I said.

He started back as though he had been stung.

"Who told you that name?" he cried. "It is a dead name. Stella, is it you? I forbade you to let it pass your lips."

"I did not speak it, father. I have never spoken it," she answered.

"Sir," I broke in, "if you will allow me I will show you how I came to know your name. Do you remember many years ago coming into the study of a clergyman in Oxfordshire and telling him that you were going to leave England for ever?"

He bowed his head.

"And do you remember a little boy who sat upon the hearthrug writing with a pencil?"

"I do," he said.

"Sir, I was that boy, and my name is Allan Quatermain. Those children who lay sick are all dead, their mother is dead, and my father, your old friend, is dead also. Like you he emigrated, and last year he died in the Cape. But that is not all the story. After many adventures I, one Kaffir, and a little girl, lay senseless and dying in the Bad Lands, where we had wandered for days without water, and there we should have perished, but your daughter, Miss . . ."

"Call her Stella," he broke in, hastily. "I cannot bear to hear that name. I have forsworn it."

"Miss Stella found us by chance and saved our lives."

"By chance, did you say, Allan Quatermain?" he answered. "There is little chance in this; such chances spring from another will than ours. Welcome, Allan, son of my old friend. Here we live as it were in a hermitage, with Nature for our only friend, but such as we have is yours, and for as long as you will take it. But you must be starving; talk no more now. Stella, it is time to eat. To-morrow we will talk."

To tell the truth I can recall very little of the events of that evening. A kind of dizzy weariness overmastered me. I remember sitting at a table next to Stella, and eating heartily, and then I remember nothing more.

I awoke to find myself lying on a comfortable bed in a hut built and fashioned on the same model as the centre one. While I was wondering what time it was, a native came bringing some clean clothes on his arm, and, luxury of luxuries, produced a bath hollowed from wood. I rose, feeling a very different man, my strength had come back again to me; I dressed, and following a covered passage found myself in the centre hut. Here the table was set for breakfast with all manner of good things, such as I had not seen for many a month, which I contemplated with healthy satisfaction. Presently I looked up, and there before me was a more delightful sight, for standing in one of the doorways which led to the sleeping huts was Stella, leading little Tota by the hand.

She was very simply dressed in a loose blue gown, with a wide collar, and girdled in at the waist by a little leather belt. In the bosom of her robe was a bunch of orange blooms, and her rippling hair was tied in a single knot behind her shapely head. She greeted me with a smile, asking how I had slept, and then held Tota up for me to kiss. Under her loving care the child had been quite transformed. She was neatly dressed in a garment of the same blue stuff that Stella wore, her fair hair was brushed; indeed, had it not been for the sun blisters on her face and hands, one would scarcely have believed that this was the same child whom Indaba-zimbi and I had dragged for hour after hour through the burning, waterless desert.

"We must breakfast alone, Mr. Allan," she said; "my father is so upset by your arrival that he will not get up yet. Oh, you cannot tell how thankful I am that you have come. I have been so anxious about him of late. He grows weaker and weaker; it seems to me as though the strength were ebbing away from him. Now he scarcely leaves the kraal, I have to manage everything about the farm; he does nothing but read and think."

Just then Hendrika entered, bearing a jug of coffee in one hand and of milk in the other, which she set down upon the table, casting a look of little love at me as she did so.

"Be careful, Hendrika; you are spilling the coffee," said Stella. "Don't you wonder how we come to have coffee here, Mr. Allan? I will tell you – we grow it. That was my idea. Oh, I have lots of things to show you. You don't know what we have managed to do in the time that we have been here. You see we have plenty of labour, for the people about look upon my father as their chief."

"Yes," I said, "but how do you get all these luxuries of civilization?" and I pointed to the books, the crockery, and the knives and forks.

"Very simply. Most of the books my father brought with him when we first trekked into the wilds; there was nearly a waggon load of them. But every few years we have sent an expedition of three waggons right down to Port Natal. The waggons are loaded with ivory and other goods, and come back with all kinds of things that have been sent out from England for us. So you see, although we live in this wild place, we are not altogether cut off. We can send runners to Natal and back in three months, and the waggons get there and back in a year. The last lot arrived quite safe about three months ago. Our servants are very faithful, and some of them speak Dutch well."

"Have you ever been with the waggons?" I asked.

"Since I was a child I have never been more than thirty miles from Babyan's Peak," she answered. "Do you know, Mr. Allan, that you are, with one exception, the first Englishman that I have known out of a book. I suppose that I must seem very wild and savage to you, but I have had one advantage – a good education. My father has taught me everything, and perhaps I know some things that you don't. I can read French and German, for instance. I think that my father's first idea was to let me run wild altogether, but he gave it up."

"And don't you wish to go into the world?" I asked.

"Sometimes," she said, "when I get lonely. But perhaps my father is right – perhaps it would frighten and bewilder me. At any rate he would never return to civilization; it is his idea, you know, though I am sure I do not know where he got it from, nor why he cannot bear that our name should be spoken. In short, Mr. Quatermain, we do not make our lives, we must take them as we find them. Have you done your breakfast? Let us go out, and I will show you our home."

I rose and went to my sleeping-place to fetch my hat. When I returned, Mr. Carson – for after all that was his name, though he would never allow it to be spoken – had come into the hut. He felt better now, he said, and would accompany us on our walk if Stella would give him an arm.

So we started, and after us came Hendrika with Tota and old Indaba-zimbi, whom I found sitting outside as fresh as paint. Nothing could tire that old man.

The view from the platform was almost as beautiful as that from the lower ground looking up to the peak. The marble kraals, as I have said, faced west, consequently all the upper terrace lay in the shadow of the great peak till nearly eleven o'clock in the morning – a great advantage in that warm latitude. First we walked through the garden, which was beautifully cultivated, and one of the most productive that

I ever saw. There were three or four natives working in it, and they all saluted my host as "Baba", or father. Then we visited the other two groups of marble huts. One of these was used for stables and out-buildings, the other as storehouses, the centre hut having been, however, turned into a chapel. Mr. Carson was not ordained, but he earnestly tried to convert the natives, most of whom were refugees who had come to him for shelter, and he had practised the more elementary rites of the church for so long that I think he began to believe that he really was a clergyman. For instance, he always married those of his people who would consent to a monogamous existence, and baptized their children.

When we had examined those wonderful remains of antiquity, the marble huts, and admired the orange trees, the vines and fruits which thrive like weeds in this marvellous soil and climate, we descended to the next platform and saw the farming operations in full swing. I think that it was the best farm I have ever seen in Africa. There was ample water for purposes of irrigation, the grass lands below gave pasturage for hundreds of head of cattle and horses, and, for natives, the people were most industrious. Moreover, the whole place was managed by Mr. Carson on the co-operative system; he only took a tithe of the produce – indeed, in this land of teeming plenty, what was he to do with more? Consequently the tribesmen, who, by the way, called themselves the "Children of Thomas", were able to accumu-late considerable wealth. All their disputes were referred to their "father", and he also was judge of offences and crimes. Some were punished by imprisonment, whipping, and loss of goods, other and graver transgressions by expulsion from the community, a fiat which to one of these favoured natives must have seemed as heavy as the decree that drove Adam from the Garden of Eden.

Old Mr. Carson leaned upon his daughter's arm and contem-plated the scene with pride.

"I have done all this, Allan Quatermain," he said. "When renounc-ing civilization, I wandered here by chance; seeking a home in the remotest places of the world, I found this lonely spot a wilderness.

Nothing was to be seen except the site, the domes of the marble huts, and the waterfalls. I took possession of the huts. I cleared the patch of garden land and planted the orange grove. I had only six natives then, but by degrees others joined me, now my tribe is a thousand strong. Here we live in profound peace and plenty. I have all I need, and I seek no more. Heaven has prospered me so far – may it do so to the end, which for me draws nigh. And now I am tired and will go back. If you wish to see the old quarry and the mouth of the ancient mines, Stella will show them to you. No, my love, you need not trouble to come, I can manage alone. Look! some of the headmen are waiting to see me."

So he went, but still followed by Hendrika and Indaba-zimbi; we turned, and, walking along the bank of one of the rivers, passed up behind the marble kraals, and came to the quarry, whence the material of which they were built had been cut in some remote age. The pit opened up a very thick seam of the whitest and most beautiful marble. I know another like it in Natal. But by whom it had been worked I cannot say; not by natives, that is certain, though the builders of these kraals had condescended to borrow the shape of native huts for their model. By the way, the only relic of those builders that I ever saw was a highly finished bronze pick-axe which Stella found one day in the quarry.

After we had examined this quarry we climbed the slope of the hill till we came to the mouth of the ancient mines which were situated in a gorge. I believe them to have been silver mines. The gorge was long and narrow, and the moment we entered it there rose from every side a sound of groaning and barking that was almost enough to deafen us. I knew what it was at once: the whole place was filled with baboons, which clambered down the rocks towards us from every direction, and in a manner that struck me as being unnaturally fearless. Stella turned a little pale and clung to my arm.

"It is very silly of me," she whispered. "I am not at all nervous, but ever since they killed Hendrik I cannot bear the sight of those animals. I always think that there is something human about them."

Meanwhile the baboons drew nearer, talking to each other as they came. Tota began to cry, and clung to Stella. Stella clung to me, while I and Indaba-zimbi put as bold a front on the matter as we could. Only Hendrika stood looking at the brutes with an unconcerned smile on her monkey face. When the great apes were quite near, she suddenly called out aloud. Instantly they stopped their hideous clamour as though at a word of command. Then Hendrika addressed them: I can only describe it so. That is to say, she began to make a noise such as baboons do when they converse with each other. I have known Hottentots and Bushmen who said that they could talk with the baboons and understand their language, but I confess I never heard it done before or since.

From the mouth of Hendrika came a succession of grunts, groans, squeals, clicks, and every other abominable noise that can be conceived, conveying to my mind a general idea of expostulation. At any rate the baboons listened. One of them grunted back some answer, and then the whole mob drew off to the rocks.

I stood astonished, and without a word we turned back to the kraal, for Hendrika was too close to allow me to speak. When we reached the dining hut Stella went in, followed by Hendrika. But Indaba-zimbi plucked me by the sleeve, and I stopped outside.

"Macumazahn," he said. "Baboon-woman – devil woman. Be careful, Macumazahn. She loves that Star (the natives aptly enough called Stella the Star), and is jealous. Be careful, Macumazahn, or the Star will set!"

CHAPTER IX
"Let Us Go In, Allan!"

It is very difficult for me to describe the period of time which elapsed between my arrival at Babyan's Peak and my marriage with Stella. When I look back on it, it seems sweet as with the odour of flowers, and dim as with the happy dusk of summer eves, while through the sweetness comes the sound of Stella's voice, and through the gloom shines the starlight of her eyes. I think that we loved each other from the first, though for a while we said no word of love. Day by day I went about the place with her, accompanied by little Tota and Hendrika only, while she attended to the thousand and one matters which her father's evergrowing weakness had laid upon her; or rather, as time drew on, I attended to the business, and she accompanied me. All day through we were together. Then after supper, when the night had fallen, we would walk together in the garden and come in at length to hear her father read aloud sometimes from the works of a poet, sometimes from history. Or, if he did not feel well, Stella would read, and when this was done, Mr. Carson would celebrate a short form of prayer, and we separated till the morning once more brought our happy hour of meeting.

So the weeks went by, and with every week I grew to know my darling better. Often, I wonder now, if my fond fancy deceives me, or if indeed there are women as sweet and dear as she. Was it solitude that had given such depth and gentleness to her? Was it the long years of communing with Nature that had endowed her with such peculiar grace, the grace we find in opening flowers and budding trees? Had she caught that murmuring voice from the sound of the streams which fall continually about her rocky home? Was it the tenderness of the evening sky beneath which she loved to walk, that lay like a shadow on her face, and the light of the evening stars that shone in her quiet eyes? At the least to me she was the realization of that dream which haunts the sleep of sin-stained men; so my memory paints her, so I hope to find her when at last the sleep has rolled away and the fevered dreams are done.

At last there came a day – the most blessed of my life, when we told our love. We had been together all the morning, but after dinner Mr. Carson was so unwell that Stella stopped in with him. At supper we met again, and after supper, when she had put little Tota, to whom she had grown much attached, to bed, we went out, leaving Mr. Carson dozing on the couch.

The night was warm and lovely, and without speaking we walked up the garden to the orange grove and sat down upon a rock. There was a little breeze which shook the petals of the orange blooms over us in showers, and bore their delicate fragrance far and wide. Silence reigned around, broken only by the sound of the falling waterfalls that now died to a faint murmur, and now, as the wavering breeze turned, boomed loudly in our ears. The moon was not yet visible, but already the dark clouds which floated through the sky above us – for there had been rain – showed a glow of silver, telling us that she shone brightly behind the peak. Stella began to talk in her low, gentle voice, speaking to me of her life in the wilderness, how she had grown to love it, how her mind had gone on from idea to idea, and how she pictured the great rushing world that she had never seen as it was reflected to her from the books which she had read. It was a curious vision of life that she had: things were out of proportion in it; it was more like a dream than a reality – a mirage than the actual face of things. The idea of great cities, and especially of London, had a kind of fascination for her: she could scarcely realize the rush, the roar and hurry, the hard crowds of men and women, strangers each to each, feverishly seeking for wealth and pleasure beneath a murky sky, and treading one another down in the fury of their competition.

"What is it all for?" she asked, earnestly. "What do they seek? Having so few years to live, why do they waste them thus?"

I told her that in the majority of instances it was actual hard necessity that drove them on, but she could barely understand me. Living as she had done, in the midst of the teeming plenty of a fruitful earth, she did not seem to be able to grasp the fact that there are millions who from day to day know not how to stay their hunger.

"I never want to go there," she went on; "I should be bewildered and frightened to death. It is not natural to live like that. God put Adam and Eve in a garden, and that is how he meant their children to live – in peace, and looking always on beautiful things. This is my idea of perfect life. I want no other."

"I thought you once told me that you found it lonely," I said.

"So I did," she answered, innocently, "but that was before you came. Now I am not lonely any more, and it is perfect – perfect as the night."

Just then the full moon rose above the elbow of the peak, and her rays stole far and wide down the misty valley, gleaming on the water, brooding on the plain, searching out the hidden places of the rocks, wrapping the fair form of nature as in a silver bridal veil through which her beauty shone mysteriously.

Stella looked down the terraced valley, she turned and looked up at the scarred face of the golden moon, and then she looked at me. The beauty of the night was about her face, the scent of the night was on her hair, the mystery of the night shone in her shadowed eyes. She looked at me, I looked on her, and all our hearts' love blossomed within us. We spoke no word – we had no words to speak, but slowly we drew near, till lips were pressed to lips as we kissed our eternal troth.

It was she who broke that holy silence, speaking in a changed voice, in soft deep notes that thrilled me like the lowest chords of a smitten harp.

"Ah, now I understand," she said, "now I know why we are lonely, and how we can lose our loneliness. Now I know what it is that stirs us in the beauty of the sky, in the sound of water and in the scent of flowers. It is Love who speaks in everything, though till we hear his voice we understand nothing. But when we hear, then the riddle is answered and the gates of our heart are opened, and, Allan, we see the way that wends through death to heaven, and is lost in the glory of which our love is but a shadow.

"Let us go in, Allan. Let us go before the spell breaks, so that whatever overtakes us, sorrow, death, or separation, we may always have this perfect memory to save us. Come, dearest, let us go!"

I rose like a man in a dream, still holding her by the hand. But as I rose my eye fell upon something that gleamed white among the foliage of the orange bush at my side. I said nothing, but looked. The breeze stirred the orange leaves, the moonlight struck for a moment full upon the white object.

It was the face of Hendrika, the Babyan-woman, as Indaba-zimbi had called her, and on it was a glare of hate that made me shudder.

I said nothing; the face vanished, and just then I heard a baboon bark in the rocks behind.

Then we went down the garden, and Stella passed into the centre hut. I saw Hendrika standing in the shadow near the door, and went up to her.

"Hendrika," I said, "why were you watching Miss Stella and myself in the garden?"

She drew her lips up till her teeth gleamed in the moonlight.

"Have I not watched her these many years, Macumazahn? Shall I cease to watch because a wandering white man comes to steal her? Why were you kissing her in the garden, Macumazahn? How dare you kiss her who is a star?"

"I kissed her because I love her, and because she loves me," I answered. "What has that to do with you, Hendrika?"

"Because you love her," she hissed in answer; "and do I not love her also, who saved me from the babyans? I am a woman as she is, and you are a man, and they say in the kraals that men love women better than women love women. But it is a lie, though this is true, that if a woman loves a man she forgets all other love. Have I not seen it? I gather her flowers – beautiful flowers; I climb the rocks where you would never dare to go to find them; you pluck a piece of orange bloom in the garden and give it her. What does she do? – she takes the orange bloom, she puts it in her breast, and lets my flowers die. I call to her – she does not hear me – she is thinking. You whisper to some one far away, and she hears and smiles. She used to kiss me some-times; now she kisses that white brat you brought, because you brought it. Oh, I see it all – all; I have seen it from the first; you are stealing her from us, stealing her to yourself, and those who loved her before you came are forgotten. Be careful, Macumazahn, be careful, lest I am revenged upon you. You, you hate me; you think me half a monkey; that servant of yours calls me Baboon-woman. Well, I have lived with baboons, and they are clever – yes, they can play tricks and know things you don't, and I am cleverer than they, for I have learnt the wisdom of white people also, and I say to you, Walk softly, Macumazahn, or you will fall into a pit," and with one more look of malice she was gone.

I stood for a moment reflecting. I was afraid of this strange creature who seemed to combine the cunning of the great apes that had reared her with the passions and skill of human kind. I foreboded evil at her hands. And yet there was something almost touching in the fierceness of her jealousy. It is generally supposed that this passion only exists in strength when the object loved is of another sex from the lover, but I confess, both in this instance and in some others which I have met with, that this has not been my experience. I have known men, and especially uncivilized men, who were as jealous of the affection of their friend or master as any lover could be of that of his mistress; and who has not seen cases of the same thing where parents and their children were concerned? But the lower one gets in the scale of humanity, the more readily this passion thrives; indeed, it may be said to come to its intensest perfection in brutes. Women are more jealous than men, small-hearted men are more jealous than those of larger mind and wider sympathy, and animals are the most jealous of all. Now Hendrika was in some ways not far removed from animal, which may perhaps account for the ferocity of her jealousy of her mistress's affection.

Shaking off my presentiments of evil, I entered the centre hut. Mr. Carson was resting on the sofa, and by him knelt Stella holding his hand, and her head resting on his breast. I saw at once that she had been telling him of what had come about between us; nor was I sorry, for it is a task that a would-be son-in-law is generally glad to do by deputy.

"Come here, Allan Quatermain," he said, almost sternly, and my heart gave a jump, for I feared lest he might be about to require me to go about my business. But I came.

"Stella tells me," he went on, "that you two have entered into a marriage engagement. She tells me also that she loves you, and that you say that you love her."

"I do indeed, sir," I broke in; "I love her truly; if ever a woman was loved in this world, I love her."

"I thank Heaven for it," said the old man. "Listen, my children. Many years ago a great shame and sorrow fell upon me, so great a sorrow that, as I sometimes think, it affected my brain. At any rate, I determined to do what most men would have considered the act of a madman, to go far away into the wilderness with my only child, there to live remote from civilization and its evils. I did so; I found this place, and here we have lived for many years, happily enough, and perhaps not without doing good in our generation, but still in a way unnatural to our race and status. At first I thought that I would let my daughter grow up in a state of complete ignorance, that she should be Nature's child. But as time went on, I saw the folly and the wickedness of my plan. I had no right to degrade her to the level of the savages around me, for if the fruit of the tree of knowledge is a bitter fruit, still it teaches good from evil. So I educated her as well as I was able, till in the end I knew that in mind, as in body, she was in no way inferior to her sisters, the children of the civilized world. She grew up and entered into womanhood, and then it came into my mind that I was doing her a bitter wrong, that I was separating her from her kind and keeping her in a wilderness where she could find neither mate nor companion. But though I knew this, I could not yet make up my mind to return to active life; I had grown to love this place. I dreaded to return into the world I had abjured. Again and again I put my resolutions aside. Then at the commencement of this year I fell ill. For a while I waited, hoping that I might get better, but at last I realized that I should never get better, that the hand of Death was upon me."

"Ah, no, father, not that!" Stella said, with a cry.

"Yes, love, *that*, and it is true. Now you will be able to forget our separation in the happiness of a new meeting," and he glanced at me and smiled. "Well, when this knowledge came home to me, I determined to abandon this place and trek for the coast, though I well knew that the journey would kill me. I should never live to reach it. But Stella would, and it would be better than leaving her here alone

ALLAN'S WIFE | **215**

with savages in the wilderness. On the very day that I had made up my mind to take this step Stella found you dying in the Bad Lands, Allan Quatermain, and brought you here. She brought you, of all men in the world, you, whose father had been my dear friend, and who once with your baby hands had saved her life from fire, that she might live to save yours from thirst. At the time I said little, but I saw the hand of Providence in this, and I determined to wait and see what came about between you. At the worst, if nothing came about, I soon learned that I could trust you to see her safely to the coast after I was gone. But many days ago I knew how it stood between you, and now things are determined as I prayed they might be. God bless you both, my children; may you be happy in your love; may it endure till death and beyond it. God bless you both!" and he stretched out his hand towards me.

I took it, and Stella kissed him.

Presently he spoke again:

"It is my intention," he said, "if you two consent, to marry you next Sunday. I wish to do so soon, for I do not know how much longer will be allowed to me. I believe that such a ceremony, solemnly celebrated and entered into before witnesses, will, under the circumstances, be perfectly legal; but of course you will repeat it with every formality the first moment it lies in your power so to do. And now, there is one more thing: when I left England my fortunes were in a shattered condition; in the course of years they have recovered themselves, the accumulated rents, as I heard but recently, when the waggons last returned from Port Natal, have sufficed to pay off all charges, and there is a considerable balance over. Consequently you will not marry on nothing, for of course you, Stella, are my heiress, and I wish to make a stipulation. It is this. That so soon as my death occurs you shall leave this place and take the first opportunity of returning to England. I do not ask you to live there always; it might prove too much for people reared in the wilds, as both of you have been; but I do ask you to make it your permanent home. Do you consent and promise this?"

"I do," I answered.

"And so do I," said Stella.

"Very well," he answered; "and now I am tired out. Again God bless you both, and good-night."

CHAPTER X

Hendrika Plots Evil

On the following morning I had a conversation with Indaba-zimbi. First of all I told him that I was going to marry Stella.

"Oh!" he said, "I thought so, Macumazahn. Did I not tell you that you would find happiness on this journey? Most men must be content to watch the Star from a long way off, to you it is given to wear her on your heart. But remember, Macumazahn, remember that stars set."

"Can you not stop your croaking even for a day?" I answered, angrily, for his words sent a thrill of fear through me.

"A true prophet must tell the ill as well as the good, Macumazahn. I only speak what is on my mind. But what of it? What is life but loss, loss upon loss, till life itself be lost? But in death we may find all the things that we have lost. So your father taught, Macumazahn, and there was wisdom in his gentleness. Ou! I do not believe in death; it is change, that is all, Macumazahn. Look now, the rain falls, the drops of rain that were one water in the clouds fall side by side. They sink into the ground; presently the sun will come out, the earth will be dry, the drops will be gone. A fool looks and says the drops are dead, they will never be one again, they will never again fall side by side. But I am a rain-maker, and I know the ways of rain. It is not true. The drops will drain by many paths into the river, and will be one water there. They will go up into the clouds again in the mists of morning, and there will again be as they have been. We are the drops of rain, Macumazahn. When we fall that is our life. When we sink into the ground that is death, and when we are drawn up again to the sky, what is that, Macumazahn? No! no! when we find we lose, and when we seem to lose, then we shall really find. I am not a Christian, Macumazahn, but I am old, and have watched and seen things that perhaps Christians do not see. There, I have spoken. Be happy with your star, and if it sets, wait, Macumazahn, wait till it rises again. It will not be long; one day you will go to sleep, then your eyes will open on another sky, and there your star will be shining, Macumazahn."

I made no answer at the time. I could not bear to talk of such a thing. But often and often in the after years I have thought of Indaba-zimbi and his beautiful simile and gathered comfort from it. He was a strange man, this old rain-making savage, and there was more wisdom in him than in many learned atheists – those spiritual destroyers who, in the name of progress and humanity, would divorce hope from life, and leave us wandering in a lonesome, self-consecrated hell.

"Indaba-zimbi," I said, changing the subject, "I have something to say," and I told him of the threats of Hendrika.

He listened with an unmoved face, nodding his white lock at intervals as the narrative went on. But I saw that he was disturbed by it.

"Macumazahn," he said at length, "I have told you that this is an evil woman. She was nourished on baboon milk, and the baboon nature is in her veins. Such creatures should be killed, not kept. She will make you mischief if she can. But I will watch her, Macumazahn. Look, the Star is waiting for you; go, or she will hate me as Hendrika hates you."

So I went, nothing loath, for attractive as was the wisdom of Indaba-zimbi, I found a deeper meaning in Stella's simplest word. All the rest of that day I passed in her company, and the greater part of the two following days. At last came Saturday night, the eve of our marriage. It rained that night, so we did not go out, but spent the evening in the hut. We sat hand in hand, saying little, but Mr. Carson talked a good deal, telling us tales of his youth, and of countries that he had visited. Then he read aloud from the Bible, and bade us good-night. I also kissed Stella and went to bed. I reached my hut by the covered way, and before I undressed opened the door to see what the night was like. It was very dark, and rain was still falling, but as the light streamed out into the gloom I fancied that I caught sight of a dusky form gliding away. The thought of Hendrika flashed into my mind; could she be skulking about outside there? Now I had said nothing of Hendrika and her threats either to Mr. Carson or Stella, because I did not wish to alarm them. Also I knew that Stella was attached to this strange person, and I did not wish to shake her confidence in her unless it was absolutely necessary. For a minute or two I stood hesitating, then, reflecting that if it was Hendrika, there she should stop, I went in and put up the stout wooden bar that was used to secure the door. For the last few nights old Indaba-zimbi had made a habit of sleeping in the covered passage, which was the only other possible way of access. As I came to bed I had stepped over him rolled up in his blanket, and to all appearance fast asleep. So it being evident that I had nothing to fear, I promptly dismissed the matter from my mind, which, as may be imagined, was indeed fully occupied with other thoughts.

I got into bed, and for awhile lay awake thinking of the great happiness in store for me, and of the providential course of events that had brought it within my reach. A few weeks since and I was wandering in the desert a dying man, bearing a dying child, and with scarcely a possession left in the world except a store of buried ivory that I never expected to see again. And now I was about to wed one of the sweetest and loveliest women on the whole earth – a woman whom I loved more than I could have thought possible, and who loved me back again. Also, as though that were not good fortune enough, I was to acquire with her very considerable possessions, quite sufficiently large to enable us to follow any plan of life we found agreeable. As I lay and reflected on all this I grew afraid of my good fortune. Old Indaba-zimbi's melancholy prophecies came into my mind. Hitherto he had always prophesied truly. What if these should be true also? I turned cold as I thought of it, and prayed to the Power above to preserve us both to live and love together. Never was prayer more needed. While its words were still upon my lips I dropped asleep and dreamed a most dreadful dream.

I dreamed that Stella and I were standing together to be married. She was dressed in white, and radiant with beauty, but it was a wild, spiritual beauty which frightened me. Her eyes shone like stars, a pale flame played about her features, and the wind that blew did not stir her hair. Nor was this all, for her white robes were death wrappings, and the altar at which we stood was formed of the piled-up earth from an open grave that yawned between us. So we stood waiting for one to wed us, but no one came. Presently from the open grave sprang the form of Hendrika. In her hand was a knife, with which she stabbed at me, but pierced the heart of Stella, who, without a cry, fell backwards into the grave, still looking at me as she fell. Then Hendrika leaped after her into the grave. I heard her feet strike heavily.

"*Awake, Macumazahn! awake!*" cried the voice of Indaba-zimbi.

I awoke and bounded from the bed, a cold perspiration pouring from me. In the darkness on the other side of the hut I heard sounds of furious struggling. Luckily I kept my head. Just by me was a chair on which were matches and a rush taper. I struck a match and held it to the taper. Now in the growing light I could see two forms rolling one over the other on the floor, and from between them came the flash of steel. The fat melted and the light burnt up. It was Indaba-zimbi and the woman Hendrika who were struggling, and, what was more, the woman was getting the better of the man, strong as he was. I rushed towards them. Now she was uppermost, now she had wrenched herself from his fierce grip, and now the great knife she had in her hand flashed up.

But I was behind her, and, placing my hands beneath her arms, jerked with all my strength. She fell backwards, and, in her effort to save herself, most fortunately dropped the knife. Then we flung ourselves upon her. Heavens! the strength of that she-devil! Nobody who has not experienced it could believe it. She fought and scratched and bit, and at one time nearly mastered the two of us. As it was she did break loose. She rushed at the bed, sprung on it, and bounded thence straight up at the roof of the hut. I never saw such a jump, and could not conceive what she meant to do. In the roof were the peculiar holes which I have described. They were designed to admit light, and covered with overhanging eaves. She sprung straight and true like a monkey, and, catching the edge of the hole with her hands, strove to draw herself through it. But here her strength, exhausted with the long struggle, failed her. For a moment she swung, then dropped to the ground and fell senseless.

"Ou!" gasped Indaba-zimbi. "Let us tie the devil up before she comes to life again."

I thought this a good counsel, so we took a reim that lay in the corner of the room, and lashed her hands and feet in such a fashion that even she could scarcely escape. Then we carried her into the passage, and Indaba-zimbi sat over her, the knife in his hand, for I did not wish to raise an alarm at that hour of the night.

"Do you know how I caught her, Macumazahn?" he said. "For several nights I have slept here with one eye open, for I thought she had made a plan. To-night I kept wide awake, though I pretended to be asleep. An hour after you got into the blankets the moon rose, and I saw a beam of light come into the hut through the hole in the roof. Presently I saw the beam of light vanish. At first I thought that a cloud was passing over the moon, but I listened and heard a noise as though some one was squeezing himself through a narrow place. Presently he was through and hanging by his hands. Then the light came in again, and in the middle of it I saw the Babyan-frau swinging from the roof, and about to drop into the hut. She clung by both hands, and in her mouth was a great knife. She dropped, and I ran forward to seize her as she dropped, and gripped her round the middle. But she heard me come, and, seizing the knife, struck at me in the dark and missed me. Then we struggled, and you know the rest. You were very nearly dead to-night, Macumazahn."

"Very nearly, indeed," I answered, still panting, and arranging the rags of my night-dress round me as best I might. Then the memory of my horrid dream flashed into my mind. Doubtless it had been conjured up by the sound of Hendrika dropping to the floor – in my dream it had been a grave that she dropped into. All of it, then, had been experienced in that second of time. Well, dreams are swift; perhaps Time itself is nothing but a dream, and events that seem far apart really occur simultaneously.

We passed the rest of the night watching Hendrika. Presently she came to herself and struggled furiously to break the reim. But the untanned buffalo hide was too strong even for her, and, moreover, Indaba-zimbi unceremoniously sat upon her to keep her quiet. At last she gave it up.

In due course the day broke – my marriage day. Leaving Indaba-zimbi to watch my would-be murderess, I went and fetched some natives from the stables, and with their aid bore Hendrika to the prison hut – that same hut in which she had been confined when she had been brought a baboon-child from the rocks. Here we shut her up, and, leaving Indaba-zimbi to watch outside, I returned to my sleeping-place and dressed in the best garments that Babyan Kraals could furnish. But when I looked at the reflection of my face, I was horrified. It was covered with scratches inflicted by the nails of Hendrika. I doctored them up as best I could, then went out for a walk to calm my nerves, which, what between the events of the past night, and of those pending that day, were not a little disturbed.

When I returned it was breakfast time. I went into the dining hut and there Stella was waiting to greet me, dressed in simple white and with orange flowers on her breast. She came forward to me shyly enough; then, seeing the condition of my face, started back.

"Why, Allan! what have you been doing to yourself?" she asked.

As I was about to answer, her father came in leaning on his stick, and, catching sight of me, instantly asked the same question.

Then I told them everything, both of Hendrika's threats and of her fierce attempt to carry them into execution. But I did not tell my horrid dream.

Stella's face grew white as the flowers on her breast, but that of her father became very stern.

"You should have spoken of this before, Allan," he said. "I now see that I did wrong to attempt to civilize this wicked and revengeful creature, who, if she is human, has all the evil passions of the brutes that reared her. Well, I will make an end of it this very day."

"Oh, father," said Stella, "don't have her killed. It is all dreadful enough, but that would be more dreadful still. I have been very fond of her, and, bad as she is, she has loved me. Do not have her killed on my marriage day."

"No," her father answered, "she shall not be killed, for though she deserves to die, I will not have her blood upon our hands. She is a brute, and has followed the nature of brutes. She shall go back whence she came."

No more was said on the matter at the time, but when breakfast – which was rather a farce – was done, Mr. Carson sent for his headman and gave him certain orders.

We were to be married after the service which Mr. Carson held every Sunday morning in the large marble hut set apart for that purpose. The service began at ten o'clock, but long before that hour all the natives on the place came up in troops, singing as they came, to be present at the wedding of the "Star". It was a pretty sight to see them, the men dressed in all their finery, and carrying shields and sticks in their hands, and the women and children bearing green branches of trees, ferns, and flowers. At length, about half-past nine, Stella rose, pressed my hand, and left me to my reflections. At a few minutes to ten she reappeared again with her father, dressed in a white veil, a wreath of orange flowers on her dark curling hair, a bouquet of orange flowers in her hand. To me she seemed like a dream of loveliness. With her came little Tota in a high state of glee and excitement. She was Stella's only bridesmaid. Then we all passed out towards the church hut. The bare space in front of it was filled with hundreds of natives, who set up a song as we came. But we went on into the hut, which was crowded with such of the natives as usually worshipped there. Here Mr. Carson, as usual, read the service, though he was obliged to sit down in order to do so. When it was done – and to me it seemed interminable – Mr. Carson whispered that he meant to marry us outside the hut in sight of all the people. So we went out and took our stand under the shade of a large tree that grew near the hut facing the bare space where the natives were gathered.

Mr. Carson held up his hand to enjoin silence. Then, speaking in the native dialect, he told them that he was about to make us man and wife after the Christian fashion and in the sight of all men. This done, he proceeded to read the marriage service over us, and very solemnly and beautifully he did it. We said the words, I placed the ring – it was her father's signet ring, for we had no other – upon Stella's finger, and it was done.

Then Mr. Carson spoke. "Allan and Stella," he said, "I believe that the ceremony which has been performed makes you man and wife in the sight of God and man, for all that is necessary to make a marriage binding is, that it should be celebrated according to the custom of the country where the parties to it reside. It is according to the custom that has been in force here for fifteen years or more that you have been married in the face of all the people, and in token of it you will both sign the register that I have kept of such marriages, among those of my people who have adopted the Christian Faith. Still, in case there should be any legal flaw I again demand the solemn promise of you both that on the first opportunity you will cause this marriage to be re-celebrated in some civilized land. Do you promise?"

"We do," we answered.

Then the book was brought out and we signed our names. At first my wife signed hers "Stella" only, but her father bade her write it Stella Carson for the first and last time in her life. Then several of the indunas, or headmen, including old Indaba-zimbi, put their marks in witness. Indaba-zimbi drew his mark in the shape of a little star, in humorous allusion to Stella's native name. That register is before me now as I write. That, with a lock of my darling's hair which lies between its leaves, is my dearest possession. There are all the names and marks as they were written many years ago beneath the shadow of the tree at Babyan Kraals in the wilderness, but alas! and alas! where are those who wrote them?

"My people," said Mr. Carson, when the signing was done, and we had kissed each other before them all – "My people, Macumazahn and the Star, my daughter, are now man and wife, to live in one kraal, to eat of one bowl, to share one fortune till they reach the grave. Hear now, my people, you know this woman," and turning he pointed to Hendrika, who, unseen by us, had been led out of the prison hut.

"Yes, yes, we know her," said a little ring of headmen, who formed the primitive court of justice, and after the fashion of natives had squatted themselves in a circle on the ground in front of us. "We know her, she is the white Babyan-woman, she is Hendrika, the body servant of the Star."

"You know her," said Mr. Carson, "but you do not know her altogether. Stand forward, Indaba-zimbi, and tell the people what came about last night in the hut of Macumazahn."

Accordingly old Indaba-zimbi came forward, and, squatting down, told his moving tale with much descriptive force and many gestures, finishing up by producing the great knife from which his watchfulness had saved me.

Then I was called upon, and in a few brief words substantiated his story: indeed my face did that in the sight of all men.

Then Mr. Carson turned to Hendrika, who stood in sullen silence, her eyes fixed upon the ground, and asked her if she had anything to say.

She looked up boldly and answered:

"Macumazahn has robbed me of the love of my mistress. I would have robbed him of his life, which is a little thing compared to that which I have lost at his hands. I have failed, and I am sorry for it, for had I killed him and left no trace the Star would have forgotten him and shone on me again."

"Never," murmured Stella in my ear; but Mr. Carson turned white with wrath.

"My people," he said, "you hear the words of this woman. You hear how she pays me back, me and my daughter whom she swears she loves. She says that she would have murdered a man who has done her no evil, the man who is the husband of her mistress. We saved her from the babyans, we tamed her, we fed her, we taught her, and this is how she pays us back. Say, my people, what reward should be given to her?"

"Death," said the circle of indunas, pointing their thumbs downwards, and all the multitude beyond echoed the word "Death".

"Death," repeated the head induna, adding, "If you save her, my father, we will slay her with our own hands. She is a Babyan-woman, a devil-woman; ah, yes, we have heard of such before; let her be slain before she works more evil."

Then it was that Stella stepped forward and begged for Hendrika's life in moving terms. She pleaded the savagery of the woman's nature, her long service, and the affection that she had always shown towards herself. She said that I, whose life had been attempted, forgave her, and she, my wife, who had nearly been left a widow before she was made a bride, forgave her; let them forgive her also, let her be sent away, not slain, let not her marriage day be stained with blood.

Now her father listened readily enough, for he had no intention of killing Hendrika – indeed, he had already promised not to do so. But the people were in a different humour, they looked upon Hendrika as a devil, and would have torn her to pieces there and then, could they have had their way. Nor were matters mended by Indaba-zimbi, who had already gained a great reputation for wisdom and magic in the place. Suddenly the old man rose and made quite an impassioned speech, urging them to kill Hendrika at once or mischief would come of it.

At last matters got very bad, for two of the indunas came forward to drag her off to execution, and it was not until Stella burst into tears that the sight of her grief, backed by Mr. Carson's orders and my own remonstrances, carried the day.

All this while Hendrika had been standing quite unmoved. At last the tumult ceased, and the leading induna called to her to go, promising that if ever she showed her face near the kraals again she should be stabbed like a jackal. Then Hendrika spoke to Stella in a low voice and in English:

"Better let them kill me, mistress, better for all. Without you to love I shall go mad and become a babyan again."

Stella did not answer, and they loosed her. She stepped forward and looked at the natives with a stare of hate. Then she turned and walked past me, and as she passed whispered a native phrase in my ear, that, being literally translated, means, "Till another moon," but which has the same significance as the French "au revoir".

It frightened me, for I knew she meant that she had not done with me, and saw that our mercy was misplaced. Seeing my face change she ran swiftly from me, and as she passed Indaba-zimbi, with a sudden movement snatched her great knife from his hand. When she had gone about twenty paces she halted, looked long and earnestly on Stella, gave one loud cry as of anguish, and fled. A few minutes later we saw her far away, bounding up the face of an almost perpendicular cliff – a cliff that nobody except herself and the baboons could possibly climb.

"Look," said Indaba-zimbi in my ear – "Look, Macumazahn, there goes the Babyan-frau. But, Macumazahn, *she will come back again*. Ah, why will you not listen to my words? Have they not always been true words, Macumazahn?" and he shrugged his shoulders and turned away.

For a while I was much disturbed, but at any rate Hendrika was gone for the present, and Stella, my dear and lovely wife, was there at my side, and in her smiles I forgot my fears.

For the rest of that day, why should I write of it? – there are things too happy and too sacred to be written of.

At last I had, if only for a little while, found that rest, that perfect joy which we seek so continually and so rarely clasp.

CHAPTER XI

Gone!

I wonder if many married couples are quite as happy as we found ourselves. Cynics, a growing class, declare that few illusions can survive a honeymoon. Well, I do not know about it, for I only married once, and can but speak from my limited experience. But certainly our illusion, or rather the great truth of which it is the shadow, did survive, as to this day it survives in my heart across all the years of utter separation, and across the unanswering gulf of doom.

But complete happiness is not allowed in this world even for an hour. As our marriage day had been shadowed by the scene which has been described, so our married life was shadowed by its own sorrow.

Three days after our wedding Mr. Carson had a stroke. It had been long impending, now it fell. We came into the centre hut to dinner and found him lying speechless on the couch. At first I thought that he was dying, but this was not so. On the contrary, within four days he recovered his speech and some power of movement. But he never recovered his memory, though he still knew Stella, and sometimes myself. Curiously enough he remembered little Tota best of all three, though occasionally he thought that she was his own daughter in her childhood, and would ask her where her mother was. This state of affairs lasted for some seven months. The old man gradually grew weaker, but he did not die. Of course his condition quite precluded the idea of our leaving Babyan Kraals till all was over. This was the more distressing to me because I had a nervous presentiment that Stella was incurring danger by staying there, and also because the state of her health rendered it desirable that we should reach a civilized region as soon as possible. However, it could not be helped.

At length the end came very suddenly. We were sitting one evening by Mr. Carson's bedside in his hut, when to our astonishment he sat up and spoke in a strong, full voice.

"I hear you," he said. "Yes, yes, I forgive you. Poor woman! you too have suffered," and he fell back dead.

I have little doubt that he was addressing his lost wife, some vision of whom had flashed across his dying sense. Stella, of course, was overwhelmed with grief at her loss. Till I came her father had been her sole companion, and therefore, as may be imagined, the tie between them was much closer than is usual even in the case of father and daughter. So deeply did she mourn that I began to fear for the effect upon her health. Nor were we the only ones to grieve; all the natives on the settlement called Mr. Carson "father", and as a father they lamented him. The air resounded with the wailing of women, and the men went about with bowed heads, saying that "the sun had set in the heavens, now only the Star (Stella) remained". Indaba-zimbi alone did not mourn. He said that it was best that the Inkoos should die, for what was life worth when one lay like a log? – moreover, that it would have been well for all if he had died sooner.

On the following day we buried him in the little graveyard near the waterfall. It was a sad business, and Stella cried very much, in spite of all I could do to comfort her.

That night as I sat outside the hut smoking – for the weather was hot, and Stella was lying down inside – old Indaba-zimbi came up, saluted, and squatted at my feet.

"What is it, Indaba-zimbi?" I said.

"This, Macumazahn. When are you going to trek towards the coast?"

"I don't know," I answered. "The Star is not fit to travel now, we must wait awhile."

"No, Macumazahn, you must not wait, you must go, and the Star must take her chance. She is strong. It is nothing. All will be well."

"Why do you say so? why must we go?"

"For this reason, Macumazahn," and he looked cautiously round and spoke low. "The baboons have come back in thousands. All the mountain is full of them."

"I did not know that they had gone," I said.

"Yes," he answered, "they went after the marriage, all but one or two; now they are back, all the baboons in the world, I think. I saw a whole cliff black with them."

"Is that all?" I said, for I saw that he had something behind. "I am not afraid of a pack of baboons."

"No, Macumazahn, it is not all. The Babyan-frau, Hendrika, is with them."

Now nothing had been heard or seen of Hendrika since her expulsion, and though at first she and her threats had haunted me somewhat, by degrees to a great extent she had passed out of my mind, which was fully preoccupied with Stella and my father-in-law's illness. I started violently. "How do you know this?" I asked.

"I know it because I saw her, Macumazahn. She is disguised, she is dressed up in baboon skins, and her face is stained dark. But though she was a long way off, I knew her by her size, and I saw the white flesh of her arm when the skins slipped aside. She has come back, Macumazahn, with all the baboons in the world, and she has come back to do evil. Now do you understand why you should trek?"

"Yes," I said, "though I don't see how she and the baboons can harm us, I think that it will be better to go. If necessary we can camp the waggons somewhere for a while on the journey. Hearken, Indaba-zimbi: say nothing of this to the Star; I will not have her frightened. And hearken again. Speak to the headmen, and see that watchers are set all round the huts and gardens, and kept there night and day. To-morrow we will get the waggons ready, and next day we will trek."

He nodded his white lock and went to do my bidding, leaving me not a little disturbed – unreasonably so, indeed. It was a strange story. That this woman had the power of conversing with baboons I knew.* That was not so very wonderful, seeing that the Bushmen claim to be able to do the same thing, and she had been nurtured by them. But that she had been able to muster them, and by the strength of her human will and intelligence muster them in order to forward her ends of revenge, seemed to me so incredible that after reflection my fears grew light. Still I determined to trek. After all, a journey in an ox

---

*For an instance of this, see Anderson's *Twenty-five Years in a Waggon*, vol. i, p. 262. – Editor

waggon would not be such a very terrible thing to a strong woman accustomed to roughing it, whatever her state of health. And when all was said and done I did not like this tale of the presence of Hendrika with countless hosts of baboons.

So I went in to Stella, and without saying a word to her of the baboon story, told her I had been thinking matters over, and had come to the conclusion that it was our duty to follow her father's instructions to the letter, and leave Babyan Kraals at once. Into all our talk I need not enter, but the end of it was that she agreed with me, and declared that she could quite well manage the journey, saying, moreover, that now that her dear father was dead she would be glad to get away.

Nothing happened to disturb us that night, and on the following morning I was up early making preparations. The despair of the people when they learned that we were going to leave them was something quite pitiable I could only console them by declaring that we were but on a journey, and would return the following year.

"They had lived in the shadow of their father, who was dead," they declared; "ever since they were little they had lived in his shadow. He had received them when they were outcasts and wanderers without a mat to lie on, or a blanket to cover them, and they had grown fat in his shadow. Then he had died, and the Star, their father's daughter, had married me, Macumazahn, and they had believed that I should take their father's place, and let them live in my shadow. What should they do when there was no one to protect them? The tribes were kept from attacking them by fear of the white man. If we went they would be eaten up," and so on. Alas! there was but too much foundation for their fears.

I returned to the huts at mid-day to get some dinner. Stella said that she was going to pack during the afternoon, so I did not think it necessary to caution her about going out alone, as I did not wish to allude to the subject of Hendrika and the baboons unless I was obliged to. I told her, however, that I would come back to help her as soon as I could get away. Then I went down to the native kraals to sort out such cattle as had belonged to Mr. Carson from those which belonged to the Kaffirs, for I proposed to take them with us. It was a large herd, and the business took an incalculable time. At length, a little before sundown, I gave it up, and leaving Indaba-zimbi to finish the job, got on my horse and rode homewards.

Arriving, I gave the horse to one of the stable boys, and went into the central hut. There was no sign of Stella, though the things she had been packing lay about the floor. I passed first into our sleeping hut, thence one by one into all the others, but still saw no sign of her. Then I went out, and calling to a Kaffir in the garden asked him if he had seen his mistress.

He answered "yes". He had seen her carrying flowers and walking towards the graveyard, holding the little white girl – my daughter – as he called her, by the hand, when the sun stood "there", and he pointed to a spot on the horizon where it would have been about an hour and a half before. "The two dogs were with them," he added. I turned and ran towards the graveyard, which was about a quarter of a mile from the huts. Of course there was no reason to be anxious – evidently she had gone to lay the flowers on her father's grave. And yet I was anxious.

When I got near the graveyard I met one of the natives, who, by my orders, had been set round the kraals to watch the place, and noticed that he was rubbing his eyes and yawning. Clearly he had been asleep. I asked him if he had seen his mistress, and he answered that he had not, which under the circumstances was not wonderful. Without stopping to reproach him, I ordered the man to follow me, and went on to the graveyard. There, on Mr. Carson's grave, lay the drooping flowers which Stella had been carrying, and there in the fresh mould was the spoor of Tota's veldschoon, or hide slipper. But where were they?

I ran from the graveyard and called aloud at the top of my voice, but no answer came. Meanwhile the native was more profitably engaged in tracing their spoor. He followed it for about a hundred yards till he came to a clump of mimosa bush that was situated between the stream and the ancient marble quarries just above the waterfall, and at the mouth of the ravine. Here he stopped, and I heard him give a startled cry. I rushed to the spot, passed through the trees, and saw this. The little open space in the centre of the glade had been the scene of a struggle. There, in the soft earth, were the marks of three pairs of human feet – two shod, one naked – Stella's, Tota's, and *Hendrika's*. Nor was this all. There, close by, lay the fragments of the two dogs – they were nothing more – and one baboon, not yet quite dead, which had been bitten in the throat by the dogs. All round was the spoor of numberless baboons. The full horror of what had happened flashed into my mind.

My wife and Tota had been carried off by the baboons. As yet they had not been killed, for if so their remains would have been found with those of the dogs. They had been carried off. The brutes, acting under the direction of that woman-monkey, Hendrika, had dragged them away to some secret den, there to keep them till they died – or kill them!

For a moment I literally staggered beneath the terror of the shock. Then I roused myself from my despair. I bade the native run and alarm the people at the kraals, telling them to come armed, and bring me guns and ammunition. He went like the wind, and I turned to follow the spoor. For a few yards it was plain enough – Stella had been dragged along. I could see where her heels had struck the ground; the child had, I presumed, been carried – at least there were no marks of her feet. At the water's edge the spoor vanished. The water was shallow, and they had gone along in it, or at least Hendrika and her victims had, in order to obliterate the trail. I could see where a moss-grown stone had been freshly turned over in the water-bed. I ran along the bank some way up the ravine, in the vain hope of catching a sight of them. Presently I heard a bark in the cliffs above me; it was answered by another, and then I saw that scores of baboons were hidden about among the rocks on either side, and were slowly swinging themselves down to bar the path. To go on unarmed as I was would be useless. I should only be torn to pieces as the dogs had been. So I turned and fled back towards the huts. As I drew near I could see that my messenger had roused the settlement, for natives with spears and kerries in their hands were running up towards the kraals. When I reached the hut I met old Indaba-zimbi, who wore a very serious face.

"So the evil has fallen, Macumazahn," he said.

"It has fallen," I answered.

"Keep a good heart, Macumazahn," he said again. "She is not dead, nor is the little maid, and before they die we shall find them. Remember this, Hendrika loves her. She will not harm her, or allow the babyans to harm her. She will try to hide her away from you, that is all."

"Pray God that we may find her," I groaned. "The light is going fast."

"The moon rises in three hours," he answered; "we will search by moonlight. It is useless to start now; see, the sun sinks. Let us get the men together, eat, and make things ready. *Hamba gachle*, Hasten slowly, Macumazahn."

As there was no help, I took his advice. I could eat no food, but I packed some up to take with us, and made ready ropes, and a rough kind of litter. If we found them they would scarcely be able to walk. Ah! if we found them! How slowly the time passed! It seemed hours before the moon rose. But at last it did rise.

Then we started. In all we were about a hundred men, but we only mustered five guns between us, my elephant *roer* and four that had belonged to Mr. Carson.

CHAPTER XII
The Magic of Indaba-Zimbi

We gained the spot by the stream where Stella had been taken. The natives looked at the torn fragments of the dogs, and at the marks of violence, and I heard them swearing to each other, that whether the Star lived or died they would not rest till they had exterminated every baboon on Babyan's Peak. I echoed the oath, and, as shall be seen, we kept it.

We started on along the stream, following the spoor of the baboons as we best could. But the stream left no spoor, and the hard, rocky banks very little. Still we wandered on. All night we wandered through the lonely moonlit valleys, startling the silence into a thousand echoes with our cries. But no answer came to them. In vain our eyes searched the sides of precipices formed of water-riven rocks fantastically piled one upon another; in vain we searched through endless dells and fern-clad crannies. There was nothing to be found. How could we expect to find two human beings hidden away in the recesses of this vast stretch of mountain ground, which no man yet had ever fully explored? They were lost, and in all human probability lost for ever.

To and fro we wandered hopelessly, till at last dawn found us footsore and weary nearly at the spot whence we had started. We sat down waiting for the sun to rise, and the men ate of such food as they had brought with them, and sent to the kraals for more.

I sat upon a stone with a breaking heart. I cannot describe my feelings. Let the reader put himself in my position and perhaps he may get some idea of them. Near me was old Indaba-zimbi, who sat staring straight before him as though he were looking into space, and taking note of what went on there. An idea struck me. This man had some occult power. Several times during our adventures he had prophesied, and in every case his prophecies had proved true. He it was who, when we escaped from the Zulu Impi, had told me to steer north because there we should find the place of a white man who lived under the shadow of a great peak that was full of baboons. Perhaps he could help in this extremity – at any rate it was worth trying.

"Indaba-zimbi," I said, "you say that you can send your spirit through the doors of space and see what we cannot see. At the least I know that you can do strange things. Can you not help me now? If you can, and will save her, I will give you half the cattle that we have here."

"I never said anything of the sort, Macumazahn," he answered. "I do things, I do not talk about them. Neither do I seek reward for what I do like a common witch-doctor. It is well that you have asked me to use my wisdom, Macumazahn, for I should not have used it again without being asked – no, not even for the sake of the Star and yourself, whom I love, for if so my Spirit would have been angry. In the other matters I had a part, for my life was concerned as well as yours; but in this matter I have no part, and therefore I might not use my wisdom unless you thought well to call upon my Spirit. However, it would have been no good to ask me before, for I have only just found the herb I want," and he produced a handful of the leaves of a plant that was unfamiliar to me. It had prickly leaves, shaped very much like those of the common English nettle.

"Now, Macumazahn," he went on, "bid the men leave us alone, and then follow me presently to the little glade down there by the water."

I did so. When I reached the glade I found Indaba-zimbi kindling a small fire under the shadow of a tree by the edge of the water.

"Sit there, Macumazahn," he said, pointing to a stone near the fire, "and do not be surprised or frightened at anything you see. If you move or call out we shall learn nothing."

I sat down and watched. When the fire was alight and burning brightly, the old fellow stripped himself stark naked, and, going to the foot of the pool, dipped himself in the water. Then he came back shivering with the cold, and, leaning over the little fire, thrust leaves of the plant I have mentioned into his mouth and began to chew them, muttering as he chewed. Most of the remaining leaves he threw on to the fire. A dense smoke rose from them, but he held his head in this smoke and drew it down into his lungs till I saw that he was exhibiting every sign of suffocation. The veins in his throat and chest swelled, he gasped loudly, and his eyes, from which tears were streaming, seemed as though they were going to start from his head. Presently he fell over on his side, and lay senseless. I was terribly alarmed, and my first impulse was to run to his assistance, but fortunately I remembered his caution, and sat quiet.

Indaba-zimbi lay on the ground like a person quite dead. His limbs had all the utter relaxation of death. But as I watched I saw them begin to stiffen, exactly as though *rigor mortis* had set in. Then, to my astonishment, I perceived them once more relax, and this time there appeared upon his chest the stain of decomposition. It spread and spread; in three minutes the man, to all appearance, was a livid corpse.

I sat amazed watching this uncanny sight, and wondering if any further natural process was about to be enacted. Perhaps Indaba-zimbi was going to fall to dust before my eyes. As I watched I observed that the discoloration was beginning to fade. First it vanished from the extremities, then from the larger limbs, and lastly from the trunk. Then in turn came the third stage of relaxation, the second stage of stiffness or *rigor*, and the first stage of after-death collapse. When all these had rapidly succeeded each other, Indaba-zimbi quietly woke up.

I was too astonished to speak; I simply looked at him with my mouth open.

"Well, Macumazahn," he said, putting his head on one side like a bird, and nodding his white lock in a comical fashion, "it is all right; I have seen her."

"Seen who?" I said.

"The Star, your wife, and the little maid. They are much frightened, but unharmed. The Babyan-frau watches them. She is mad, but the baboons obey her, and do not hurt them. The Star was sleeping from weariness, so I whispered in her ear and told her not to be frightened, for you would soon rescue her, and that meanwhile she must seem to be pleased to have Hendrika near her."

"You whispered in her ear?" I said. "How could you whisper in her ear?"

"Bah! Macumazahn. How could I seem to die and go rotten before your eyes? You don't know, do you? Well, I will tell you one thing. I had to die to pass the doors of space, as you call them. I had to draw all the healthy strength and life from my body in order to gather power to speak with the Star. It was a dangerous business, Macumazahn, for if I had let things go a little further they must have stopped so, and there would have been an end of Indaba-zimbi. Ah, you white men, you know so much that you think you know every-thing. But you don't! You are always staring at the clouds and can't see the things that lie at your feet. You hardly believe me now, do you, Macumazahn? Well, I will show you. Have you anything on you that the Star has touched or worn?"

I thought for a moment, and said that I had a lock of her hair in my pocket-book. He told me to give it him. I did so. Going to the fire, he lit the lock of hair in the flame, and let it burn to ashes, which he caught in his left hand. These ashes he mixed up in a paste with the juice of one of the leaves of the plant I have spoken of.

"Now, Macumazahn, shut your eyes," he said.

I did so, and he rubbed his paste on to my eyelids. At first it burnt me, then my head swam strangely. Presently this effect passed off, and my brain was perfectly clear again, but I could not feel the ground with my feet. Indaba-zimbi led me to the side of the stream. Beneath us was a pool of beautifully clear water.

"Look into the pool, Macumazahn," said Indaba-zimbi, and his voice sounded hollow and far away in my ears.

I looked. The water grew dark; it cleared, and in it was a picture. I saw a cave with a fire burning in it. Against the wall of the cave rested Stella. Her dress was torn almost off her, she looked dreadfully pale and weary, and her eyelids were red as though with weeping. But she slept, and I could almost think that I saw her lips shape my name in her sleep. Close to her, her head upon Stella's breast, was little Tota; she had a skin thrown over her to keep out the night cold. The child was awake, and appeared to be moaning with fear. By the fire, and in such a position that the light fell full upon her face, and engaged in cooking something in a rough pot shaped from wood, sat the Baboon-woman, Hendrika. She was clothed in baboon skins, and her face had been rubbed with some dark stain, which was, however, wearing off it. In the intervals of her cooking she would turn on Stella her wild eyes, in which glared visible madness, with an expression of tenderness that amounted to worship. Then she would stare at the poor child and gnash her teeth as though with hate. Clearly she was jealous of it. Round the entrance arch of the cave peeped and peered the heads of many baboons. Presently Hendrika made a sign to one of them; apparently she did not speak, or rather grunt, in order not to wake Stella. The brute hopped forward, and she gave it a second rude wooden pot which was lying by her. It took it and went. The last thing that I saw, as the vision slowly vanished from the pool, was the dim shadow of the baboon returning with the pot full of water.

Presently everything had gone. I ceased to feel strange. There beneath me was the pool, and at my side stood Indaba-zimbi, smiling.

"You have seen things," he said.

"I have," I answered, and made no further remark on the matter. What was there to say?* "Do you know the path to the cave?" I added.

He nodded his head. "I did not follow it all just now, because it winds," he said. "But I know it. We shall want the ropes."

"Then let us be starting; the men have eaten."

He nodded his head again, and going to the men I told them to make ready, adding that Indaba-zimbi knew the way. They said that was all right, if Indaba-zimbi had "smelt her out", they should soon find the Star. So we started cheerfully enough, and my spirits were so much improved that I was able to eat a boiled mealie cob or two as we walked.

We went up the valley, following the course of the stream for about a mile; then Indaba-zimbi made a sudden turn to the right, along another kloof, of which there were countless numbers in the base of the great hill.

On we went through kloof after kloof. Indaba-zimbi, who led us, was never at a loss, he turned up gulleys and struck across necks of

---

* For some almost equally remarkable instances of Kaffir magic the reader is referred to a work named *Among the Zulus*, by the late David Leslie. – Editor

hills with the certainty of a hound on a hot scent. At length, after about three hours' march, we came to a big silent valley on the northern slope of the great peak. On one side of this valley was a series of stony koppies, on the other rose a sheer wall of rock. We marched along the wall for a distance of some two miles. Then suddenly Indaba-zimbi halted.

"There is the place," he said, pointing to an opening in the cliff. This opening was about forty feet from the ground, and ellipse-shaped. It cannot have been more than twenty feet high by ten wide, and was partially hidden by ferns and bushes that grew about it in the surface of the cliff. Keen as my eyes were, I doubt if I should ever have noticed it, for there were many such cracks and crannies in the rocky face of the great mountain.

We drew near and looked carefully at the place. The first thing I noticed was that the rock, which was not quite perpendicular, had been worn by the continual passage of baboons; the second, that something white was hanging on a bush near the top of the ascent.

It was a pocket-handkerchief.

Now there was no more doubt about the matter. With a beating heart I began the ascent. For the first twenty feet it was comparatively easy, for the rock shelved; the next ten feet was very difficult, but still possible to an active man, and I achieved it, followed by Indaba-zimbi. But the last twelve or fifteen feet could only be scaled by throwing a rope over the trunk of a stunted tree, which grew at the bottom of the opening. This we accomplished with some trouble, and the rest was easy. A foot or two above my head the handkerchief fluttered in the wind. Hanging to the rope, I grasped it. It was my wife's. As I did so I noticed the face of a baboon peering at me over the edge of the cleft, the first baboon we had seen that morning. The brute gave a bark and vanished. Thrusting the handkerchief into my breast, I set my feet against the cliff and scrambled up as hard as I could go. I knew that we had no time to lose, for the baboon would quickly alarm the others. I gained the cleft. It was a mere arched passage cut by water, ending in a gully, which led to a wide open space of some sort.

I looked through the passage and saw that the gulley was black with baboons. On they came by the hundred. I unslung my elephant gun from my shoulders, and waited, calling to the men below to come up with all possible speed. The brutes streamed down the gloomy gulf towards me, barking, grunting, and showing their huge teeth. I waited till they were within fifteen yards. Then I fired the elephant gun, which was loaded with slugs, right into the thick of them. In that narrow place the report echoed like a cannon shot, but its sound was quickly swallowed in the volley of piercing human-sounding groans and screams that followed. The charge of heavy slugs had ploughed through the host of the baboons, of which at least a dozen lay dead or dying in the passage. For a moment they hesitated, then they came on again with a hideous clamour. Fortunately by this time Indaba-zimbi, who also had a gun, was standing by my side, otherwise I should have been torn to pieces before I could re-load. He fired both barrels into them, and again checked the rush. But they came on again, and notwithstanding the appearance of two other natives with guns, which they let off with more or less success, we should have been overwhelmed by the great and ferocious apes had I not by this time succeeded in re-loading the elephant gun. When they were right on to us, I fired, with even more deadly effect than before, for at that distance every slug told on their long line. The howls and screams of pain and rage were now something inconceivable. One might have thought that we were doing battle with a host of demons; indeed in that light – for the overhanging arch of rock made it very dark – the gnashing snouts and sombre glowing eyes of the apes looked like those of devils as they are represented by monkish fancy. But the last shot was too much for them; they withdrew, dragging some of their wounded with them, and thus gave us time to get our men up the cliff. In a few minutes all were there, and we advanced down the passage, which presently opened into a rocky gulley with shelving sides. This gully had a water-way at the bottom of it; it was about a hundred yards long, and the slopes on either side were topped by pre-cipitous cliffs. I looked at these slopes; they literally swarmed with baboons, grunting, barking, screaming, and beating their breasts with their long arms, in fury. I looked up the water-way; along it, accompanied by a mob, or, as it were, a guard of baboons, ran Hendrika, her long hair flying, madness written on her face, and in her arms was the senseless form of little Tota.

She saw us, and a foam of rage burst from her lips. She screamed aloud. To me the sound was a mere inarticulate cry, but the baboons clearly understood it, for they began to roll rocks down on to us. One boulder leaped past me and struck down a Kaffir behind; another fell from the roof of the arch on to a man's head and killed him. Indaba-zimbi lifted his gun to shoot Hendrika; I knocked it up, so that the shot went over her, crying that he would kill the child. Then I shouted to the men to open out and form a line from side to side of the shelving gully. Furious at the loss of their two comrades, they obeyed me, and keeping in the water-way myself, together with Indaba-zimbi and the other guns, I gave the word to charge.

Then the real battle began. It is difficult to say who fought the most fiercely, the natives or the baboons. The Kaffirs charged along the slopes, and as they came, encouraged by the screams of Hendrika, who rushed to and fro holding the wretched Tota before her as a shield, the apes bounded at them in fury. Scores were killed by the assegais, and many more fell beneath our gun-shots; but still they came on. Nor did we go scathless. Occasionally a man would slip, or be pulled over in the grip of a baboon. Then the others would fling themselves upon him like dogs on a rat, and worry him to death. We lost five men in this way, and I myself received a bite through the fleshy part of the left arm, but fortunately a native near me assegaied the animal before I was pulled down.

At length, and all of a sudden, the baboons gave up. A panic seemed to seize them. Notwithstanding the cries of Hendrika they thought no more of fight, but only of escape; some even did not attempt to get away from the assegais of the Kaffirs, they simply hid their horrible faces in their paws, and, moaning piteously, waited to be slain.

Hendrika saw that the battle was lost. Dropping the child from her arms, she rushed straight at us, a very picture of horrible insanity. I lifted my gun, but could not bear to shoot. After all she was but a mad thing, half ape, half woman. So I sprang to one side, and she landed full on Indaba-zimbi, knocking him down. But she did not stay to do any more. Wailing terribly, she rushed along the gully and through the arch, followed by a few of the surviving baboons, and vanished from our sight.

CHAPTER XIII
What Happened to Stella

The fight was over. In all we had lost seven men killed, and several more were severely bitten, while but few had escaped without some tokens whereby he might remember what a baboon's teeth and claws are like. How many of the brutes we killed I never knew, because we did not count, but it was a vast number. I should think that the stock must have been low about Babyan's Peak for many years afterwards. From that day to this, however, I have always avoided baboons, feeling more afraid of them than of any beast that lives.

The path was clear, and we rushed forward along the watercourse. But first we picked up little Tota. The child was not in a swoon, as I had thought, but paralysed by terror, so that she could scarcely speak. Otherwise she was unhurt, though it took her many a week to recover her nerve. Had she been older, and had she not remembered Hendrika, I doubt if she would have recovered it. She knew me again, and flung her little arms about my neck, clinging to me so closely that I did not dare to give her to any one else to carry lest I should add to her terrors. So I went on with her in my arms. The fears that pierced my heart may well be imagined. Should I find Stella living or dead? Should I find her at all? Well, we must soon learn now. We stumbled on up the stony water-course; notwithstanding the weight of Tota I led the way, for suspense lent me wings. Now we were through, and an extraordinary scene lay before us. We were in a great natural amphitheatre, only it was three times the size of any amphitheatre ever shaped by man, and the walls were formed by precipitous cliffs, ranging from one to two hundred feet in height. For the rest, the space thus enclosed was level, studded with park-like trees, brilliant with flowers, and having a stream running through the centre of it, that, as I afterwards discovered, welled up from the ground at the head of the open space.

We spread ourselves out in a line, searching everywhere, for Tota was too overcome to be able to tell us where Stella was hidden away. For nearly half an hour we searched and searched, scanning the walls of rock for any possible openings to a cave. In vain, we could find none. I applied to old Indaba-zimbi, but his foresight was at fault here. All he could say was that this was the place, and that the "Star" was hidden somewhere in a cave, but where the cave was he could not tell. At last we came to the top of the amphitheatre. There before us was a wall of rock, of which the lower parts were here and there clothed in grasses, lichens, and creepers. I walked along it, calling at the top of my voice.

Presently my heart stood still, for I thought I heard a faint answer. I drew nearer to the place from which the sound seemed to come, and again called. Yes, there was an answer in my wife's voice. It seemed to come from the rock. I went up to it and searched among the creepers, but still could find no opening.

"Move the stone," cried Stella's voice, 'the cave is shut with a stone."

I took a spear and prodded at the cliff whence the sound came. Suddenly the spear sunk in through a mass of lichen. I swept the lichen aside, revealing a boulder that had been rolled into the mouth of an opening in the rock, which it fitted so accurately that, covered as it was by the overhanging lichen, it might well have escaped the keenest eye. We dragged the boulder out; it was two men's work to do it. Beyond was a narrow, water-worn passage, which I followed with a beating heart. Presently the passage opened into a small cave, shaped

244 | Hunter Quatermain's Story

like a pickle bottle, and coming to a neck at the top end. We passed through and found ourselves in a second, much larger cave, that I at once recognized as the one of which Indaba-zimbi had shown me a vision in the water. Light reached it from above – how I know not – and by it I could see a form half sitting, half lying on some skins at the top end of the cave. I rushed to it. It was Stella! Stella bound with strips of hide, bruised, torn, but still Stella, and alive.

She saw me, she gave one cry, then, as I caught her in my arms, she fainted. It was happy indeed that she did not faint before, for had it not been for the sound of her voice I do not believe we should ever have found that cunningly hidden cave, unless, indeed, Indaba-zimbi's magic (on which be blessings) had come to our assistance.

We bore her to the open air, laid her beneath the shade of a tree, and cut the bonds loose from her ankles. As we went I glanced at the cave. It was exactly as I had seen it in the vision. There burnt the fire, there were the rude wooden vessels, one of them still half full of the water which I had seen the baboon bring. I felt awed as I looked, and marvelled at the power wielded by a savage who could not even read and write.

Now I could see Stella clearly. Her face was scratched, and haggard with fear and weeping, her clothes were almost torn off her, and her beautiful hair was loose and tangled. I sent for water, and we sprinkled her face. Then I forced a little of the brandy which we distilled from peaches at the kraals between her lips, and she opened her eyes, and throwing her arms about me clung to me as little Tota had done, sobbing, "Thank God! thank God!"

After a while she grew quieter, and I made her and Tota eat some food from the store that we had brought with us. I too ate and was thankful, for with the exception of the mealie cobs I had tasted nothing for nearly four-and-twenty hours. Then she washed her face and hands, and tidied her rags of dress as well as she was able. As she did so by degrees I drew her story from her.

It seemed that on the previous afternoon, being wearied with packing, she went out to visit her father's grave, taking Tota with her,

and was followed there by the two dogs. She wished to lay some flowers on the grave and take farewell of the dust it covered, for as we had expected to trek early on the morrow she did not know if she would find a later opportunity. They passed up the garden, and, gathering some flowers from the orange trees and elsewhere, went on to the little graveyard. Here she laid them on the grave as we had found them, and then sitting down, fell into a deep and sad reverie, such as the occasion would naturally induce. While she sat thus, Tota, who was a lively child and active as a kitten, strayed away without Stella observing it. With her went the dogs, who also had grown tired of inaction; a while passed, and suddenly she heard the dogs barking furiously about a hundred and fifty yards away. Then she heard Tota scream, and the dogs also yelling with fear and pain. She rose and ran as swiftly as she could towards the spot whence the sound came. Presently she was there. Before her in the glade, holding the screaming Tota in her arms, was a figure in which, notwithstanding the rough disguise of baboon skins and colouring matter, she had no difficulty in recognizing Hendrika, and all about her were numbers of baboons, rolling over and over in two hideous heaps, of which the centres were the unfortunate dogs now in process of being rent to fragments.

"Hendrika," Stella cried, "what does this mean? What are you doing with Tota and those brutes?"

The woman heard her and looked up. Then Stella saw that she was mad; madness stared from her eyes. She dropped the child, which instantly flew to Stella for protection. Stella clasped it, only to be herself clasped by Hendrika. She struggled fiercely, but it was of no use – the Babyan-frau had the strength of ten. She lifted her and Tota as though they were nothing, and ran off with them, following the bed of the stream in order to avoid leaving a spoor. Only the baboons who came with her, minus the one the dogs had killed, would not take to the water, but kept pace with them on the bank.

Stella said that the night which followed was more like a hideous nightmare than a reality. She was never able to tell me all that occurred in it. She had a vague recollection of being borne over rocks and along kloofs, while around her echoed the horrible grunts and clicks of the baboons. She spoke to Hendrika in English and Kaffir, imploring her to let them go; but the woman, if I may call her so, seemed in her madness to have entirely forgotten these tongues. When Stella spoke she would kiss her and stroke her hair, but she did not seem to understand what it was she said. On the other hand, she could, and did, talk to the baboons, that seemed to obey her implicitly. Moreover, she would not allow them to touch either Stella or the child in her arms. Once one of them tried to do so, and she seized a dead stick and struck it so heavily on the head that it fell senseless. Thrice Stella made an attempt to escape, for sometimes even Hendrika's giant strength waned and she had to set them down. But on each occasion she caught them, and it was in these struggles that Stella's clothes were so torn. At length before daylight they reached the cliff, and with the first break of light the ascent began. Hendrika dragged them up the first stages, but when they came to the precipitous place she tied the strips of hide, of which she had a supply wound round her waist, beneath Stella's arms. Steep as the place was the baboons ascended it easily enough, springing from a knob of rock to the trunk of the tree that grew on the edge of the crevasse. Hendrika followed them, holding the end of the hide reim in her teeth, one of the baboons hanging down from the tree to assist her ascent. It was while she was ascending that Stella bethought her of letting fall her handkerchief in the faint hope that some searcher might see it.

By this time Hendrika was on the tree, and grunting out orders to the baboons which clustered about Stella below. Suddenly these seized her and little Tota who was in her arms, and lifted her from the ground. Then Hendrika above, aided by other baboons, put out all her great strength and pulled the two of them up the rock. Twice Stella swung heavily against the cliff. After the second blow she felt her senses going, and was consumed with terror lest she should drop Tota. But she managed to cling to her, and together they reached the cleft.

"From that time," Stella went on, "I remember no more till I woke to find myself in a gloomy cave resting on a bed of skins. My legs were bound, and Hendrika sat near me watching me, while round the edge of the cave peered the heads of those horrible baboons. Tota was still in my arms, and half dead from terror; her moans were pitiful to hear. I spoke to Hendrika, imploring her to release us; but either she has lost all understanding of human speech, or she pretends to have done so. All she would do was to caress me, and even kiss my hands and dress with extravagant signs of affection. As she did so, Tota shrunk closer to me. This Hendrika saw and glared so savagely at the child that I feared lest she was going to kill her. I diverted her attention by making signs that I wanted water, and this she gave me in a wooden bowl. As you saw, the cave was evidently Hendrika's dwelling-place. There are stores of fruit in it and some strips of dried flesh. She gave me some of the fruit and Tota a little, and I made Tota eat some. You can never know what I went through, Allan. I saw now that Hendrika was quite mad, and but little removed from the brutes to which she is akin, and over which she has such unholy power. The only trace of humanity left about her was her affection for me. Evidently her idea

was to keep me here with her, to keep me away from you, and to carry
out this idea she was capable of the exercise of every artifice and cunning. In that way she was sane enough, but in every other way she
was mad. Moreover, she had not forgotten her horrible jealousy.
Already I saw her glaring at Tota, and knew that the child's murder
was only a matter of time. Probably within a few hours she would be
killed before my eyes. Of escape, even if I had the strength, there was
absolutely no chance, and little enough of our ever being found. No,
we should be kept here guarded by a mad thing, half ape, half
woman, till we perished miserably. Then I thought of you, dear, and
of all that you must be suffering, and my heart nearly broke. I could
only pray to God that I might either be rescued or die swifty.

"As I prayed I dropped into a kind of doze from utter weariness,
and then I had the strangest dream. I dreamed that Indaba-zimbi
stood over me nodding his white lock, and spoke to me in Kaffir,
telling me not to be frightened, for you would soon be with me, and
that meanwhile I must humour Hendrika, pretending to be pleased
to have her near me. The dream was so vivid that I actually seemed to
see and hear him, as I see and hear him now."

Here I looked up and glanced at old Indaba-zimbi, who was sitting near. But it was not till afterwards that I told Stella of how her
vision was brought about.

"At any rate," she went on, "when I awoke I determined to act on
my dream. I took Hendrika's hand, and pressed it. She actually
laughed in a wild kind of way with happiness, and laid her head upon
my knee. Then I made signs that I wanted food, and she threw wood
on the fire, which I forgot to tell you was burning in the cave, and
began to make some of the broth that she used to cook very well, and
she did not seem to have forgotten all about it. At any rate the broth
was not bad, though neither Tota nor I could drink much of it. Fright
and weariness had taken away our appetites.

"After the meal was done – and I prolonged it as much as possible
– I saw that Hendrika was beginning to get jealous of Tota again. She
glared at her and then at the big knife which was tied round her own

body. I knew the knife again; it was the one with which she had tried to murder you, dear. At last she went so far as to draw the knife. I was paralysed with fear, then suddenly I remembered that when she was our servant, and used to get out of temper and sulk, I could always calm her by singing to her. So I began to sing hymns. Instantly she forgot her jealousy and put the knife back into its sheath. She knew the sound of the singing, and sat listening to it with a rapt face; the baboons, too, crowded in at the entrance of the cave to listen. I must have sung for an hour or more, all the hymns that I could remember. It was so very strange and dreadful sitting there singing to mad Hendrika and those hideous man-like apes that shut their eyes and nodded their great heads as I sang. It was like a horrible nightmare; but I believe that the baboons are almost as human as the Bushmen.

"Well, this went on for a long time till my voice was getting exhausted. Then suddenly I heard the baboons outside raise a loud noise, as they do when they are angry. Then, dear, I heard the boom of your elephant gun, and I think it was the sweetest sound that ever came to my ears. Hendrika heard it too. She sprang up, stood for a moment, then, to my horror, swept Tota into her arms and rushed down the cave. Of course I could not stir to follow her, for my feet were tied. Next instant I heard the sound of a rock being moved, and presently the lessening of the light in the cave told me that I was shut in. Now the sound even of the elephant gun only reached me very faintly, and presently I could hear nothing more, straining my ears as I would.

"At last I heard a faint shouting that reached me through the wall of rock. I answered as loud as I could. You know the rest; and oh, my dear husband, thank God! thank God!" and she fell weeping into my arms.

CHAPTER XIV

Fifteen Years After

Both Stella and Tota were too weary to be moved, so we camped that night in the baboons' home, but were troubled by no baboons. Stella would not sleep in the cave; she said the place terrified her, so I made her up a kind of bed under a thorn-tree. As that rock-bound valley was one of the hottest places I ever was in, I thought that this would not matter; but when at sunrise on the following morning I saw a veil of miasmatic mist hanging over the surface of the ground, I changed my opinion. However, neither Stella nor Tota seemed the worse, so as soon as was practicable we started homewards. I had already on the previous day sent some of the men back to the kraals to fetch a ladder, and when we reached the cliff we found them waiting for us beneath. With the help of the ladder the descent was easy. Stella simply got out of her rough litter at the top of the cliff, for we found it necessary to carry her; climbed down the ladder, and got into it again at the bottom.

Well, we reached the kraals safely enough, seeing nothing more of Hendrika, and, were this a story, doubtless I should end it here with – "and lived happy ever after". But alas! it is not so. How am I to write it?

My dearest wife's vital energy seemed completely to fail her now that the danger was past, and within twelve hours of our return I saw that her state was such as to necessitate the abandonment of any idea of leaving Babyan Kraals at present. The bodily exertion, the anguish of mind, and the terror which she had endured during that dreadful night, combined with her delicate state of health, had completely broken her down. To make matters worse also, she was taken with an attack of fever, contracted no doubt in the unhealthy atmosphere of that accursed valley. In time she shook the fever off, but it left her dreadfully weak, and quite unfit to face the trial before her.

I think she knew that she was going to die; she always spoke of my future, never of *our* future. It is impossible for me to tell how sweet she was; how gentle, how patient and resigned. Nor, indeed, do I wish to tell it, it is too sad. But this I will say, I believe that if ever a woman drew near to perfection while yet living on the earth, Stella Quatermain did so.

The fatal hour drew on. My boy Harry was born, and his mother lived to kiss and bless him. Then she sank. We did what we could, but we had little skill, and might not hold her back from death. All through one weary night I watched her with a breaking heart.

The dawn came, the sun rose in the east. His rays falling on the peak behind were reflected in glory upon the bosom of the western sky. Stella awoke from her swoon and saw the light. She whispered to me to open the door of the hut. I did so, and she fixed her dying eyes on the splendour of the morning sky. She looked on me and smiled as an angel might smile. Then with a last effort she lifted her hand, and, pointing to the radiant heavens, whispered:

"*There, Allan, there!*"

It was done, and I was broken-hearted, and broken-hearted I must wander till the end. Those who have endured my loss will know my sorrow; it cannot be written. In such peace and at such an hour may I also die!

Yes, it is a sad story, but wander where we will about the world we can never go beyond the sound of the passing bell. For me, as for my father before me, and for the millions who have been and who shall be, there is but one word of comfort. "The Lord gave, and the Lord hath taken away." Let us, then, bow our heads in hope, and add with a humble heart, "Blessed be the name of the Lord."

I buried her by her father's side, and the weeping of the people who had loved her went up to heaven. Even Indaba-zimbi wept, but I could weep no more.

On the second night from her burial I could not sleep. I rose, dressed myself, and went out into the night. The moon was shining brightly, and by its rays I shaped my course towards the graveyard. I drew near silently, and as I came I thought that I heard a sound of moaning on the further side of the wall. I looked over it. Crouched by Stella's grave, and tearing at its sods with her hands, as though she would unearth that which lay within, was *Hendrika*. Her face was wild and haggard, her form was so emaciated that when the pelts she wore slipped aside, the shoulder-blades seemed to project almost through her skin. Suddenly she looked up and saw me. Laughing a dreadful maniac laugh, she put her hand to her girdle and drew her great knife from it. I thought that she was about to attack me, and prepared to defend myself as I best could, for I was unarmed. But she made no effort to do so. Lifting the knife on high, for a moment she held it glittering in the moonlight, then plunged it into her own breast, and fell headlong to the ground.

I sprang over the wall and ran to her. She was not yet dead. Presently she opened her eyes, and I saw that the madness had gone out of them.

"Macumazahn," she said, speaking in English and in a thick difficult voice like one who half forgot and half remembered; "Macumazahn, I remember now. I have been mad. Is she really dead, Macumazahn?"

"Yes," I said, "she is dead, and you killed her."

"I killed her!" the dying woman faltered, "and I loved her. Yes, yes – I know now. I became a brute again and dragged her to the brutes, and now once more I am a woman, and she is dead, and I killed her – because I loved her so. I killed her who saved me from the brutes. I am not dead yet, Macumazahn. Take me and torture me to death, slowly, very slowly. It was jealousy of you that drove me mad, and I have killed her, and now she never can forgive me."

"Ask forgiveness from above," I said, for Hendrika had been a Christian, and the torment of her remorse touched me.

"I ask no forgiveness," she said. "May God torture me for ever, because I killed her; may I become a brute for ever till she comes to find me and forgives me! I only want her forgiveness." And wailing in an anguish of the heart so strong that her bodily suffering seemed to be forgotten, Hendrika, the Baboon-woman, died.

I went back to the kraals, and, waking Indaba-zimbi, told him what had happened, asking him to send some one to watch the body, as I proposed to give it burial. But next morning it was gone, and I found that the natives, hearing of the event, had taken the corpse and thrown it to the vultures with every mark of hate. Such, then, was the end of Hendrika.

A week after Hendrika's death I left Babyan Kraals. The place was hateful to me now; it was a haunted place. I sent for old Indaba-zimbi and told him that I was going. He answered that it was well. "The place has served your turn," he said; "here you have won that joy which it was fated you should win, and have suffered those things that it was fated you should suffer. Yes, and though you know it not now, the joy and the suffering, like the sunshine and the storm, are the same thing, and will rest at last in the same heaven, the heaven from which they came. Now go, Macumazahn."

I asked him if he was coming with me.

"No," he answered, "our paths lie apart henceforth, Macumazahn. We met together for certain ends. Those ends are fulfilled. Now each one goes his own way. You have still many years before you, Macumazahn; my years are few. When we shake hands here it will be for the last time. Perhaps we may meet again, but it will not be in this world. Henceforth we have each of us a friend the less."

"Heavy words," I said.

"True words," he answered.

Well, I have little heart to write of the rest of it. I went, leaving Indaba-zimbi in charge of the place, and making him a present of such cattle and goods as I did not want.

Tota, I of course took with me. Fortunately by this time she had almost recovered the shock to her nerves. The baby Harry, as he was afterwards named, was a fine healthy child, and I was lucky in getting a respectable native woman, whose husband had been killed in the fight with the baboons, to accompany me as his nurse.

Slowly, and followed for a distance by all the people, I trekked away from Babyan Kraals. My route towards Natal was along the edge of the Bad Lands, and my first night's outspan was beneath that very tree where Stella, my lost wife, had found us as we lay dying of thirst.

I did not sleep much that night. And yet I was glad that I had not died in the desert about eleven months before. I felt then, as from year to year I have continued to feel while I wander through the lonely wilderness of life, that I had been preserved to an end. I had won my darling's love, and for a little while we were happy together. Our happiness was too perfect to endure. She is lost to me now, but she is lost to be found again.

Here on the following morning I bade farewell to Indaba-zimbi.

"Good-bye, Macumazahn," he said, nodding his white lock at me. "Good-bye for a while. I am not a Christian; your father could not make me that. But he was a wise man, and when he said that those who love each other shall meet again, he did not lie. And I too am a wise man in my way, Macumazahn, and I say it is true that we shall meet again. All my prophecies to you have come true, Macumazahn, and this one shall come true also. I tell you that you shall return to Babyan Kraals and shall not find me. I tell you that you shall journey to a further land than Babyan Kraals and shall find me. Farewell!" and he took a pinch of snuff, turned, and went.

Of my journey down to Natal there is little to tell. I met with many adventures, but they were of an every-day kind, and in the end we arrived safely at Port Durban, which I now visited for the first time. Both Tota and my baby boy bore the journey well. And here I may as well chronicle the destiny of Tota. For a year she remained under my charge. Then she was adopted by a lady, the wife of an English colonel, who was stationed at the Cape. She was taken by her adopted parents to England, where she grew up a very charming and pretty girl, and ultimately married a clergyman in Norfolk. But I never saw her again, though we often wrote to each other.

Before I returned to the country of my birth, she too had been gathered to the land of shadows, leaving three children behind her. Ah me! all this took place so long ago, when I was young who now am old.

Perhaps it may interest the reader to know the fate of Mr. Carson's property, which should of course have gone to his grandson Harry. I wrote to England to claim the estate on his behalf, but the lawyer to whom the matter was submitted said that my marriage to Stella, not having been celebrated by an ordained priest, was not legal according to English law, and therefore Harry could not inherit. Foolishly enough I acquiesced in this, and the property passed to a cousin of my father-in-law's; but since I have come to live in England I have been informed that this opinion is open to great suspicion, and that there is every probability that the courts would have declared the marriage perfectly binding as having been solemnly entered into in accordance with the custom of the place where it was contracted. But I am now so rich that it is not worth while to move in the matter. The cousin is dead, his son is in possession, so let him keep it.

Once, and once only, did I revisit Babyan Kraals. Some fifteen years after my darling's death, when I was a man in middle life, I undertook an expedition to the Zambesi, and one night outspanned at the mouth of the well-known valley beneath the shadow of the great peak. I mounted my horse, and, quite alone, rode up the valley, noticing with a strange prescience of evil that the road was overgrown, and, save for the music of the waterfalls, the place silent as death. The kraals that used to be to the left of the road by the river had vanished. I rode towards their site; the mealie fields were choked with weeds, the paths were dumb with grass. Presently I reached the place. There, overgrown with grass, were the burnt ashes of the kraals, and there among the ashes, gleaming in the moonlight, lay the white bones of men. Now it was clear to me. The settlement had been fallen on by some powerful foe, and its inhabitants put to the assegai. The forebodings of the natives had come true; Babyan Kraals were peopled by memories alone.

I passed on up the terraces. There shone the roofs of the marble huts. They would not burn, and were too strong to be easily pulled down. I entered one of them – it had been our sleeping hut – and lit a candle which I carried with me. The huts had been sacked; leaves of books and broken mouldering fragments of the familiar furniture lay about. Then I remembered that there was a secret place hollowed in the floor and concealed by a stone, where Stella used to hide her little treasures. I went to the stone and dragged it up. There was something within wrapped in rotting native cloth. I undid it. It was the dress my wife had been married in. In the centre of the dress were the withered wreath and flowers she had worn, and with them a little paper packet. I opened it; it contained a lock of my own hair!

I remembered then that I had searched for this dress when I came away and could not find it, for I had forgotten the secret recess in the floor.

Taking the dress with me, I left the hut for the last time. Leaving my horse tied to a tree, I walked to the graveyard, through the ruined garden. There it was, a mass of weeds, but over my darling's grave grew a self-sown orange bush, of which the scented petals fell in showers on to the mound beneath. As I drew near, I heard a crash and a rush. A great baboon leapt from the centre of the graveyard and vanished into the trees. I could almost believe that it was the wraith of Hendrika doomed to keep an eternal watch over the bones of the woman her jealous rage had done to death.

I tarried there a while, filled with such thoughts as may not be written. Then, leaving my dead wife to her long sleep where the waters fall in melancholy music beneath the shadow of the everlasting mountain, I turned and sought that spot where first we had told our love. Now the orange grove was nothing but a tangled thicket; many of the trees were dead, choked with creepers, but some still flourished. There stood the one beneath which we had lingered, there was the rock that had been our seat, and *there on the rock sat the wraith of Stella, the Stella whom I had wed!* Ay! there she sat, and on her upturned face was that same spiritual look which I saw upon it in the hour when we first had kissed. The moonlight shone in her dark eyes, the breeze wavered in her curling hair, her breast rose and fell, a gentle smile played about her parted lips. I stood transfixed with awe and joy, gazing on that lost loveliness which once was mine. I could not speak, and she spoke no word; she did not even seem to see me. I drew near. Now her eyes fell. For a moment they met mine, and their message entered into me.

Then she was gone. She was gone; nothing was left but the tremulous moonlight falling where she had been, the melancholy music of the waters, the shadow of the everlasting mountain, and, in my heart, the sorrow and the hope.